APRIL FOOL

BY

JOY WOOD

Thankyou for your
Support Richard

Best wishes
Joy Wood
x

Acknowledgements

As always, there is a list of people who I'd like to thank that have enabled me to write this book. First and foremost is my husband whose support is unwavering. He juggles all the other balls while I sit and write. More often than not he is head gardener, chef, food-shopper, driver and anything else that needs doing! Without him, there wouldn't be any books, so thank you, John, from the bottom of my heart for everything you do to enable me to write. Our life together is such a joy - long may it continue.

I am extremely fortunate to be blessed with truly wonderful friends, far too many to mention but they know who they are. They are always there for me jollying me along. What a dull life it would be without them in it. And they like my books, so that's a bonus!

To my beta readers, Jacqui Barwell, Maxine McCormick and Julie Popplewell. You are all brilliant at spotting the grammatical errors, and often finding those little tiny mistakes that aren't evident to me. I read the manuscript how I think I've written it . . . not how it actually is. So to have it fine-tuned is more than helpful. And of course your support with the story, I know you'd all say if it didn't work.

To my editor, John Hudspith – thank you, Johnny, you make my words shine. Writing books is one thing, sharing them requires your skill. Thank goodness I have you in my corner, long may our writing relationship continue.

2018 has been a year of numerous opportunities for me to give my talk, "From Bedpan to Pen" to WI's, book clubs and luncheons. I wish I had words other than thank you to convey how grateful I am to every single person that has purchased my books or downloaded Kindle copies. It is such a delight to have so many enthusiastic readers who genuinely want me to do well.

Finally to all my readers – I couldn't do it without you. Every review, email or message I receive saying you've enjoyed reading one of my books makes all the blood, sweat and edits worth it. Thank you most sincerely. While you continue to take pleasure from them . . . I'll continue to write them (God willing!).

Dedication

To my dear husband John for belicving in me.
None of my success would mean a thing without you in
my life.

Table of Contents

Chapter 1

"Sign here."

April took the chewed-up pen from the prison officer and signed along the dotted line to acknowledge she'd received her meagre belongings.

"Print your name in full underneath."

The lack of pleasantries was no surprise. To them it was just a job, one inmate leaving only to be replaced by another prisoner by the end of the day. She signed her name and tossed the pen down.

"Right, follow me."

She matched the prison officer's brisk pace as she headed to what would be their eventual destination, the exit. This particular part of the open prison wasn't completely new to her. She'd walked through the area when she'd arrived twelve weeks ago.

Each unit was separated by an electronic door. It wasn't like on television where the prison officer had a bunch of keys, and opened and closed each door behind them. It was a swipe card and fingerprint recognition which allowed access into each area.

There wasn't any communication from the miserable sod walking alongside her, known to the inmates as Dr Death. Her cell mate, Julia, had explained the name had stuck due to two unexpected deaths in the prison, and on both occasions this particular prison officer had been on duty. Julia reckoned one look at her ugly face was enough for anyone to commit hari-kiri.

They continued in silence with only the background music from one of the rest areas in the distance.

Dr Death didn't like her, and April new exactly why. She'd been fortunate to have inherited her mother's beautiful looks, which on occasions had been an obstacle with other females. So often in her young life she'd used her appearance to her advantage with the opposite sex, but some women hated her for it, particularly fat overweight ones like Dr Death who denied overeating, and blamed their weight on their metabolic rate, their underactive thyroid gland, or some other obscure health condition, opposed to the reality that they were stuffing their faces at every available opportunity.

They reached the final door - the exit.

"Is someone outside to meet you?" Dr Death asked with a smirk on her face as if she knew there wouldn't be.

She wasn't going to tell her anything. "I'm not entirely sure."

"You've money to get a bus, or a taxi to the station; do you know the area and how to get to town?"

"Yes, it isn't far, I understand."

"No. Basically you turn right out of the prison and just keep walking. But here," she handed her a card, "if you'd prefer to call a taxi. This is a local one the inmates use."

April shook her head refusing the card, "I think a walk might be good."

Dr Death shrugged and turned to press in the final code which would mean her release. She didn't rush. It was almost as if she was prolonging the moment on purpose.

April watched as the door to freedom slowly opened, squinting until her eyes became accustomed to the bright sunshine.

Eighty-five long days she'd been incarcerated. And every single tortuous one of them, she'd meticulously ticked off on a calendar. Visually seeing them disappear gave her the momentum to get through another laborious day.

She stepped forward to make her way through the big oak prison door, and deliberately didn't look back. There was no way she was going to acknowledge Dr Death by shaking her hand on the way out. Prison officers weren't friends or acquaintances. They had a bit of power because of the nature of the job, but boy did that go to their heads. Not all of them, some were reasonably okay, but not this one. She'd been hateful.

If Dr Death had known who April really was, then she wouldn't have been quite so punitive and given her such a hard time. And there was a time she would have made her pay for the way she'd treated her, but not anymore.

Nothing was going to get in her way. Certainly not revenge on a jumped-up prison officer. To get to where she was right now had required meticulous planning and attention to detail. The new identity, the change in her appearance, and the stretch in prison had all been absolutely necessary to assist her as she was about to embark on the biggest pay day of all.

Chapter 2

Dylan Rider was trying desperately to keep his temper in check and calm his itchy fingers, which right now prickled with the urge to clout his seventeen-year-old son.

"I'm warning you, Henry, any more drugs and I swear you'll be out of here on your arse. I've paid a ridiculous amount of money for the clinic to get you straight, but that's it. No more." He glared, "Do you understand?"

His son, sitting opposite him looked as sullen as ever. Despite trying not to raise his voice, Dylan couldn't help it. "Well, do you?"

"Yes," Henry grunted, contempt etched all over his acne-covered face.

"It would help if you looked at me when I was speaking to you."

Henry never looked directly at him, or anybody for that matter, unless he was forced.

He waited until he did turn his face towards him.

"I've provided you with a car, and I expect you to use it to find work. You've made it clear you don't want to go to college, despite what I want, so you need to get a job. Tomorrow, go down to the job centre and speak to someone, to see if you could be considered for some sort of apprenticeship. There must be something you can do along those lines. Look at," he hesitated trying to think of something that might be suitable, "engineering or plumbing . . . anything that might be useful?"

His son's whole persona smacked of boredom, and his tone was insolent as he sneered, "Have you finished?"

What was the point?

"For now, yes, and remember what I've said, no more drugs. Not even cannabis. If I as much as suspect you're going down that road again, I mean it, that's it. You'll be out."

Henry got up, and even after he'd left the room, Dylan continued to stare.

Why is he so bloody awkward?

He blew out a frustrated breath and went to the drinks cabinet. He selected a Glenmorangie whisky and poured a generous measure. He could do with some ice, but couldn't be bothered to go to the kitchen to get it. The thick amber liquid burnt his throat as he gulped a mouthful, and he savoured the heat as it travelled down his chest. He sat down on the sofa and flopped his head back onto the headrest, perching the crystal glass on his abdomen.

How had he ended up with a delinquent son? Plenty of kids had divorced parents and made something of their lives, Christ he'd had to. Okay, so nobody expected Henry's mother to die at thirty six, and he had to take some responsibility for not being the best father in the world, but whose fault was that? What bloke wants a kid at twenty? He was just having a good time with Alicia. Marriage and kids was well down the line, if ever.

He recalled with clarity the night she dropped the bombshell she was pregnant eighteen years earlier. It was etched on his mind as one of the biggest shocks of his young life. Until then, he'd been footloose and fancy free. Her announcement changed all that.

They were in a trendy cocktail bar and he'd asked her what she wanted to drink expecting her to go for an expensive cocktail, and she asked for a lime and soda. His antenna went up straight away. Alicia could drink, she was a good match for any bloke.

"Lime and soda?" he'd asked, "What's up with you?"

"Get the drinks while I grab a seat, and then I'll tell you."

He honestly thought she'd eaten something and felt queasy. What a bloody shock when she told him she was eight weeks pregnant. He'd prayed it might be a false alarm, even though she'd done a test and it was positive. She'd given him some mumbo-jumbo about the contraceptive pill she'd been taking not working, but his cynical mind knew that wasn't the case.

Alicia had trapped him.

He recalled the shame he felt when his father raged at him for being such a bloody fool for not wearing a condom, and did he not realise that women like Alicia would see the bigger picture. Wealth.

They'd hurriedly married, and on his wedding day he wanted to turn around and run. It felt like the biggest mistake of his life, and that had quickly become apparent during their first year of marriage. They were only kids themselves and certainly not ready to deal with the stresses of living together in the same house with a child. Prior to that, they'd only dated and hadn't spent much time in each other's company. They were so young.

The marriage must have been the fastest one on record, and the only good thing that had come out of their union, was the absolute certainty he was never going down that road again. So, since the divorce, women were compartmentalised in his life and that's the way he liked it.

His phone buzzed in his pocket. He reached for it and saw his brother's name come up.

"Hi, Vic."

"Hi. I've had J on the phone."

Dylan knew who he meant. He and Vic never discussed names of anyone on the phone. Their business was too delicate for intruder's ears.

"What the hell's he doing calling?"

"Getting twitchy."

"What's new?"

"Yeah, I know. He wants the merchandise offloading sooner rather than later."

"Did you tell him we're not ready?"

"I've told him exactly that."

"Why's he getting twitchy now, for Christ's sake?"

"He just is, but don't worry, we're not going to be rushed."

"I'm pleased to hear it."

"We call the shots, not him. I've warned him not to ring anymore, and I'll be in touch with him when *we're* ready."

"Too bloody right."

"We can talk more on Friday, are we still on for dinner?"

"Sure."

"Good. How's Henry?"

"Sulking."

"You collected him then?"

"Yep. Tempting though it was to leave him at the clinic, I didn't fancy paying another grand for his so-called *in-house therapy.*"

"I don't blame you, at least he's home."

"Yeah, and I've given him the gypsy's warning, any more crap and he'll be out on his ear. And I mean it, Vic. He's bloody stupid getting involved in drugs."

"Hopefully he won't anymore. He's been through a lot with his mother dying; it's not been that long."

"Yeah, well, we all have shit to deal with."

"Cut him some slack, Dyl, I'm sure he'll behave himself now."

"I hope you're right. I've told him to try and get some sort of apprenticeship. He refuses to discuss college. Come to think of it, he doesn't discuss very much at all."

"Give him time. He's got his autism to deal with, it can't be easy."

"Autism? As far as I can see that's just bullshit for being a sullen and awkward little git."

"Yeah, you could be right," Vic sympathised, "but he does have some odd tendencies, and his behaviour is strange at times."

"You're telling me. He gets on my bloody nerves skulking around the house all the time."

"Give him a break. Can't you remember being an awkward seventeen-year-old and not really fitting in? I can."

"I tell you what, Mr Sympathetic, how about he stays at yours and you can parent him?"

"No thanks, matey, kids have never been on my agenda."

"No, me neither, but it looks like I'm stuck with one." He checked his watch. "Listen, I'm going to have to get off, Vic, I've got a date."

"Probably just what you need now, to relieve some of that tension."

"You could be right there, bro," he laughed, "cheers, see you Friday."

"See ya."

Dylan drained the last of the whisky and made his way upstairs to his bathroom. He discarded his clothes, stepped into the shower and turned the therapeutic massage jets on, welcoming the warm water cascading down his body.

Right now, a fuck was exactly what he needed to relieve the tension, and he'd get a good one with no-strings-Ingrid. It suited him that she was married as he didn't need to engage in all the usual clap trap of wining and dining her to get her into bed, or spending heaps of money on her. They met occasionally for a drink, but being married meant she couldn't get away that often. And he saw her at the gallery every day, so they had plenty of opportunities to screw.

Guilt wasn't an emotion that affected him, he was an opportunist, and it wasn't his fault her husband couldn't get it up. He was more than happy to oblige. Ingrid was fit for her age, and always gagging for it. In fact, he hardly had to work at it, she was like a dog on heat.

But even with on-tap sex, he was bored and yearned for something different. A contrast from his usual choices, maybe a woman who wasn't fixated on how she looked, how much food she ate, or if she was wearing the latest designer outfit.

What would it be like to have a decent conversation with a woman not fawning over him because he was Dylan Rider.

Did such a woman exist?

He vigorously rubbed the shower gel over his torso and underneath his arms.

Nah, they were all the same.

Chapter 3

If April thought the prison bed had been uncomfortable, it had nothing on the cheap mattress she was currently laid on. But at least she was out of prison now, and the reward had been a substantial monetary package courtesy of the police and the insurance company for being locked up for twelve weeks.

Money had been the first thing she'd negotiated before agreeing to anything. Both services had coughed and spluttered at the amount she suggested, gone away and came back to negotiate, but she stood her ground. Their plan couldn't have moved forward without her, and she knew it.

Her eyes flicked around the sparsely furnished room. It was adequate for the task ahead. Exactly the sort of place an ex-con would live. The walls were a manky taupe colour, but she suspected they were originally much lighter, maybe a sort of warm biscuity-beige opposed to a dingy dirty one. The whole room was in desperate need of a lick of paint.

The thought of a shower in the grimy room that passed as a bathroom made her shudder, and her thoughts drifted back to her beautiful white bathroom in her own home with her Elemis Frangipani shower scrub and body cream invitingly waiting on the shelf. If she tried really hard, she could close her eyes and imagine the smell. It had been so long since she'd had decent cosmetics. Even the moisturiser she now used was a regular store brand and not the Clarins she usually favoured.

How long before she would get back to it?

She reached for her watch from the coffee-stained bedside table. When she'd arrived yesterday, a letter had been waiting for her on the Formica table in the tiny kitchen. It said very little.

Monday 20th March   11am, @ 7, East Hill, Bethnal Green, E2 9JE.

Appointment with your parole officer, Tom Campbell. Give your name at the desk when you arrive.

The shower had been surprisingly warm, and there was heating in the flat which she was grateful for. She selected a pair of jeans and a jumper from the drawer she'd emptied her few items of clothes into the previous evening. There was a full length mirror on the inside of the wardrobe door, but to look at herself, she had to negotiate a crack running down its centre.

Her cropped hair made her appear younger somehow and reminded her of being a teenager. A time when she'd been a scrawny sixteen-year-old and she and her sister, Chloe were living with foster carers. The Crawford's had been lovely people, and she knew with absolute certainty their chaotic lives would have been enhanced greatly had they been placed with them when they were younger. The years of being in the care of the local authority, and some dodgy foster carers, had been a significant struggle for both of them.

Her once-tight blue jeans hung off her hips. It wasn't just the diet of prison food that was responsible, she'd always been slim, but looking at herself properly, she realised she needed to beef out a bit. And she would, soon, if everything went according to plan. Hopefully then she'd be dining out on the finest food, but for now, plain and simple was good. A reformed prisoner was the part she needed to play, and she would play it well.

She had to.

There'd be no second chances.

She opened the dirty-white front door of the flat, and fished in her bag for a reel of black cotton. She snapped a short length off and moistened it with saliva before bending down and placing it in a straight line on the dirty carpet that looked speckled, but in reality was filthy ground-in muck. She took a photo on her phone, and gently closed to the door behind her.

Not the most sophisticated trap in the world, but it would be evident if the cotton had moved that someone had been in the flat.

She trusted nobody.

Chapter 4

April gave her alias to the receptionist, "Gemma Dean to see Tom Campbell." She glanced at her watch, "Sorry, I'm a bit early, my appointment isn't until eleven."

The shrill of the telephone interrupted them.

"That's fine," the receptionist smiled, "have a seat. I'll just take this call and see if he's free."

She sat down on the well-used settee and gazed around the room wondering if the offices were only used for probation and parole services. The building was archaic, but with modern touches such as the doors with disability access, and the huge fire-exit signs. She ran her hand along the old radiator. Even though heat was blasting out, the room felt cold. It most probably had been built in the early part of the nineteenth century with its huge ceilings and wide door frames, a time when indoor heating wasn't part of life.

She tightened her jacket around her.

The door opened and a man in his mid-fifties walked towards the desk and handed the receptionist two envelopes as she hung up the phone.

"Can you put them in the post please, Emma?"

"Yes, of course," the receptionist took the envelopes from him. "Miss Dean's here to see you," she gestured with her head towards the seating area.

He turned and took two steps towards her, holding out his hand. April stood up and took it. It was a feeble handshake for a man.

"Hi. I'm Tom Campbell, pleased to meet you."

"Likewise," she smiled. So this was her parole officer. She hadn't been sure what to expect, it wasn't like she'd ever needed one before.

"Would you like to follow me," he instructed, and turned towards the receptionist. "Hold any calls for the next hour or so please, Emma."

"Will do," Emma answered, quickly taking another call.

They walked the endless corridors side by side. It seemed like his office was the furthest away from the reception area. The silence between them was interrupted occasionally by someone passing by, addressing him pleasantly.

"Here we are," he said eventually. He opened the door to his office and indicated she went in before him, "please take a seat." He nodded to a small area away from the desk which appeared to be set up as a meeting area with less formal chairs and a low coffee table.

It was a dismal old office which clearly hadn't seen a decorator for twenty years or so. It still appeared that whoever had occupied the office smoked at least twenty a day. Even the office furniture looked antiquated.

"Can I get you a coffee? It's only instant, I'm afraid."

"No, thank you," she sat down on the worn padded chair, lifted her satchel bag over her head and placed it on the floor beside her, "I'm fine. I just had one before I left home. But please, you go ahead."

"I've already had my quota this morning. I'm one of those people that can't function without coffee, so by mid-morning, I've had quite enough."

A tap on the door made them both turn their heads. Even before the door opened, April knew exactly who it was.

Today was all part of a well-rehearsed plan.

The last three months had been working towards this particular moment.

Chapter 5

"Looking good, April, how've you been?" her boss of the last three years asked as he took the seat opposite her and Tom.

Superintendent Paddy Frodsham hadn't changed in the three months since she'd last seen him. Still as portly, more so in fact, and his whisky nose looked marginally redder and puffed up from the copious amounts he most definitely was partial to.

"Not brilliant considering I've been locked up for the past twelve weeks," she answered flippantly.

He had the grace to look sympathetic. "No, I'm sure that must have been difficult, but it has been a necessary evil. Without that spell inside, we couldn't have moved forward."

It had been months since they'd initiated the undercover process. She knew exactly what was supposed to happen, but wasn't entirely sure how much had been shared with the parole officer. She moved her eyes sideways towards Tom Campbell on her left, silently asking the question about how much he'd been briefed.

Her boss read her thoughts. "Tom's up to speed about everything. He's going to be your parole officer in every sense of the word. As you know, he's assisted us with undercover work before."

It was reassuring to hear everything was in place, so they could move forward straight away. Spending so long incarcerated had been a real endurance test when all her adult life had been about enforcing the law. To have to appear to totally disregard her police officer training in prison had been the stuff nightmares were made of. Frustration didn't even come close.

"Do you want to explain your part," Paddy instructed the parole officer.

Tom took his cue. "Everything's set. Tomorrow I take you to the Carson Rider Gallery, and introduce you to the staff supervisor who'll complete the necessary paperwork. All being well you'll start work there the following day."

April knew the plan. It had been a painstakingly slow process to get to the stage they were at now, and while there were no guarantees they could pull it off, she was confident she could. Failure wasn't a word in her vocabulary.

"How long do you think we give it before I try my luck with Rider?" she asked her boss.

Paddy's eyebrows knitted together. "I think that very much depends on when the opportunity arises," he turned his attention to Tom, "we know Rider has a weakness for beautiful women," he smiled affectionately at her, "and they don't come any more beautiful than April. But we also know he's no fool. We need to take our time, we can't rush this."

"How often do I meet with you?" she asked Tom.

"For the first couple of weeks, once a week, and then we can go to fortnightly all being well. It's important that we do at least have telephone conversations. Parole officers are busy people, we don't have the time or the resources to be visiting every ex-con."

Even though her boss has said the sting couldn't be rushed, she needed some clarification. She'd been away from her family for so long already.

"How soon realistically do you think we can have this all wrapped up?"

"As I said . . ."

"I know what you said, Paddy," she interrupted, "but I need to have a time frame in my mind, even if it's just ballpark."

"We can't put a time frame on it, April, you know that. We have to find out where he's stashed the painting. As soon as we know, you're out of there."

That was easier said than done. The beautiful Magdalena Portillo portrait had been stolen four months earlier during the transportation from the airport to the National Gallery. There were absolutely no direct leads whatsoever, but intelligence had supported Dylan Rider being behind it. The police, along with the insurance company had examined cases over a number of years and suspected that he, and his brother, were more than likely behind heists of valuable artefacts. The difficulty was proving it. Each operation they carried out was very slick, and while they suspected Dylan and his brother had most definitely masterminded each robbery, it was going to be a considerable challenge getting the evidence to confirm it. To all intents and purposes, both brothers were affluent businessmen with not a hint of criminality between them.

Tom cleared his throat. "Far be it for me to pour water on a strategy the police force and insurance company have devised, but could I just say, while I understand this elaborate plan, and the lengths you are going to so you can expose this man, what makes you think Dylan Rider is going to spill the beans?" He gave a puzzled frown, "Okay, so he likes beautiful women, and even if April does entice him, he's not going to tell her where he's stashed one of the most expensive paintings in the world. Are you even sure he has it?"

"He has it alright," Paddy replied curtly, "and others too. Not as valuable as the Portillo, but we're confident that he's got a stash of them and he's not displaying those in that gallery of his, that's for sure. It's finding out where they are right now, and linking him to the initial robbery that's going to prove difficult."

"But you must have considered this could end up being a complete waste of time and resources? And to have April incarcerated for so long," he looked directly at her, "I take it they paid you well for that."

"She was paid well enough," Paddy snapped, "and don't call her April. From now on, she's Gemma. Gemma Dean," he emphasised, "have you got that?"

Tom nodded.

"You too," he repeated to April. "You need to remember the importance of being Gemma from now on. Don't think of yourself as April anymore, not for the next few weeks, at least."

"I do know that, Paddy," she glared, "I've been Gemma Dean for three months already."

Did he not realise how convincing she'd had to be to play the part of a prisoner?

"Good," he continued, "you don't need me to remind you, not only do we need to get Rider from a legal perspective, the insurance company are paying millions to get the painting back. This has to work, and I have every confidence it will if we all stick to the plan." He looked at Tom, "If it was anyone other than *Gemma,*" he emphasised the pseudonym, "then I'd share your concerns, but I know she will make it happen. There's nobody better than her at this."

April took a deep breath in. He was right, she'd done these stings before, but this would be her last. Not that she was going to tell them that. She always played her cards close to her chest, that's why she was good at what she did.

Paddy began rounding things up. "Right, so everything seems to be in place."

"Have you got my mobile phone?" she asked. She had the crap pay as you go one, but she wanted her own iPhone with all her contacts in.

"It's in the flat. In the bedroom, there's an ottoman. If you take the rug up, the floor boards lift. There's a handbag in there with your own personal bits in it. It's all been wiped though and replaced with fake stuff."

Wiped?

Shit.

"Is my sister's number still stored in it?"

"Yes, we've left that. You'll find it under, Molly Tym. And there's a small laptop with a fictitious Facebook account on it with photos of you as Gemma Dean. The password is all one word, MollyTym18. It's all there in the handbag."

She raised an eyebrow. "The police department are giving out handbags now are they? It's not a Michael Kors by any chance, is it?"

"Rest assured, it isn't," Paddy replied curtly, "domestic staff cleaning toilets at an art gallery don't as a rule, carry Michael Kors handbags."

"Yeah," she sighed, "point taken. What about the cover story, is that set up on the internet?"

"Yes, that's been there a while. You worked for Forrest Mount Accountants in Wales and stole some money from the firm with your accomplice, David Grange. He went to jail for five years, you for two. You've spent the last twelve weeks in Colverton open prison pending your release; it's all there for anyone to see."

"What about the stolen money?"

"It's written that David Grange's assets were frozen so the implication is the money was retrieved. You both got your prison sentences and your transfer to Colverton fits in perfectly as a way of rehabilitation for you, ready for your release. He's supposedly still inside, and the accountants went into liquidation. As you know, that's why we chose that particular company."

"That's good. They'll definitely be checking it all out."

"They will if they've got any sense. Dylan Rider's no dummy. He'll know everything there is to know about you before you even set foot in the gallery. Remember also, the last girl who went to clean there as part of a rehabilitation programme from prison, has since disappeared. We're sure they got her involved in something illegal. We know when she left the UK, and she's certainly not come back as yet. We have a customs alert to flag when she does."

April turned to Tom. "What time do I need to be at the gallery tomorrow?"

"Five p.m. They like the gallery cleaning in the evening. I'll introduce you to Ingrid Ruth, the supervisor. She's had ex-cons before, but I need to warn you, she's a strange one. Keep your head down, and don't whatever you do get on the wrong side of her, otherwise she'll have you out of there and you'll not be retrieving any paintings, that's for sure."

Paddy stood up and moved towards the door. "Give me five minutes before you leave. Remember, Tom's your point of contact. It's more legitimate this way. It will be expected he'll be keeping in touch with you. I'll see you at eleven on Saturday at Victoria Park. And don't rush this," he warned, "we've come this far, we need to take our time."

"That's easy for you to say," she replied cynically, "you haven't been locked up in prison for the last three months, and now stuck in a grotty flat for God knows how long."

She thought about her beautiful home and how desperately she longed to be back sitting in her lounge, listening to music and clutching a glass of red.

"Yeah, but you'll reap the rewards when the lot of them are banged up. That's the police officer in you . . . *Gemma*. See you Saturday."

"And good luck," he said quietly as he closed the door behind him.

She stared at the closed door and then, and purely for her own benefit, she spoke out loud.

"This is it then. Goodbye April Masters . . . hello Gemma Dean."

***

He was pissed off waiting.

Boredom had made him chew that much gum, his jaw ached. The car was becoming claustrophobic despite the window being open, and his eyes almost ached from staring at the back door of the parole office building.

He'd watched Paddy Frodsham slip in, and waited for him to leave about thirty minutes later. He knew April would give her boss time to get away before she left also, and, as he predicted, he used the back door.

He started the engine and put the car into gear. He wanted to be at the front of the building when she came out. It only took a minute or so and he found a space far enough away, but with a good view of the entrance for when she came out.

He fixed his eyes on the front door of the draconian building.

It had been twelve weeks and three long days since he'd last seen her.

Seconds later, she emerged and stood on the steps. He watched her scrunch her beautiful green eyes up at the bright sunlight, and reach inside her bag to pull out a pair of oversized sunglasses and put them on.

His gut thumped. From a distance she was as stunning as he remembered. Only she could make cheap chain store sunglasses, look sexy.

As she made her way down the street, he watched every step she took. She was graceful, like a gazelle with her long slender legs moving quickly as she hurriedly walked along the pavement.

He started the car and followed her until she stopped at the bus stop.

Where was she off to now?

She appeared every inch a woman without money in her faded jeans, oversized jumper and cap on top of her head. He couldn't quite make out the logo as he was too far away. It'd be something cryptic no doubt.

Only he knew that underneath that ordinary exterior, was a beautiful young woman who effortlessly slipped into the role of a commuter.

Nobody in the bus queue would have any idea the woman stood alongside them was a highly decorated police officer.

Chapter 6

April hated buses. There was something about being closely confined with other people she didn't like. Maybe that was the police officer in her which saw members of the public as trouble because her whole working life had been responding to their needs. She much preferred the solitary quietness of her car to get from A to B, and she silently vowed that once this job was finished, she'd not use public transport again.

A bus passed by, going the other way, and she observed the miserable faces of those that were sat on it looking out of the windows. Buses reminded her of a time in her life when she had nothing. Those days all she would dream about was making a better life.

She'd spent most of her childhood in care, and her greatest desire once she was old enough to realise there was a way out, was to become a police officer. It was that which saw her through the endless years of foster homes she and her beloved sister had been placed in.

Her sister was the complete opposite to her. Chloe spent most of her life being a victim in some form or another. Although they changed schools frequently, Chloe was always on the receiving end of someone who was determined to make her life hell. At college she was excluded from groups and it wasn't long before she had left college, using the excuse she wanted to work rather than spend her time in the classroom.

Their young lives had been shaped to a certain extent by their drug addict mother who had injected herself once too often with dodgy heroine that eventually killed her, which meant for the two girls, years of being under the care of the local authority.

Since their mother had died, she'd become a surrogate mother to Chloe. It happened naturally as she'd been the much stronger and forceful of the two, which didn't just stem from her being older by eighteen months; it was more that she was an achiever. Sadly, Chloe wasn't.

They'd been fortunate with their final placement with foster carers who encouraged them both with academic work. But while she thrived on it, Chloe was miserable. Most of their early childhood, she'd managed to protect Chloe from the bullying, even though it became increasingly more difficult as they got to secondary school. She had been academically able, whereas Chloe struggled. As a consequence, they were segregated by ability and spent most of the time in different areas of the school which caused Chloe a lot of distress.

No-one would dare bully April Masters; they'd be too fearful of what they might get in return. Her whole persona had been one of toughness, which had pushed her in the direction of the police force at the age of eighteen. Following two years of police training, and the mandatory probationary period, she'd been told by her superiors she was an exceptional police officer, but she already knew that. Not once had she ever hidden behind a male officer. Initially, when she'd completed her police training, she was put on traffic duties, and during that period she booked more motorists for offences than any other officer. As she progressed in the force, she gained the respect of colleagues. April Masters was one to look up to. If there was a domestic violence call, she was the first in the house; if there was an attempted robbery at a late-night off-license; she was the first in the shop. Her career was about succeeding, and when she was on duty, the criminals needed to look out. Failure wasn't an option to her. She was dedicated and focussed, so she swiftly went through the ranks from police officer to sergeant, inspector and to detective inspector.

Eventually, the force offered her two options, either the Police Armed Division, or undercover work. She chose the latter. She liked the idea of pitting her wits against the criminal fraternity, and better still, bringing them to justice. And she did just that. It didn't matter how long each sting took, she made it happen.

Nobody scared her. She wasn't fearful of anyone, or anything.

The one thing in her favour had been her looks which she used to her advantage on many occasions. Why not? There was no point in looking like she did, and not using that. It wasn't about being vain, far from it, she wasn't bothered what she looked like. If she had been, she'd have been gutted to have cut her long thick blonde hair short. On some women, the cropped look would be too harsh, but she had the bone structure to carry it off. It suited her. And if the occasion arose, which it undoubtedly would shortly, she would be able to dress up like the rest of them. A bit of gel on her fingers, and a quick fluff up at the roots, and she'd look like a trendy fashion model. And even though the vast majority of men loved women with long flowing hair, she knew she was beautiful however she wore her hair. She'd never been short of admirers, but she kept men compartmentalised in her life. As far as she was concerned, she used them like they used her.

She stood up and pressed the bell to notify the bus driver she wanted to get off, before making her way down the aisle to the exit door.

The task ahead now was to bring Dylan Rider down, and she was going to succeed.

Nothing was more certain.

Failure wasn't a word in her vocabulary.

Chapter 7

Just as Paddy had said, the handbag was there under the ottoman. April delved into the black leather bag and removed a laptop and her mobile phone. The laptop would be one issued by the tech department and she knew it would contain material a single woman would have. All the emails and Facebook account would be in the name of her alias, Gemma Dean. Even her iPhone had been set up.

She clicked on a couple of the text messages. They were innocuous girly chats with people she didn't even know, but for anyone finding the phone, it wouldn't look amiss.

She pressed her sister's number as the coded Molly Tym that Paddy had told her. Even if she didn't utter a word, she would know it was Chloe when she answered as invariably music would be playing in the background. If it wasn't, something would be wrong.

The melody of Sam Smith's, *Stay with Me* lingered in the background as Chloe answered. "April! Thank God!" she shrieked.

"Hi Chlo."

Her sister's voice went up in pitch, "Where the hell have you been? We haven't heard from you for months?"

"I know, I'm sorry, I've been on an extended work thing."

"Where? Didn't you get my messages?"

Chloe had every right to be angry, but how could she have phoned? She couldn't allow her cover to be broken. The spell in prison had been the longest time ever she'd not spoken to her beloved sister. But she was out now, so would make up for it as soon as this last job was over.

"I couldn't get back to you; I've been out of the country." Although she'd been expecting Chloe's wrath, it still felt uncomfortable. "It's been a difficult time, I've really missed you."

"Where've you been that you couldn't have sent a text? I've been worried sick. You could have at least let me know you were okay."

"I know and I've said I'm sorry. It was a one off and it won't happen again, I promise. Tell me about Noah, how's he doing?"

Chloe was easily distracted. Noah, her four year old son, was her life.

"He's fine," her voice softened, "we've got another fundraising on Saturday night at the club. We've raised twenty-five thousand so far."

April sighed. That was nowhere near the hundred grand needed to take Noah to Missouri for treatment. It wasn't just the surgery, there was the aftercare, all the physiotherapy and learning to walk, and there would need to be accommodation while her sister and husband stayed in the US with Noah. Probably the one hundred thousand pounds was an underestimate.

"Twenty-five grand, that's amazing, well done. I'll be able to add to that soon, I'll be getting a pay-out at the end of this job I'm doing, so I can send you some."

"Oh, April, you've given us more than you can afford to, you need your money."

"Noah needs it more. I want to help, I've missed him so much."

"He misses you too. He's always asking when you are coming. I don't know what bloody job you're doing, but surely you can visit, even if it's just for the day. Please say you'll come."

Her sister's plea wrenched at her gut, but there was no way she could go right now. At the end of this job, she'd have plenty of time to see them.

"I can't, Chlo, I would if I could. But I promise you, this will be my last job, and then I'll have all the time in the world to visit you. In fact, I might even move. I don't need to be in the city once I'm no longer working."

"Yeah, right. Like you're gonna give up the job you love. You thrive on it. It's all you've ever wanted to do since you were a little girl."

"I know but I'm not going to give up completely. I'll just go into security or something like that. I'll do anything that will allow me to be in my own bed each night."

"Can you afford to do that? You've got a lot of years ahead of you to work?"

"I think so, I'll have to see. But like I said, this is the last job."

"How long is it going to be? Is this a one-off conversation like the last time, and I won't hear from you for three months?"

Yes, it was exactly like that. She might be able to manage an odd phone call, but it wouldn't be any more than that for the foreseeable future. She actually preferred to work without any interruptions. When she did a job, which invariably entailed becoming an alias, she liked to concentrate on just that. She couldn't have any distractions.

"I'll do my best to keep in touch," she reassured, "but you know how it is."

"Oh, I know all right. Your work always comes first, your family second."

"Don't be like that. I'll make it up to you, I promise. Can I speak to my gorgeous nephew, is he there?"

Chloe sighed, "I'll put him on, but I want to speak to you before you go. Don't be hanging up."

"I won't."

"Just a sec, then."

She waited. It had been so long since she'd spoken to Noah, her heart was actually racing.

She heard Chloe in the background, "It's Auntie April, say hello."

A tiny voice came through, "Hello."

"Hello, my favourite soldier, how are you?"

"I've just been for an ice cream."

"Have you? Was it one of those big white whippy ones with a cone?"

"Yeah, and I had a chocolate flake."

"Oh, you lucky boy, I love those."

"You can come next time if you want to." His sweet voice pained her heart. How long before she would be able to?

"Can I? I'd love that. I'm going to come and see you soon, or maybe you can visit me. Would you like that?"

"With Mummy?"

"Yes of course with Mummy."

"Can we go to the cinema again?"

"Why not? We liked it last time, didn't we? Your mummy told us off for eating too much chocolate, can you remember?"

He giggled. "When can we go?"

"Soon my darling I promise. Right now I've got to go to work, but I'm going to post a little present for you. So, in two days, look out for the postman, and see what he brings you. Will you do that?"

"How many sleeps?"

"Well, let's say three to be on the safe side, and then you should get something from me."

"Okay."

"Alright, put Mummy back on so I can say goodbye to her. And don't forget, even when I can't get to see you, I'm always thinking about you. I love you very much, sweetheart."

He didn't reply but she knew he was nodding his little head.

"I'll get Mummy. Bye bye."

"Bye bye, my darling. Love you loads."

Chloe took a while, but eventually came back on the phone. "What have you promised him? He's on about the postman coming."

"I've just said I'll put a little something in the post for him. I told him to watch out for the postman."

"Thanks for that," she replied sarcastically, "he'll be plaguing me to death every day now."

A smile twitched April's lips, she knew exactly what he'd be like. "What about you, Chlo, are you okay?"

"Yeah, fine. Gavin might be getting a promotion at work, nothing definite, but he thinks he might be in with a chance. It will mean a bit more money coming in which we could do with. If he does get it, he says the first thing he's going to do is a makeover in Noah's bedroom."

"Aw, that sounds lovely; I'll keep everything crossed for him."

She thought about her brother-in-law, Gavin. Not the sharpest tool in the box, but a hardworking man. And he loved Noah so much. He'd walk to the ends of the earth for him. Nobody could do more for their disabled son than he did. Her sister wouldn't have been able to cope without him.

Her and Chloe were a real chalk and cheese mix. It was hard to believe they were sisters really, they were so different. Chloe was highly strung and worried about everything, whereas she didn't have a nervous bone in her body.

"Right, I'd better get off, Chlo, look after yourself and I'll be in touch when I can."

"Okay." April could hear the disbelief in her sister's voice, "Watch what you're doing. I have no idea what these secret jobs are, but for goodness' sake take care. I'm sure there must be some risks involved."

"Hey, don't you be worrying like that, the jobs are nothing of that nature," she reassured. It's just a bit of undercover work, that's all, and as I said, this is the last one I'm doing."

How could she tell her sister that every job she did had danger attached to it?

"I'll believe that when I see it," Chloe replied. "Oh, before you go, I haven't told you. Noah goes to school on the bus now instead of me taking him. There's a driver and a designated lady, Moira, who helps the children get on and off the bus."

"That's brilliant. It'll be good for him to get a bit of independence."

"Yes, he loves it. I just get freezing now waiting at the bus stop. I go in the car sometimes if it's really cold, even though it's only round the corner."

"I don't blame you, I would too. Give him a big kiss from me, won't you?"

"Of course I will. You will call again? Promise me it won't be another three months."

"I promise," she reassured and repeated the childhood saying which they always did at the end of their conversations, "love you to the moon and back."

She knew her sister was smiling, "You too. Please take care."

"I will, I promise. Bye for now."

She placed the phone in the handbag and lent forward to carefully place it in the hole below the floorboards. The small rug hid the loose floorboards and she dragged the ottoman over the top. The cheap pay as you go phone would suffice for now. It would look odd having the latest iPhone for the part she was about to play. She had to continue with the deception of being poor.

She stretched out on the uncomfortable bed with a lumpy mattress that should have been thrown out years ago, and picked up the glossy brochure Tom had given her about the Carson Rider gallery. There was a sleek picture of the charismatic owner, Dylan Rider, but no mention of his brother, Victor, who she knew was more of a silent partner.

It appeared that the gallery was founded by their father in the eighties.

Each page was impressive with the vast amount of paintings exhibited. She knew all there was to know from studying it prior to her time inside, but it was good to refresh her memory.

The ground floor of the gallery was open to the public. It was tastefully decorated with the wide walk-through areas and strategic seating which would allow people to sit and enjoy the paintings on show. There were a number of valuable paintings listed, with a brief description of the history of each one.

As part of her rehabilitation programme, her job was going to be cleaning. Seemingly, Dylan Rider liked to give ex-prisoners the chance to rehabilitate. She was, with the support of her parole officer, to spend three months working there. The rent on her flat was being paid, and she'd receive a salary with an increment from the prison rehabilitation programme. So, to all intents and purposes, her rehabilitation was state funded. In reality, the police force was paying her, and the insurance company once the Portillo was recovered.

Over the last twelve weeks in the open prison, she had got used to being prisoner, Gemma Dean. She had supposedly been transferred there from Campden female prison, having served two years for fraud. Any online searches done on her which the police knew would be likely to happen, would all come up with Gemma Dean. There was even a birth certificate and passport in the name of Gemma Dean.

The worst part of the operation up to now had been the stay in prison. Every single day inside had dragged. She'd tried working in the laundry initially which was okay, but eventually got a move to the kitchens which were more to her liking. There she met Julia, and they became friends. Julia made her prison stretch bearable.

There was a hierarchy amongst the prisoners which they'd tried to enforce on her. Each cluster group amongst the prisoners had a menacing leader, and the inmates fitted into one of the groups. April fitted into none, and she had no intention of doing so.

She was more of a loner, which clearly annoyed Irene Ball, one of the ring-leaders. It started out when she was asked to do small things such as lending an inmate some money or smuggling extra food out of the kitchens. She didn't smoke so couldn't share cigarettes, but they were always wanting stuff from her. Initially, when she ignored them, they left her alone, most probably as they weren't entirely sure if she would conform. But like any bullies, Irene and her gang needed to find a weakness. When she refused to comply, things started to happen. Toiletries went missing from her cell, and a couple of photos were defaced, which didn't bother her too much as they were fake anyway. But the final straw was finding urine in her bed.

Her temper had raged.

Undercover or not, she was having none of that.

She'd made her way to the recreation room and asked her friend Julia to distract the prison guard. Irene Ball was watching television with her buddies sat around fawning over her.

April went up to her chair and from behind, trapped her head in a headlock.

She glared at the cronies sat alongside, "Don't any of you move a fucking muscle."

They stared but didn't attempt to intervene.

Through gritted teeth, she told Irene, "I know exactly how to break your neck if I want to, so you'd better keep still. Got it?"

She tightened her grip, making it difficult for Irene to breathe let alone speak. Irene got the message and nodded with her eyes.

"You've put piss on my bed, so I'll tell you what we're going to do now. We are going to your cell and we are swapping mattresses. You're having the one with piss on, and I'm having yours."

April dragged Irene out of the chair still with her hands locked around her neck. She fixed her eyes on the group of women ready to spring off their chairs. She spoke quietly so she didn't attract any of the prison officers.

"I'm going to release my arms and this fat bitch and I are walking together to our cells. Don't any of you dare try and alert the guards. If anyone does, they'll have me to answer to. Have you morons all got that?"

The cronies had nodded in unison, surprise etched all over their well-worn faces that someone, who up until then had been largely solitary, had dared to tackle Irene of all people.

She'd released her arms from around Irene's neck and linked an arm through hers.

"You as much as itch your fucking nose, and you'll be sorry," she'd warned.

They'd walked out of the recreation room and past the prison guard. If it looked like they were going to their cell for some intimacy, she didn't care.

Irene's eyes had been filled with hatred, furious at being humiliated in front of her cronies, no doubt. But all bullies relied on compliance, and Irene knew she'd met her match with April.

For the rest of her sentence, April continued to be solitary, but by attacking the leader of the pack who the inmates all looked up to, she'd gained credence and respect.

She sighed, thank God that part of her life was now over. She stared at the dingy off-white ceiling that must have last seen paint twenty-five years ago, and contemplated how long she would have to be there. Prison had been necessary; but part two of the plan started right now.

Tomorrow she would finally be one step closer to Dylan Rider.

Softly, softly catches the monkey.

Chapter 8

April would have preferred to have met Tom, her parole officer at the gallery, but he'd insisted she was to come to the office and he would take her and introduce her to Ingrid Ruth the cleaning supervisor, who would be her boss for the next three months.

Although she didn't know Tom Campbell personally, she knew enough about him from the file the police held. She was one of those lucky individuals that could retain information. If she was asked, she could recite verbatim exactly how his life had panned out from university to his current position as a highly regarded parole officer. She'd researched every single detail about everyone she was to come into contact with to bring Rider to justice.

Tom put the car into gear and moved away to the car park exit.

"How you getting along with public transport?" he asked. "You must be more used to nipping around in a Volkswagen Golf or something, rather than the local bus service?"

"Yeah," she nodded, "but I think they might smell a rat if I turned up in a flash car for a cleaning job."

"I'm sure you're right," he agreed, turning his head from left to right as he edged the car out of the car park onto the main road. "How are you feeling, nervous?"

"Nope. Keen to get started. It's been a long time getting to this point."

"Tell me," he asked, "why does a beautiful young woman like you want to get involved in this? You're not telling me it isn't without risks."

She didn't answer. What business was it of his?

"Is it just the money?" he pressed.

"Mmm, something like that." She turned to stare out of the window, hoping he'd get the message and shut up. He did for a few minutes but when he stopped at traffic lights, he asked, "Isn't there some bloke out there wanting you at home with him?"

It's probably easier to verbally shut him up.

She turned her face towards him as he concentrated on his driving and the road ahead.

"Tom, the less you know about me, the better. Any why, what, who or where, has nothing to do with you. I can't stress enough that it's absolutely necessary for you to be my parole officer, nothing more. I understand you have been chosen due to your ability to be of assistance to us, so I need you to forget who I am, just treat me as one of your ex-cons." She widened her eyes questioningly, "I'm hoping that won't be too difficult for you."

She waited for him to nod he understood where she was coming from. She carried on, "And please don't try and second guess me. I have this covered, but only if you go along with what I say. Don't be thinking you can save me . . . I'm just a young woman . . . I need protecting. I don't. I'm an experienced police officer, and while I'm quite sure things may unexpectedly change from the plan, I'm more than adequately prepared for that. What I don't need is you deviating from your part. You treat me as you would anyone else released from prison."

"Okay," he nodded, "I've got it. I'm your parole officer. No slipping out of that. If that's what you want."

"That's exactly what I want, and what you're being paid to do. The last thing I need is for my cover to be blown. One mistake could mean it's all over."

"You can rely on me," he reassured, "they're paying me enough to pull this off. With a bit of luck, when this is all finished, I'll be able to take early retirement."

"Let's hope it's not going to take too long, then."

"Well, like I already said, it could be over before it begins if you get on the wrong side of the cleaning supervisor, Ingrid Ruth. We've had ex-prisoners start their rehabilitation here before, but they never last long. She sees to it they don't. I don't profess to know the working ways of a woman's mind, but I do know the ones that look anything like you, don't last." He lifted his eyebrows, "So whatever happens, don't get on the wrong side of her."

She knew all there was to know about Ingrid Ruth. She didn't need advice from him.

"Thanks, I won't."

"Right, we'll get you started in there, the rest is up to you. You've got my number in your phone, haven't you?"

"Yes."

"Use it if you have to. It's perfectly legitimate for you to have problems initially which may result in you contacting me."

"Thank you, I will."

Shut up now for Christ's sake.

"Can I ask you one thing?"

She widened her eyes as if to say, yes, only one more though.

"What makes you think you can pull this off? I mean, Dylan Rider's no fool, and neither is that brother of his, Victor. They have a reputation of being a formidable pair. What makes you think you've got what it takes to bring them down?"

He turned into the gallery car park and pulled into one of the vacant designated staff spaces. She waited until he applied the brake and cut the engine so that she had his complete attention.

"Just stick to your part of the plan," she emphasised, "that's all you need to do. As for me, I have precisely what it takes, and from now on, you're going to see a different side of me. I'll be playing a part, you need to remember to play yours and treat me exactly the same as any other ex-con."

She rested her hand on the door handle but didn't open it.

With a determined look on her face, and calmness in her voice, she emphasised, "And just so you know, I will bring Dylan Rider down. Nothing's more certain than that."

Chapter 9

Dylan Rider checked his watch. He needed to make a move to get to the restaurant on time to meet Victor. They had a lot to discuss, and he preferred to do that while dining on fine food. Walls had ears, so the conversation they needed to have was better done under the guise of a family meal.

They needed to move the Portillo. Jit Monks and the gang wanted paying. They'd agreed in the beginning there would be a period of time when they couldn't move the painting, but they would need to shift it in the next couple of months. The last thing anyone wanted was to be caught in possession of it.

He'd spoken to the contact in France, and suggested a couple more months before they needed to think about moving it. He'd share that with Victor over dinner tonight.

They'd managed to pay off the small fry initially involved in the robbery, but Jit wanted his money. The plan was to move the painting across the channel where they had a buyer for it.

Things had certainly died down in the media, the robbery was hardly mentioned now. When they'd first stolen it, the cops were everywhere, not to mention the insurance company.

Fortunately, no-one suspected him and Victor; there was nothing to link them to it. That's how he and Vic operated. They'd masterminded heists, with virtually nothing that could tie them to each one. They were seen as legitimate buyers in the art world. Victor was in gem merchandise, while he managed the art side of the business.

He reached for his sports jacket and looked out of the office window which overlooked the back of the gallery. A male and a female stood at the back entrance. The door was heavily secured and only ever opened by the security man, Joey Jacobs. He liked Joey. Although he hadn't been at the gallery that long, he was a hard worker, polite, and Dylan felt he was loyal. Loyalty was important to him.

He checked his Rolex. It was almost six, his usual time for leaving. He liked to be around when the cleaners arrived to start their work at five. Ingrid stayed to supervise them until they finished at eight. Although he had a secretary to support him, he paid Ingrid to oversee the staff, which included the caretakers, reception staff, the security staff and the cleaners.

The gallery had to have security personnel at all times, even overnight. The burglar alarms were part funded by a generous contribution from the insurers. And even though they were as sophisticated as money could buy, there had to be in-house security as well. Joey did the late afternoon and evening shift, and his other security bloke, Robert did the morning shift. He also employed night security men.

You couldn't be too careful.

He knew only too well the intricacies of security.

He made it his business to.

He watched the two people waiting to be let into the gallery, a middle-aged bloke and a young woman. Ingrid had told him earlier a new cleaner would be starting that evening at six, so he deduced this must be her. She wasn't very old, he knew that from the information had had on her. Twenty-nine, which made her younger than the last girl, but this one was beautiful if her photograph was anything to go by. She had to be easy on the eye; any future plans would only succeed if she was attractive. He'd approved her probation because of her looks, and of course the criminal background.

That was essential.

Almost as if she knew she being watched, the young woman's eyes drifted up towards his window. As quickly as she saw him, she looked away. No doubt distracted by the door being opened in front of her.

She wouldn't last long. These prison ones never did. They started out with this positive attitude of not returning to prison . . . they were never going to get on the wrong side of the law again, yet invariably they did. Lawlessness was innate in them, which is precisely why he provided them with an opportunity to at least try and go straight. But if they wished to continue down the deviant path, then they were in the right place.

She disappeared from his view.

It didn't matter for now. He'd find out from Ingrid what she was like in a week or two.

It was far too early to speculate if she might be useful.

Chapter 10

April rubbed the hand basin taps with a clean cloth to make them shine. She'd been cleaning at the gallery three nights and had barely got out of the toilets. Every evening was the same. Her first job was the toilets on the top floor adjacent to the offices, then she moved down a floor to the first floor and cleaned the public toilets, and finally the ground floor. Once she'd done them and passed Ingrid Ruth's rigorous inspection, she was then sent to the staff kitchen to clean that area, which was a significant challenge. Quite how the daytime staff could make so much mess was a mystery. There can't have been that many of them working there.

The toilet door opened, "Coffee time," her cheerful cleaning colleague Rachel smiled, "I've made you one."

Rachel was a lovely girl. What she lacked in intelligence, she made up for in personality. She was a breath of fresh air, always smiling and giggling. She was a pretty, petite young thing which seemed to make her all the more endearing. It was surprising she was actually forty as she could easily pass for early thirties. Rachel had made cleaning toilets bearable, and even though she'd only just met her, April warmed to her.

She flung her rubber gloves down. "Great, I'm ready for it. Do we have Ingrid's approval?" She followed Rachel and they walked together down the back stairs. Ingrid didn't like them using the lifts.

"She never minds us having a break, she just doesn't want us to take too long. She knows I need a ciggy, she smokes herself."

"I haven't seen her."

Rachel shook her head, "No, I haven't either."

"How do you know, then?"

"I just do. When you smoke, you can tell those that do, and I know she's a smoker."

They collected their coffees from the staff room and headed for the back door where the security guard was waiting to let them out. He'd introduced himself to her the first night as Joseph Jacobs, but to call him Joey, as everyone did, apart from his mother he'd added with a wink which had amused her.

Joey was a smoker too.

He joined them for their break as they needed him to let them in and out of the building. Nobody managed that without him. He let them in at five when they arrived for their shift each evening, and out of the building again at eight.

"Alright, ladies," Joey greeted them, clutching his own drink. "How are you two hot chicks this evening?"

He tapped in a code number and held up his badge for scanning.

The door opened. Only he and Ingrid had the code.

"Excited," Rachel answered as the door closed behind them. "I've got a date after I finish here tonight."

Joey grinned and passed her a cigarette out of his packet and held his lighter towards it to light hers before his own. He inhaled a deep breath of the nicotine. "I thought you looked a bit glam when you arrived tonight," he puffed smoke into the air.

April sipped her coffee, watching him. He was a good-looking man, so she could easily see why Rachel was attracted to him. Mid-thirties, and he seemed reasonably fit underneath his security uniform. His dark hair was cut short, and his neck showed muscle that no doubt shaped his entire body. He had a firm chest and his abdomen looked perfectly flat, so he obviously worked out. His eyes were a warm brown colour, framed by neat brows. A prominent, well-defined nose dominated his face, but it suited him. His chin was obscured by a fuzzy thin beard.

"Who's the lucky man?" Joey asked Rachel.

"His name is Jonathon Hall and he's a lifeguard."

"Oh, right, you swim a lot in your spare time, do you?" Joey grinned.

"No, stupid," she rolled her eyes, "I met him at a pub, actually."

"What pub? Have you bombed mine out, then?"

"No. If I get a second date with Jonathon, I'll bring him. Hey, why don't you ask Gemma to join you? She might fancy a night out."

April held her hand up in protest, "Err, no thank you," she smiled apologetically at Joey, "I don't want to be going out at the moment."

"Why's that then?" Rachel blew smoke out of her mouth, "You're single, aren't you?"

"Yes, and that's the way I want to stay."

"You're not on the other bus, are you?" Joey asked.

She shook her head. "I'm not looking for a date, that's all. What about you, which bus are you on?" she asked cheekily.

"Oh God, Gemma, don't get him on that," Rachel laughed, "Joey's really homophobic."

"No, I'm not," Joey replied indignantly, "I don't get it, that's all. I wouldn't persecute anyone who was that way inclined."

"Why do you call them shirt-lifters then? That's homophobic."

"It isn't," he grinned, "it's my opinion, nowt wrong with that. I just don't get why blokes fancy men when there are stacks of gorgeous women around."

"Shame you can't find one that likes you, then." Rachel squeezed his cheek playfully, "You'll end up on the shelf you will, you're that choosy."

"I'd rather be on the shelf than stuck with a woman and be miserable."

Rachel scrunched up her nose, "Yeah, but you must get lonely on your own all the time?"

Joey shrugged.

"What about you, Gemma, don't you get lonely?" Rachel asked her.

"No, not really."

"Well, if you ever are," Joey interjected, "let me know. You can come and join a bunch of us at the pub I go to. They're a great crowd."

"Yeah, you should, Gemma," Rachel added enthusiastically, "I've been a few times. Joey's friends are a real laugh. It gets you out if you're a bit fed up."

"Thanks, I'll remember that. Maybe in a few weeks I'll get out on the social scene a bit more. I don't mind my own company actually."

"God," Rachel pulled a face, "I can't stand being on my own. I have to go out, I'd go crackers in my flat every night. Plus," she winked, "you do need to find something to keep you warm at night if only to save on the heating bills."

Joey rolled his eyes.

"I don't know why you're pulling a face, Joey, you're always out. And you're not telling me you aren't on the pull."

"I'm not telling you anything," he grinned, putting his cigarette out against the wall and placing the stub back in the packet. "Right, we'd better get back otherwise we'll have Ingrid on our backs. I swear she has eyes in the back of her head, she'll know exactly what time we came outside."

"You're right," Rachel agreed, "I think she has some sort of special powers as she seems to know about stuff I haven't even told her. God knows how. Maybe she has a tracking device on us with a microphone attached."

"Christ, I'll have to watch what I say then," April smiled, enjoying their banter.

"Yeah, you specially, she'll have her eye on you, that's for sure." Rachel suddenly looked pained as if she'd dropped a huge gaff, "Sorry, I didn't mean anything . . ."

"It's okay," April reassured, "I know they'll be watching me like a hawk. I've got to work on earning people's trust. This job's actually a stop-gap for me. I want to make a fresh start and as soon as I can . . . you know, move on with a different job where nobody knows about my past."

"Good for you. We had another girl like you, Lilly, she came to us from prison, but she disappeared suddenly. I really liked her. I was disappointed when she just left without a goodbye. I thought she was my friend."

"Aw, that's a shame." They walked back into the building together, and Joey secured the door behind them.

"Yeah, I wish she'd have kept in touch, I'd love to know how she's doing."

"Maybe Ingrid might know where she's gone. Have you asked her?"

"Only once, but she didn't seem to know. She wasn't bothered," she lowered her voice, "more worried about the inconvenience of having to find a replacement."

April knew exactly where Lilly O'Brian had gone. She'd certainly left the country; the police knew that much about her. They just didn't have the evidence that the Rider brothers had assisted her with the finances to do so.

Yet.

Chapter 11

It was week two of cleaning toilets, and still no result. April sprayed the vanity mirror and vigorously polished it working hard to make sure there weren't any smears. She stared back at herself. Minimal eye make-up, just enough to enhance her eyes which were deep green today, but some days looked a completely different colour depending on what she was wearing. Because her hair was now short, she had small decorative ear-rings to enhance the cropped look and make herself look more attractive. She quite liked what she saw. Understated, but pretty. Hopefully it would be enough to catch Dylan Rider's eye. She'd seen him in the distance a few times before he left each evening, usually from behind, but had not yet spoken to him directly. Ingrid Ruth saw to that. Every time she turned around, Ingrid seemed to be there giving her yet another cleaning job.

She knew with absolute certainty Ingrid didn't like her. It was more sensing it than anything else because she was used to it. Most of her adult life she came across females who didn't like her. She was tough in her police officers role, she had to be to succeed at the level she worked at in the male dominated profession. But it wasn't the toughness that was currently off-putting as the part she was playing made her submissive and compliant. It was the fact that women like Ingrid saw her as a threat. And she was exactly the same as any other woman; apart from one thing . . . Ingrid wanted Dylan Rider for herself. That was the gut feeling of the police officer within her. She'd seen Ingrid come out of his office one night, flushed and heading for the toilet. Her intuition told her they'd just had sex. It certainly hadn't been a long session though; April had timed her going in and coming out. It couldn't have been more than a quick wham bam.

An unexpected bonus of being at the gallery each evening was seeing Rachel and Joey. She loved the banter with them, they were a real laugh and thoroughly decent people. She didn't come across too many of those in her job.

Rachel had confided in her that she liked Joey, but he'd never made any advances towards her. She still persisted that he might be gay, likening him to a closet one as he gave the impression he favoured women. April dismissed that. Joey didn't appear one bit gay to her.

Even though Rachel had seemingly set her sights on him, she clearly wasn't the type to linger if she wasn't making headway, although none of the men she met seemed to work out. She was a good-looking woman, so could certainly attract blokes, but it sounded as if her encounters never got past the one-night stand phase. Not that it deterred her. After each knock back, she seemed to be up again for the next challenge.

April was getting impatient now to make some headway with Dylan Rider, even if it was just to meet him. She tied a knot in the two black bags of rubbish and glanced around the toilets; the surfaces sparkled, and the dirty grout between the tiles, now looked much cleaner. She'd taken in a toothbrush, and worked her way along the grimy tiles, scrubbing a bit each evening to remove the ground-in dirt. There was something about cleaning that she liked. It was a purpose with an end result. Very task orientated. She knew she was doing a good job, and even though Ingrid didn't like her, she seemed pleased with her work.

She dropped one of the bags to open the door, and held it ajar with her foot.

A male voice startled her. "Here, let me."

Dylan Rider moved towards the door and held it open for her.

Halleluiah!

The moment she'd been waiting for.

The pictures and VT's she'd seen of him had demonstrated how attractive he was, but nothing had prepared her for him up close. Dressed in a navy suit that had quality written all over it, he looked every inch, a wealthy man. He was breathtakingly handsome with his olive skin and dark hair which was cropped short, but it was naturally thick and tiny curls had started to sprout which was most probably due to being the end of the day. She'd wager a bet it would be much slicker first thing in a morning when he'd just washed it and probably used products to settle it down. His thick angular jaw had a day's growth darkening it. No doubt that too wouldn't be evident first thing in a morning either. The end-of-the-day look suited him. He appeared incredibly masculine causing an unexpected flutter to spread through her.

"Thank you," she smiled and walked through the door with the two bags, one in each hand.

"Shall I take those?" he asked.

"There's really no need," she said, "I'm only going to the exit with them. I can manage."

Go on, ask me again. That's how it works.

"I'm sure you can, but I'm going that way anyway."

"Then thank you," she met his warm friendly eyes with her own, "that would be a great help."

She walked alongside him.

"We've not been properly introduced; I'm Dylan Rider, the owner."

She smiled an acknowledgment, "Yes, I know who you are."

He made a move towards the lift, causing her to hesitate.

"Erm, I'm afraid I can't take the rubbish in the lift. I have to take it down the back stairs."

His beautiful dark eyes, enhanced by thick dark lashes, completely wasted on a man, crinkled at the edges. "Oh, I think on this occasion, we can bend the rules. The bags are heavy, after all," he winked.

Heavy? They only had used paper towels in them.

He pressed the call button for the lift and the door opened. He gestured with his head for her to go in first and he followed, resting the bags down before pressing the ground-floor button.

The door closed.

It felt uncomfortably intimate to be in an enclosed space with him. She caught his cologne, a mixture of smooth vanilla and fresh lemon. It hadn't been recently applied, but it was subtly there; an invigorating freshness befitting his masculine confidence.

"How are you getting on?" he asked politely, breaking the silence.

"Fine," she smiled.

Maybe she should add more?

"Everyone seems really nice."

"Yes, I'm lucky with all the staff. They work hard and are loyal. I like that in a person. I think it's an important quality, don't you?"

Was that a threat with her prison record?

"Yes, of course."

She found his powerful aroma and nearness, intoxicating. Without warning, it gave a powerful kick to her dormant libido.

He changed the subject. "Do you live locally?"

"Not far. I only need one bus to get here."

"That's not too bad, then. Have you always done cleaning jobs?"

"I've done allsorts in the past."

"Like what?"

He'd have a file on her, she knew that. And she knew exactly what false information was in it.

"Admin mostly, but I've done a bit of retail."

"I see. Well I hope you get on here. Ingrid says you are proving to be a hard worker, which I'm pleased to hear."

Yeah, she should bloody well say that. She'd worked her arse off in the couple of weeks she'd been there.

"That's kind of her to say. I do try to do a good job," she smiled, "a good day's work for a good day's pay, and all that." Her eyes purposely met his.

He stared at her with an expression on his face that she couldn't fathom. He was much more charismatic than she'd imagined. Sex appeal was oozing out of every pore.

Fill the silence.

"I'm very grateful for you for giving me this opportunity. I won't let you down."

"Good, I'm pleased to hear that."

The lift door opened and they walked towards the exit.

"Thank you again," she reached for the rubbish bags he was still holding.

Ingrid was heading towards them. "There you are, Gemma. Can you get a move on to the toilets on one? There seems to be a bit of a flood that needs cleaning up."

"Yes, of course." She placed the bags next to the exit door ready for Joey to take outside, and walked away. Without looking back, she knew Dylan Rider was watching her.

And so it begins.

Chapter 12

Dylan pounded the treadmill in the basement of his Kensington flat. Each morning without fail he ran for five miles and then lifted weights. A sweaty work-out first thing was part of his daily routine, he rarely missed it. If he was away on business he didn't bother, but at home, it had become a ritual which he enjoyed.

Exercise always made him feel better. He was still fuming with Henry after yet another set-to the previous evening. Despite his instruction that his son needed to find a job, the little shit was doing very little as far as he could see. Communication was a real problem between them; he'd even had to ask the housekeeper if he actually ate food in the house as he never saw him eat. Probably feasting on junk food by the look of his dreadful skin.

After their altercation, he'd hooked up with an old flame and taken her out to dinner. Sex quickly followed, which relaxed him, but much to her dissatisfaction, he'd come home afterwards so he could sleep in his own bed and do his morning workout. If the truth be told, he didn't particularly like sleeping alongside a woman. He'd never felt the need for the after-sex bonding, it just wasn't him. He enjoyed the act, but that was it. Nor had he the urge to stick to one woman either, he liked variety and made that clear to any woman he met. Time and time again he told them not to get attached to him, marriage wasn't on his agenda, he liked being single. But would they listen? No. They all wanted the piece of him he wouldn't commit to.

Maybe his father who had been a serial womaniser, had influenced him. His mother had loved him so much and was with him for ten years until he replaced her with a younger model, just as she'd once been his other woman. His mother had been his secretary, and he'd left his first wife for her. His half-brother Victor was a result of his father's first marriage.

He'd slept badly, which wasn't unusual. If he managed five hours, that was good. He'd woken up suddenly and the image in his head was of the cleaner at the gallery. She could be a model with her figure and looks. It really was the luck of the draw. He'd been born with a silver spoon in his mouth. Never wanting for anything, even when his father divorced his mother, he still generously provided for him and Victor, the only children he had. Well, the only two legitimate children; he wouldn't have been surprised if his old man hadn't fathered other children along the way. None came forward when he died though, and you would have expected that there would have been.

His thoughts drifted back to the cleaner. When he spoke to her briefly yesterday, something shifted inside him. He couldn't put his finger on it, but when he looked into her stunningly green eyes, he wanted more, which he quickly chastised himself for. He was being ridiculous. She was a cleaner and as well as that, a cleaner with a criminal record. He shouldn't be remotely interested on her.

But he was.

He knew every detail there was about her from the file he'd obtained. The only reason he'd agreed to her working at the gallery was he'd sussed out she could be exactly what he and Victor needed. Whether or not she'd be interested, he had yet to find out. That last one, Lilly, she was perfect, and she was now happily ensconced in Spain on her generous cut. But he'd not been remotely interested in her, only what she could do for them.

This cleaner was different.

Would she play ball?

He hoped so.

And if he got to screw her along the way, all the better.

He headed for the shower and stripped off his clothes. Thinking about the hot little cleaner in that tight black uniform neatly encasing those generous tits, had his cock at full-mast.

Standing against the hot jets of water he pressed his head against the tiles and squeezed his dick, working its length. He imagined the cleaner naked on top of him, and those pert tits thumping up and down as she rode him, hard and fast, until she was screaming his name, over and over again. His hips jerked, and his balls tightened.

With a hiss, he spilled his load over the wall.

Chapter 13

Against her better judgement, April had allowed Rachel and Joey to drag her to the pub. Despite not wanting to go, she was actually enjoying it. She couldn't relax and let her guard down so was going easy on the lager, but it was infinitely better than sitting in the flat on her own for yet another night.

She had her first meeting with Paddy the following day and she was hoping to have something to feedback, so anything she could glean would be helpful.

As yet another karaoke singer took to the tiny area that served as a stage, Rachel asked her, "Can you sing?"

"Me, sing?" April sniggered, "You must be joking. If I got up there, the place would empty in seconds." She drained the last dregs of the lager, "What about you?"

"Only when I'm truly pissed, then I can give a good rendition of Gloria Gaynor's, I Will Survive."

"Oh, really? We must get you pissed then, I'd love to hear that."

Joey returned clutching three drinks and April took two from him and put them down on the table. "Rachel was just telling me she does karaoke occasionally. What about you, can you sing?"

"I have been known to if I've had a few," he grinned, "did she tell you we once did a mean Sonny and Cher, *I got you babe*."

"Really," she laughed, "this gets better. I'd love to see that."

"Aw, shut up, Joey. I'm not doing that ever again." Rachel widened her eyes playfully, "Have you told Gemma about your speciality performance?"

"Nah, she doesn't want to hear about that. Anyway, it was just a one-off to help out a mate."

"What. Tell me?" April asked enthusiastically.

"Go on, tell her, Joey."

"Bloody hell, Rachel, that was ages ago. It was just for a laugh."

"I'll tell you if he won't," Rachel giggled, "they did the full Monty."

April widened her eyes at Joey.

"They were fabulous," Rachel continued, "you should have seen them all. They came on dressed as policemen and looked so hot in their uniforms. And they did it all, everything came off. They had the balloons in strategic places but surprised us all by popping them. We well and truly got the full Monty, which was okay in some cases, but definitely not in others." She screwed her face up, "It made you realise how men are all very different. Some were at the front of the queue when they gave out . . . you know . . . vital tackle, while others were most definitely at the back."

"Where was I then?" Joey asked cheekily, "you know, when they gave it out?"

Rachel took a mouthful of wine, "Err, I'm leaning more towards the back."

He rolled his eyes, "Cheers."

Rachel put her arm around him, pulled him towards her and kissed his head. "Aw, sweetie pie, I'm only joking. You're just right." She winked at Rachel, "Not that I've ever seen it up close."

Joey grinned, "Say the word and you can have access anytime you want."

April took a mouthful of her lager and watched them both interacting. Joey clearly liked Rachel; they seem to have a natural rapport and a mutual respect for each other.

She checked her watch, it was time she left and got the bus home before it was too late. Travelling on public transport at night didn't make her nervous. Her police training and extensive self-defence classes prepared her for any eventualities, but the part she was playing insisted she displayed caution.

"I'm going to make a move and leave you two to it, if you don't mind before it gets too late. It's been a great night and I've really enjoyed it."

"Aw, don't go, Gemma, have another quick one, it's early yet. You can stay at mine if you want to?"

"No, I'm fine honestly, I'd rather get off. And I couldn't stay over as I'm not allowed out all night. I'll have to ask Tom, my parole officer, when the ban will be lifted. He did say to sleep in my flat initially, so I'd better do as I'm told."

"That'll be the key," Joey chipped in, "they want to see you complying, then you'll have more freedom."

"Yeah, I'm sure you're right," she agreed gulping down the last of her drink.

She stood and took her denim jacket off the back of the chair.

"They can't keep you locked up though, surely," Rachel frowned, "what if you meet someone?"

"I think I just need to ask, that's all. Best to make sure I'm not breaking any of the rules."

Joey stood up and leant forward to give her a kiss on her cheek. "You'll be okay getting home on your own?"

"Course I will. It's not that late." She reached across and hugged Rachel. "Right, I'll see you both on Monday night."

"You sure will," Rachel smiled.

"Hey, I meant to ask you," Joey cut in, "did Dylan Rider catch up with you?"

"Catch up with me?" she repeated.

"Yeah, he asked me where you were earlier on when we were at the gallery. I told him you'd be on the ground floor. He seemed to want you for something?"

"Well he never came and found me," she frowned, "I can't imagine what he'd want me for?"

"Maybe he likes you," Rachel widened her eyes, "I did see him watching you from behind the other night. And you are really attractive."

"Yeah, right. Like a millionaire playboy is going to be interested in a jailbird cleaner. I don't think so somehow, do you?"

Rachel crinkled her nose. "Maybe you're right. Wonder what it was though?"

"It'll be something and nothing, you'll see. I probably haven't left enough toilet rolls out in the gents, or something like that."

"I can't imagine you doing that. You're like cleaner of the year the way you clean."

April did a mock curtsey, "Why thank you, ma'am, you are very kind," and bent down and picked up her bag from the floor.

"It's true. You're really thorough, and very quick."

"I'm trying. I do need this job so I can get back on my feet."

"Well, you've got it, hun, they won't be getting rid of you any time soon. You work too hard. Now me, they wouldn't be bothered if I went or not."

"I bet that's not true," she dismissed throwing her decorative scarf around her neck. "Right you two, thanks for a great evening, enjoy the weekend." She blew them both a kiss as she walked away.

Why had Dylan Rider been looking for her?
What did he want?

Chapter 14

April was coming out of the toilets and walking past Dylan's office when he spotted her. "Ah, Gemma, have you got a minute please?"

Here goes.

He held the door, "Please, come in a moment."

She entered the office and stood in front of him. She was tall for a female, but he must have been six-two as her nose was level with his tie knot. His invigorating, fresh vanilla aftershave, gave a kick reminding her sex had been such a long time ago.

"I wonder if you could help me out?" he asked. "The girl that cleans my house has injured her wrist and I asked Ingrid if she could get me a temporary cleaner. She contacted the agency, but they can't place anyone at short notice for a few days. My housekeeper, Mrs Lile, is doing as much as she can, but she has arthritis and needs some help with the bigger jobs. I suggested to Ingrid that we might ask you."

"Me?"

Christ, she had more than enough cleaning the bloody gallery.

"Yes. Apparently Rachel has another job in the daytime so can't help, but I wondered if you could. It would only be for a couple of days. And I'd pay you, of course."

Don't say yes straight away. He likes a challenge.

"I'll have to check with my parole officer."

"Of course. I thought if you could come in the morning for a couple of hours, then it wouldn't interfere with your cleaning job in the evening here."

"Can I let you know when I've made a phone call?"

"That's fine. Here," he opened his wallet and handed her a business card, "If you could ring me as soon as you know, then I can give you directions and let Mrs Lile know you're coming."

She looked at the glossy embossed card.

Slick, just like him.

"Okay," she agreed, "I'll ring you tomorrow."

"Good. I'll make sure you're paid with your gallery money. Unless . . ." he hesitated, "unless you'd prefer cash? It is only for a day or two. Would that be acceptable?"

Snap his hand off, you're poor.

"It would, yes. Thank you."

"No, thank you," he smiled, "you haven't seen what you're letting yourself in for yet. My son's bedroom will be a significant challenge, I can assure you."

Their eyes met but they both remained silent, staring at each other.

The office door opened, and together they turned their heads to look at the tall dark male entering. April knew exactly who he was.

"Sorry, am I interrupting?"

"Not at all, Vic, come in," Dylan said. "This is Victor, my brother," he introduced proudly, his tone full of respect, "and this is Gemma, one of the new gallery cleaners."

"Hello," she nodded politely at Victor, and watched his lips as they formed a courteous smile which didn't quite reach his eyes.

"Hopefully Gemma will be helping me out at home as my cleaner's sick," Dylan told Victor.

Victor attempted to look interested.

Time to go.

"I better get on then . . . if there's nothing else?" she questioned Dylan.

"No that's all," he replied warmly, "I'll wait to hear from you, tomorrow."

"Yes," she smiled, and nodded to Victor, "nice to meet you."

"You too," he replied.

She walked towards the door and closed it behind her.

Bingo!

What a surprise.

She certainly hadn't expected to have access to his house quite so quickly.

Chapter 15

"What do you think?" Dylan asked his brother, "She's a looker isn't she? Far too attractive to be a cleaner, that's for sure."

Victor knocked back the last of his whisky and placed the glass on the desk. "For Christ's sake, haven't you got enough women falling at your feet? The last thing you should be doing is screwing the hired help."

"I know, but I can't help being curious about her. She seems . . . oh, I don't know, too beautiful to be a cleaner. She could be a model if she wanted to. It makes you think, doesn't it, about heritage and birth-right. If she had the right background, with her looks, she could have become so much more."

"Yeah and she could quite easily *become so much more* by hooking up with you. Many an attractive woman has gone on to a better standard of living by bagging a rich bloke," Victor added cynically, "so you've been warned."

"You don't need to tell me that. Every woman I've ever met is a wife-to-be predator, but I've not got to this age by falling for anyone's charms just yet." He scowled, "Apart from the once that is, but if I was thinking about becoming snared, which I'm not, it wouldn't be with a jailbird, that's for sure."

"Pleased to hear it. What was she inside for?"

"Fraud."

"Right. So is your regular cleaner really off for a few days, or have you engineered that to get her round to yours?"

"You're a cynical bastard, aren't you?"

"No, just a realist."

"Well, for your information, my cleaner is off and I do need the extra help. Mrs Lile is great as my housekeeper, but she doesn't like getting her hands dirty. She's more suited to organising and planning."

"So, the jailbird doing the cleaning is all you're interested in?"

Dylan smirked, "Unless she's up for extras. I'm not going to knock her back if she comes onto me."

"She didn't look like the type to be coming onto anyone."

"Ah, but you haven't seen the way she looks at me. There's definitely something between us."

"So, you're not thinking she has the potential to be brought into the fold?"

"There's potential in all of them, you know that. That's why we give these jailbirds an opportunity."

Chapter 16

It was the third day of cleaning Dylan Rider's house, and April was determined to make a start on his son's bedroom. Elizabeth Lile, the housekeeper, had told her to only give it a lick and a promise as Henry Rider hated anyone touching anything of his.

They should be paying me extra for all this work on top of surveillance.

The whole house was immaculate so to see the unsightly mess of the son's bedroom, irritated her. April hated mess of any kind. She was almost obsessive with cleanliness in her own home. She lived her life like that. Ordered and organised.

The room was a typical teenagers room, the difference being this was a bigger than average bedroom. The bed was a super king-size, and in a normal room would be overpowering, but not in this one. There was so much space. The décor was neutral, and the furniture contemporary. A long, what appeared to be, purpose-built desk dominated the full length of one of the walls, with an array of computer equipment spread out along it. It wasn't your average hardware suitable for a teenager either. Thousands of pounds worth of sophisticated equipment pointed towards a computer geek.

The bed looked as if at least three people had slept in it; either that or it was never made properly. She ripped the duvet and bedclothes off and diligently replaced them all, straightening and tucking the sheets with neat envelope corners to secure them without creases. She turned the bedclothes back tidily and fluffed up the pillows. It wasn't quite to a shop display standard, but it was infinitely better. The silky sheets were pure quality, an eight hundred thread count at the very least. Definitely not the thread count on her thin bedding, that was for sure.

There were two doors leading off from the bedroom. She peered in one to the left of the bed, and her eyes swept around a dressing room which was a complete mess. Despite rows of hanging space, there were heaps of jeans, tee shirts and underpants discarded on the floor. Looking at the hanging space, she could see at some stage the clothes had been segregated, so the jackets were clustered together, and there was a space for trousers. It was the same with the shirts, although there was an equal amount on the rails as there looked to be on the floor.

She moved towards the other door to the right of the bed which was the ensuite. Again, it was about as tidy as his dressing area. There was a selection of shower gels and colognes, many of them with their tops discarded. She noticed there was an assortment of products for the treatment of acne. High-end face washes, toners, a couple of jars of moisturiser, and a tube of spot concealer for men. Many were replicated more than once with a particular brand. There must have been hundreds of pounds worth lined up on the shelf.

The bath and washbasin were clean apart from some toothpaste stains which appeared recent. It was apparent whoever had the job of cleaning his bedroom and bathroom, only did the minimum.

She sighed at the task ahead.
More bloody sinks and toilets to clean.

She made a start, spraying the shower cubicle and scrubbing the standing area which was engrained with dirty foot marks. Once she was satisfied it was cleaner, she then turned her attention to the washbasin and scoured it until it gleamed, and finally moved onto cleaning and disinfecting the toilet.

It didn't appear as if the huge corner bath was in use, so she left that. There was more than enough to clean without doing unnecessary jobs.

She folded the thick fluffy towels, and placed them on the chrome towel rail. Glancing around at her handiwork, she was pleased with how nice it looked, but whether an untidy teenager would see it quite that way, she wasn't sure.

She closed the ensuite door behind her and headed for the dressing room. It was a mess she was determined to sort. Each item of clothes she placed onto a hanger, and all the underwear strewn all over the floor, whether dirty or not, was tossed in the wash-basket. It didn't matter how much Dylan Rider paid her, it wasn't enough to distinguish which items were clean and which had been used.

As she stood back admiring how much better it was, she became aware of someone in the dressing room doorway.

She turned towards the gangly male glaring at her.

"Who the fuck are you?" he snarled.

So this was the son.

Arrogant little sod.

"The cleaner. Who the fuck are you?"

"Henry Rider. This is my room and you've no business being in here." He didn't have the grace to look embarrassed by his tone.

"Haven't I? That's odd then as your father specifically asked me to clean in here. Said it was untidy," she moved her head around the room, "I'd say he was being a tad polite, it's actually a tip."

"So?"

"So, someone's got to clean it. I think it looks much better now, don't you?"

"Like I give a shit what you think," he scowled, as he walked away into the bedroom.

He took a seat at his computer desk with his back to her.

Ignorant little git.

She followed him. "No, I don't suppose you do care what I think, but here's the thing; I'm paid to clean this house for the next few days, but to be honest, I feel I'm getting my money under false pretences as every where's so tidy. That is except your pit. So I thought I'd earn my money and try and get your dressing room into some sort of order. Sorry if that offends you, maybe if you kept it right, I wouldn't need to."

He turned in his swivel chair to face her. Irritation was written all over his face.

"Where's . . .?" he frowned, struggling to remember the cleaner's name. That is if he ever actually knew it.

"Sick," she brushed her hands across the bed to smooth a non-existent crease in the duvet, "so, until she's better, you've got me."

"Well, you've done that now, so you can go."

"Can I?" she tilted her head, "that's very gracious of you." She picked up her holdall of cleaning utensils and looked directly at him, but he averted his eyes. There was no mistaking it was Dylan Rider's son, they looked alike, but unlike his handsome fit father, his face was covered in carbuncles and spots with huge heads on them which no amount of products would clear. She remembered Chloe as a teenager, her skin was exactly the same until they'd got a sympathetic GP who'd referred her to a skin specialist.

Despite him glancing everywhere around the room but at her, she continued. "I'll be back tomorrow to clean again, and the next day. In fact, I'll be in here every day unless your dad tells me otherwise. So don't leave any more of your shitty boxers lying around. I'm not paid enough to pick those filthy things up."

His brow furrowed and he shook his head, "Yeah, whatever."

She was determined to have the final say with the little git. At the door, she paused.

"By the way, all the products in the world won't get rid of your acne. You need to see a skin specialist and get a prescription for Roaccutane. That's the only thing that'll clear it up, those other products won't. They're a waste of money."

Mrs Lile was coming along the landing towards her as she closed Henry's door.

"There's a coffee for you in the kitchen when you're ready, Gemma," she smiled, "I'm just popping out to the post office. I'll only be ten minutes."

"Thank you. I'm coming down, I've finished up here."

"Did you see Henry?" Mrs Lile asked cautiously, as if she already knew he'd have given her a hard time.

"Yes, I did. Charming, isn't he?"

They walked down the huge ornate staircase together.

Elizabeth Lile puffed out her cheeks, "Between you and I, he's a bit of a troubled soul."

"Why, what's the matter with him?"

She lowered her voice which was completely unnecessary as they were alone. "He's a bit odd, that's all. Not quite all there, if you get my drift. I think these modern-day people call it autism or something like that."

"Oh, right. I did think it a bit strange that he didn't look me in the eye when I was talking to him. He sort of looked past me."

"He never does," she scowled, "you didn't tidy his room, did you? I did say he doesn't like things moving about."

"I didn't do much, just picked a few things up and made his bed."

"That's good. He goes off on one if anyone tidies his room. He can be a little touchy."

"A little touchy?" April rolled her eyes, "I think that's an understatement."

She made a mental note to read up more on autism. When they'd started the process of planning the investigation, the son didn't even live at the house, but now he was part of the equation, she needed to find out more about him.

Chapter 17

April continued along the huge hallway toward the kitchen to have the coffee Elizabeth had made her. The front door opened and she turned around.

Dylan Rider's infectious smile greeted her.

"Hello, Gemma, how are you getting on?"

"Oh, hello." She hadn't expected him to be in the house while she was cleaning. "Mrs Lile's just nipped out."

"Has she," he shrugged, placing his car keys on the elegantly polished console table.

Should she have her coffee now he was here? It'd be an opportunity to move things along.

"Yes, she's made me a coffee in the kitchen. Would you like me to make you one?"

"Coffee sounds good, but I'll make it. Come on."

She followed him towards the kitchen.

"Your son's home . . . he's in his room," she added, to keep the conversation going.

"Best place for him. He's not the sociable type."

He made his way towards the coffee machine. Her coffee was perched on the draining board, which he saw and threw down the sink.

"You don't want that instant crap. I'll make you a proper coffee." He proceeded to open a cupboard and lift a box of coffee pods down. "What do you fancy, latte, cappuccino, Americano?"

"I was fine with the instant one."

"Well, I'm not. Come on, humour me, this machine makes great coffee. What's your poison?"

"In that case," she smiled, "a latte would be lovely, thank you."

As she watched him fill the coffee maker with milk, her eyes were drawn to his hands. They were groomed as if he had them manicured regularly, which he probably did as his hands would be on display with his line of work.

But it wasn't his perfect nails that held her attention. It was the fine hairs jutting out from underneath his cuffs. They were dark, just like him. She always found dark-haired men attractive, and they didn't come much darker than Dylan Rider.

Her pussy clenched at his virility.

Why couldn't he have been blonde and ugly?

That would have made things so much easier.

She needed to distract herself from the way her thoughts were drifting. Why wasn't he making his son a drink? Okay, she knew enough about teenagers to know sitting down and chatting wasn't what they did, but she thought he could at least have shouted up to see if he wanted anything?

"So tell me a bit more about yourself," he said, folding his arms and leaning against the unit as the coffee machine burbled away behind him.

"Nothing much to tell, really," she dismissed.

"How about where you live? You never did say."

So he'd remembered she didn't answer his question when he'd asked at the gallery.

"Notting Dale."

"Ah, not too far from here or the gallery." It was a statement rather than a question that needed answering.

"And are you settling in at the gallery? I've asked Ingrid and she seems to think you are."

"Yes, I've been made very welcome."

"Good. You must yell out if there is anything. The same goes for here, too. Have you met Henry, my son?"

"Just."

"And you survived that?" he enquired, with a raised eyebrow.

"I think so. He's certainly not a conversationalist, is he?"

He threw his head back and laughed. "You could say that."

Dylan was a handsome man anyway, but when he laughed, it somehow made him fifty times more attractive. She watched as his dextrous fingers fiddled with the machine.

"Do you mind me asking," he didn't wait for her to reply, "have you got a boyfriend?"

She feigned surprise by widening her eyes, as if she was perturbed. It had the desired effect.

"Sorry, I'm being far too personal, ignore me."

She hadn't really taken offence, but she was playing a part. Several kiss-and-tell articles all labelled him as being keen on the chase, but once he'd won, he quickly lost interest.

"It's okay," she reassured. "It feels a bit awkward that's all, here in your house when I'm supposed to be cleaning and instead I'm in your kitchen drinking coffee when you're paying me to work."

"Don't feel awkward, there's really no need," he said, "you are entitled to a coffee break, you know. And you'll still get paid, I promise you. Here . . ."

He passed her a steaming coffee with a layer of frothy milk, in a beautiful glass mug.

"Thank you." She took a sip and placed it on the work surface. He'd been right, the coffee machine did make fabulous coffee.

Get him talking.

"You have a beautiful home."

"Thank you. It is rather nice, isn't it? I like it."

"It certainly is. You're very lucky."

"Yes, I suppose I am." He took a sip of his coffee, "At the risk of me speaking out of turn again, you didn't answer as to whether or not you have a boyfriend. It's important I know before I ask my next question?"

She took a deep breath in, "No."

"Really? That does surprise me. I would have thought they'd be queuing up to take you out."

"Nope," she shook her head, "I've not seen any queues. Not the last time I looked, anyway."

He smiled. "That's good, because I wanted to ask if you would like to go out for dinner one evening?"

"With you?" she asked incredulously.

"Yes, with me. I don't bite," he grinned cheekily, "unless I'm asked."

Tempting as it was to give a flirty reply, it was too soon.

"You must have your pick of women to take out?"

He didn't answer the question, just ploughed ahead. "I thought dinner would be nice, if you're up for it."

She shook her head, "I really don't think so." She gulped another mouthful of her coffee. "Now if you'll excuse me, I'd better crack on."

"Why? I'm only talking about dinner if that's what you're worried about."

"I'm not worried about anything," she said, "I don't feel it's appropriate going out with my boss, that's all."

"I won't tell if you won't," he said with a glint in his eye, "I know a quiet little bistro which I'm sure you'd like. They do a mean fillet mignon. If you like meat, that is."

"I do, but I'd rather not, thank you."

She took her coffee cup over to the sink and ran some water into it.

Keep him interested.

She pulled an apologetic face. "I think it's best if we keep things strictly as employer and employee."

"Is it your parole officer you're worried about? I could have a word if that would help."

"Please don't. It's nothing personal . . . you're an attractive man, but I'm really not interested in . . . dating, dinner or anything. I'll be moving on shortly, I'd hate things to be awkward at the gallery between us."

"Okay," he nodded, as if he understood. But she could tell he wasn't about to give up.

"I get you don't want to be seen out with me, even though I'm an," he did air quotes with his fingers, "eligible bachelor with no ties. How about eating in then? You do eat dinner, don't you?"

"Yes, of course."

"How about dinner here? Unless you'd rather I came to yours, I could bring take-away?"

She cringed. God, if he saw how she was living right now.

"I'd rather not do either. But thank you for asking me. She made a hasty retreat out of the kitchen, grateful he didn't attempt to follow her.

Keep asking, won't you?
And I will eventually say yes.

Chapter 18

It was Saturday morning. April was walking slowly alongside Paddy by the duck pond in the park. They'd met to discuss her progress. She linked her arm in his as they'd agreed. To anyone watching them, they'd appear like father and daughter walking around the busy park amongst the children playing ball games and running about, and couples laid about reading and enjoying the freedom of the weekend.

"So, Rider's asked you out. Why am I not surprised?"

"I've said no."

"But he'll ask again?"

"I think so. Or at least he should do. I know Dylan Rider better than he knows himself. He's in it for as long as the chase goes on."

"Have you managed to find out anything more at the house?"

"No, nothing. I've flicked through a few drawers and things, but I can't get into his study yet. His housekeeper cleans that. I'm more the beds, toilets and bathroom girl," she looked down at her hands, "which my hands can vouch for. They're so bloody dry, now."

"Maybe he keeps his house separate from the gallery and *other* work?"

"I'm guessing he keeps everything stored at the gallery, although he does have a huge safe in his bedroom at the house."

"Do you think you could get access to it, you know, somehow get the number?"

"I doubt it. I reckon I'd have to sleep with him first to get that."

Paddy quickly turned his head to look at her.

"I'm only joking," she reassured, "I'm good at my job, but I draw the line at that."

He looked relieved. Paddy wouldn't expect that of her.

"Can you get near anything at the gallery?"

"I'm working on it. I'm getting close to Rachel, the girl that cleans the offices. I've been out with her socially, and my intention is to somehow get rid of her, so I can get in that office myself to clean and have a good scout round."

"How will you manage to get rid of her?"

"I'll slip something in her drink that'll make sure she's off work the next day."

His expression darkened.

"Hey, don't be looking like that. I'm talking about something to give her the runs."

"And you think if she's off one night, they'd let you clean his office?"

"Why not? Ingrid, the lazy supervisor will want the work done, she won't care who does it. And besides, anything of interest will be locked away. Rider's not the type to be leaving stuff lying around."

"Be careful," he warned, "we've got a lot riding on this. He'll have to move that painting soon. We need to know where it's stored, and link him to it. Then we'll have you out of there. It's gone on long enough."

"Yes, it is slow," she sighed, "but I'm sure I can locate it."

"Me too. If anyone can, you can. There's no-one better than you." He smiled affectionately at her, "No wonder you've turned Rider's head, you're a stunning girl, far too beautiful really to be a police officer."

"Why thank you, kind sir," she joked, "on that note I'd better get going. There's more cleaning to be done," she rolled her eyes, "I should be getting double, I've never had an undercover job like this before," she twisted her hands upwards, "I've developed calluses with all this bloody cleaning."

"You get Rider, and you'll be eligible for a huge bonus," he smiled, "but watch your back, won't you?"

"I will do."

She gave him a hug which felt a bit awkward. They'd decided in the beginning it would be more realistic if they did so for the benefit of anyone watching. "Bye, then," she smiled as he walked away.

She watched as he made his way to his exit.

She'd lied to him.

She would sleep with Dylan Rider if she had to. In fact, she was expecting to.

She'd told the parole officer she would bring Dylan down, and she would. Nothing was more certain than that.

If that meant having sex with him, then so be it.

It had been that long, she might even enjoy it.

***

He'd stood a safe distance away so he couldn't be spotted, and watched her talking as she walked leisurely around the lake.

It was a beautiful day, perfect for a stroll. They looked so innocent, just a father walking with his daughter.

You could tell it was her even from a distance. April Masters held herself in a graceful, poised way. The new short-cropped hairstyle would look butch on some women, perhaps more suited to a gay woman, but on her it was incredibly sexy. It exposed her long graceful neck.

She was wearing jeans which hung off her hips and clung to her race-horse legs. His eyes were drawn to her boots which were full-length, like riding boots. Oh, how he'd love to be riding her in only those boots and nothing else.

The conversation between the two of them looked intense. To anyone passing by, they weren't interacting like a casual encounter. But he knew what they were discussing was serious.

It hadn't been long before they said their goodbyes.

He knew exactly what they'd been talking about.

The question was, could she pull off such an elaborate plan?

Only time would tell.

Chapter 19

April checked her personal iPhone and saw a missed call from her sister. She called Chloe, impatiently waiting while it rang.

"Come on, pick up," she muttered to herself. It was unusual to see her sister come up as a missed call. Chloe knew not to ring. She'd told her often enough to text first and she would ring her back. On the last ring her sister picked up.

"Chloe, is everything okay?" she blurted.

"Noah's been admitted to hospital. His lungs are congested so he's got to be nebulised and have some physio. We're at Great Ormond Street, is there any chance you can come?"

God, she didn't need this right now. She couldn't afford to blow her cover.

"Are you still there?" Chloe asked anxiously.

"Yeah, sorry. How's Noah doing?"

"Okay. You know what he's like, he won't be kept down for long. He's tired though, but they've started him on steroids so that'll boost him. When he's picked up a bit, he's going to have more physio to clear his chest properly. Will you be able to come?"

She shouldn't go. Not while she was in the middle of a massive police sting, but wild horses wouldn't keep her away. Noah was sick and she needed to be there.

"I'll see if I can get away."

"Will you?" Chloe exclaimed in a relieved voice, "I can't wait to see you. Gavin can come in the evenings, but work are funny about too much time off in the day. He'll be here at the weekend, thank God."

"Okay, I'll go now and try and arrange something. I'll ring you in the morning and let you know which day I can come."

"That'll be brilliant. It will be lovely to see you, and Noah will be thrilled too. He'll perk up when you get here, I bet."

Her tummy tightened.

"God love him. Give him a big kiss from me and tell him I'll be there as soon as I can."

"I will do. Love you to the moon and back."

"Me too."

April ended the call. It was early days, nobody was suspicious about her, so she would be able to go visit Noah. She could get there and back in time for the gallery cleaning at six, but the problem was she was supposed to be cleaning Dylan's house during the day. How could she get out of that? She couldn't use being sick as an excuse, but then manage to clean the gallery. Maybe she could have a full day off. That's what she'd have to do. Ring Tom, before anyone else and he'd clear her being off. She could go with a diarrhoea bug which would just last a day.

Yes, she'd pull a sicky. Only for a day though, she couldn't afford any longer.

Noah was such a precious little boy. April was his birth mother, and her sister's husband, Gavin was his genetic father. All it had taken was a basting stick, several months, and Noah had been conceived.

April spent many hours, days and months analysing why she'd agreed to be a surrogate for her sister. If a psychiatrist was to study her and Chloe's relationship, it wouldn't take much effort to come to the conclusion that she had an unhealthy desire to compensate for any failings in her sister's life. As if it was her responsibility to fix them. It stemmed from her mother dying which left her, a young child herself, trying to compensate for things Chloe missed out on.

Chloe had been married almost as soon as she left school. She'd got a job in a local department store and soon met Gavin who worked as a delivery driver. They were married within months, boasting about the large family they were going to have. By the time they underwent lengthy fertility investigations, it became apparent Chloe wouldn't conceive due to a gynaecological medical condition. The doctors tried to be encouraging, saying there was a small chance, but it was unlikely as her fallopian tubes were blocked with endometriosis.

Chloe and Gavin were devastated. Their dream was in shreds, and her sister had taken the news badly. She became depressed and required medication to lift her mood. They didn't have immediate family so there was nobody else to turn to. April desperately wanted to help and when the first couple of NHS IVF treatments failed, she'd loaned them the money to go privately. The IVF took its toll and Chloe became more and more disheartened. By this time she couldn't face work as the vast majority of her co-workers were young females and many were on their second and third babies. It all got too much for Chloe and she became even more withdrawn.

An article April read in a GP surgery while she was waiting for a smear test first gave her the idea of becoming a surrogate. It took a month until she approached them both with the idea she would have a baby for them. They'd spent several hours discussing the what-ifs, and the pitfalls, of which there were many, but eventually they came to the decision - it was doable.

And so the process began. It was a bit awkward, but they managed it. She would visit Chloe and Gavin during the fertile period of her cycle each month, and inseminate herself with Gavin's sperm. She would spend time on her back with her pelvis tilted on a pillow to encourage the sperm to travel. She loved those times laid on the bed with Chloe by her side. It was their time together. They talked about their mother, and April got to the point where she wasn't sure if their recollections were actually real, or if it was just make-believe. All she knew was, those moments together were special and etched on her mind.

She remembered vividly the time when she did her own test in her flat and it confirmed she was pregnant. It had been a massive surprise as she had been doubtful the insemination would actually work. And once she became accustomed to the idea, another emotion she wasn't expecting, surfaced; the overwhelming desire to protect the little thing growing inside of her.

The early days flew by, and when she reached fourteen weeks, she took a sabbatical from work for a year. The uneventful pregnancy progressed, and she kept very trim with a healthy diet and regular exercise. It wasn't a case of concealing the pregnancy; it was more that it wasn't obvious to anyone.

It was decided between the three of them, they were going to be open about the surrogacy, but not until the baby was much older, then they would have the discussion as a family.

The biggest surprise for April had been how attached she became to Noah during the pregnancy. Becoming emotionally involved was something she hadn't expected. She'd gone into the arrangements with her eyes wide open, but nothing had prepared her for the maternal feelings she had towards the little baby growing inside her. Despite barely glancing at the scans, and ignoring the little fellow as he kicked continually each evening, well into the night when she wanted to sleep, somehow along the way, she fell in love with him.

The pregnancy had been completely text book, she'd sailed through it. Labour was hard, but Chloe was there, holding her hand, and the joy was immeasurable when Noah had been born.

Keeping him had been a consideration. She'd fleetingly weighed up the option of taking him away and bringing him up as a single parent. But that would mean alienating herself from Chloe and she couldn't bring herself to do that. Chloe and Gavin were all ready to take this precious little baby and bring him up as theirs, and they could offer all the things she couldn't. They'd always be there for him. They'd be up with him in the night when he was poorly, proudly there watching each milestone he achieved such as learning to walk and talk, riding a bike and starting school, and eventually see that he grew up into a fine young man. And she would be part of all that, too. It wasn't like a random family was adopting him and she'd never get to see him. She'd have regular contact with him, and vowed she'd be the best auntie in the world. So the way she saw it was, he'd be such a lucky little boy to have three people that would love him dearly and look out for him.

But the hardest part had been handing her precious little baby over. It was the most difficult thing she'd ever had to do, and it broke her new hormonal, maternal heart. She had held him all night before she parted with him. His little face was etched in her mind; his perfect head, his beautiful blue tiny eyes, and his little pug nose with a layer of sweat as he took his feed. But she knew she had to let Chloe and Gavin bring him up, and forget all about being his mummy.

So she'd walked away, and thrown herself back into the only role she knew. It would all work out for the best, she told herself over and over again. She would grow up being his auntie and had to be content with that. Her focus had always been about being a police officer, anyway. Children had never been on her agenda, she didn't have time to raise a child, and her track record in the romance department was poor.

It was a health visitor that first alerted Chloe that Noah wasn't developing quite how they anticipated. He didn't appear to have the co-ordination they would expect. April went with Chloe and Gavin to see the paediatrician, and after numerous tests, Noah was diagnosed with spastic diplegic cerebral palsy. The prognosis wasn't good. He'd be unlikely to ever walk, or if he did, he would need the aid of a walking frame.

They were all devastated, but if God had any influence in which parents were to have a disabled child, then Chloe and Gavin had been selected for a reason. Noah was given so much love and encouragement. They were completely devoted to him.

The health bods seemed reluctant to offer odds on Noah's future. The family were supported well by Great Ormond Street Hospital, but Noah's hips were too far out of position for surgeons to operate in this country. It wasn't until Noah reached four that the suggestion was made that a surgeon in St Louis Children's Hospital, Missouri, USA might be able to help.

The lengthy surgery involved a neurosurgical technique to treat the spasticity in the lower limbs. It was explained to them that it involved opening the lower vertebrae to release the spinal cord which contains the neurones of the central nervous system. Neurones, the consultant had explained, were a bundle of nerve fibres, which carried messages between the brain and different areas of the body. During the procedure, electrical stimulation is used to identify and divide the sensory and motor nerves, sort of unscrambling the mixed messages the brain takes to the muscles.

They were warned there were no guarantees. Months, if not years of physiotherapy would be required after the surgery to retrain the legs.

Devastating as the news was, they finally had something to work towards, however, the cost of the surgery made it completely prohibitive.

April only had a few grand of equity in her flat. She'd saved so hard for a deposit to get a mortgage, and even if she sold it, there wouldn't have been enough for the treatment and the rehabilitation that would be needed. Chloe would need to stay in the US while Noah underwent his treatment which could take anything from six months to a year.

One night, after a lengthy meeting with the consultant, Chloe came up with the idea she would start a fundraising campaign to try and get the money to facilitate the surgery. The process was slow, and deeply frustrating. April generously donated from her salary, but it quickly became apparent it was a long road ahead. Initially people gave generously at the fund-raising events, but eventually the support became less and less.

Undercover work paid well, but however much she gave, they were far short of their target. The American consultant advised there were no tangible benefits of considering the surgery until after Noah's fifth birthday. So currently, all they had was time.

And April was determined Noah was going to get the surgery he needed.

It didn't matter how much it cost.

Chapter 20

April looked at herself in the cracked full-length mirror. Her chain store Debenhams dress was flattering and clung in all the right places. The animal print suited her; it somehow made her eyes seem a deeper shade of green than they actually were.

She'd given into Dylan's request for dinner the third time he'd asked. He'd been like a man on a mission since the first time she'd turned him down. She knew he would be. Nobody said no to Dylan Rider. There wasn't anything she didn't know about him. Even though the police had issued her with a complete resume on him, she'd also done her own research and read anything that had ever been written about him. By the time she'd finished, she knew more about him than his own mother.

He'd been born with a silver spoon in his mouth and had a privileged upbringing. He attended the best schools, and initially when he left university, he'd gone into banking and was doing relatively well until his brother Victor had relinquished overseeing the gallery, and he'd been the natural successor.

Seemingly, the Rider gallery had thrived when Dylan took the helm. His charm and good looks made him a natural with potential customers. Newspapers used the analogy of selling ice to Eskimos. Artists wanted their work exhibited at the prestigious Carson Rider gallery. It seemed to be the in place for paintings to be seen, and had a reputation for attracting the big buyers in the art world.

April ran the brush through her thick short hair and then applied some gel with her fingers. The intention was to lift her soft fringe and for a more sophisticated evening look. Even though her hair was short, she could achieve many different looks. Men like Dylan Rider's preference would be women with long flowing hair, she knew that. But she also knew that very few women could wear their hair as she did and still look good. It wasn't vanity, she didn't buy into that, but she was a realist and learnt over the years, she had something men desired.

She stared back at herself. Her long elegant neck and sharp facial features showed the short hair off to perfection. She flattened a few stray hairs behind her ears so that she could expose her tiny ear lobes and added some small inexpensive earrings which enhanced her appearance, but she didn't really need them.

Even a no-nonsense police officer liked to dress up and look girlie, so she'd applied a moderate amount of make-up. Large smoky green eyes stared back at her, which were down to a makeup palate which made them seem bigger than they actually were, and she applied layers of mascara to complete the look. It was her green eyes that separated her from other women. Green was the rarest of colours, and they become more green, grey or blue dependant on her mood, surroundings and what she was wearing.

She thought about her life away from work. It had been such a long time since she'd been in her beautiful home. How she longed to open the door of her flat and shut the world out as she closed it behind her. To kick her shoes off, strip off her clothes and have a long soak in the enormous bath she'd had put in. And then pour herself a glass of red and relax in her conservatory, listening to some classical music. The whole image was heart-warming, and a far cry from her run-down bedsit.

Her kitten-heeled shoes completed the look. The dress reached above her knee and her legs look slender and toned with a dusting of fake-tan.

The sooner she got the job done, the better. Dylan Rider was interested, overly interested really. She wasn't stupid, she knew he was only after one thing, and however receptive she was towards him, that didn't involve telling her where the Portillo was.

But her ace card was the knowledge he needed to move it from the UK soon.

And her job was to link him to it.

The whole charade depended on it.

She'd followed Dylan into the dining room of his house. The table looked stunning with a silver-coloured runner and expensive placemats. The various array of crystal glasses were no doubt for a multitude of different wines. Men like Dylan Rider didn't do casual.

"Please take a seat. Can I get you a glass of white or red? We're having lamb, so I'm having red."

"Then I will too if you've opened the bottle. No sense in opening two."

"You're sure? You can have white if you prefer," he grinned, "I think I can stretch to two bottles." His eyes crinkled at the edges. He was so handsome, too bloody handsome. No wonder the tabloids chased him trying to find out who his latest conquest was. Invariably it was a model of some description. Always stunningly beautiful, but then he seemed to surround himself by beauty.

"Excuse me for a moment," he said and left the room.

She gazed around the huge dining room that would easily seat twenty people comfortably.

Everything about Dylan Rider was classy. Even his house was elegant and tastefully decorated. The walls had a collection of stunning pictures on them, most contemporary, but there were some older prints.

She thought about the tabloid newspapers. *What would they make of Dylan Rider entertaining a jailbird?*

"Here you are," he interrupted her train of thought and handed her a drink.

She took it from him, allowing her fingers to touch his for a second. "Thank you."

He sat down opposite and lifted his own glass. "Now then, what shall we drink to?" His brown eyes glistened, "How about, new friends?"

"Sounds good to me." She lifted her glass, "New friends," they both said in unison.

She savoured a sip of wine. "This is nice."

"Glad you like it. I think it's got a fruity body, and doesn't leave a bitter after taste."

"You're right, it doesn't. Not that I'm an expert on wine. I have no idea really what I'm drinking, but I do know when I don't like a wine. This one's lovely."

"Good, because we've got plenty to get through," he nodded towards the kitchen, "I've got another one opened and breathing."

"Not for me I hope, wine goes straight to my head. I'd be flat out if I had too much."

His eyes glinted with playfulness, "Maybe that's my intention."

"Then you're going to be disappointed as it isn't mine," she told him firmly but with a cheeky smile.

A tap on the dining room door made her turn her head. A young girl gently opened the door.

"Are you ready to start, Mr Rider?"

"Yes please, Zian."

The girl nodded and closed the door behind her.

"Zian is the little gem that caters for me when I have guests. She's a fantastic cook. I've asked her to do my favourite starter, salt beef hash cake with a quail egg and rhubarb ketchup. It's to die for. You'll see exactly what I mean when you try it."

"Sounds wonderful. Does she have her own business?"

"Yes. It's called Love at First Bite, an online company run by her and her sister. They prepare meals in clients' homes, and they do corporate functions. I use her for anything at the gallery. It's a relatively new company they've set up, and as far as I can see, they're doing brilliantly."

The door opened and Zian came in carrying two dishes which she placed in front of them.

"Thank you," Dylan acknowledged, "I was just telling Gemma about your business and how well you're doing."

Zian smiled affectionately at him and then looked at April, "A lot of that's down to Mr Rider. He has put plenty of business our way."

"That's because your food it too gorgeous not too," he looked at April, "which you're going to find out any minute now."

Zian nodded, "Hopefully yes. I'll leave you to it then. Bon appetite."

Dylan hadn't been wrong. The starter was amazing. April savoured every mouthful.

"I told you," he said, "she's such a fantastic cook."

"You're telling me. Delicious doesn't come close to describing it."

"You'll run out of adjectives before long. Everything tastes as good as this, you'll see."

As he took a sip of his wine, her eyes were drawn to his Adam's apple protruding as he swallowed. He was really hot, and smelled so good. His spicy, citrusy aftershave played havoc with her senses, and she felt her pussy twitch as his tongue licked the surplus wine off his lips.

He put his glass down, "Now, tell me more about yourself."

"I'd rather not," she scrunched her nose up, "I'm sure your life is much more interesting than mine. You tell me about yourself, I'd enjoy that."

"Okay, but you're not getting away that easily. How about we take turns and I'll start."

He began to describe his life in detail from junior school to the present time. Nothing he said she didn't know from his file, but she made encouraging noises and smiled in all the right places. If only he knew. She could have told him all of that.

During the conversation, they'd eaten the braised lamb breast. Every mouthful was a gourmet delight. It wasn't saturated in a rich sauce hiding the flavour of the meat, just a simple jus and the accompaniment of fresh garden vegetables, were perfect. Whichever way Zian had cooked the lamb, she'd done an amazing job. It was delicious.

Zian came in to clear their plates and Dylan asked for a bit of a breather before they had dessert.

He leant back against his chair. "Right, your turn now."

"I'm not sure I can follow that. Mine's a bit mundane, I'm afraid."

"Go on, I like mundane."

"Okay then," she placed her wine down, "don't say I didn't warn you."

She started on the fictitious personal life she knew off by heart. She spoke about her school life then her parents emigrating to New Zealand, and her father's heart attack and eventual death at forty-five. She lied about being an only child and her uneventful life of school, college and finally work. She spoke jovially about it all, until the time came to inject some sadness into her voice.

"And then I fell in love. I'd been feeling vulnerable after my parents emigrated to New Zealand, and it's the old story about a charismatic older man coming into my life and literally sweeping me off my feet."

"Were you together long?"

"Too long, really. He was an accountant at the firm I worked for and he took me under his wing, so to speak. I was on a training scheme which would have eventually meant if I passed all the exams, I'd be a qualified accountant."

"Go on," he encouraged, sipping his wine.

She put a pained expression on her face, as if she was struggling to tell the rest.

"Not much to tell really. Only that I was very much in love and would have done anything for him. In fact, I did, and that's why I ended up where I am right now." She took a huge gulp of wine for effect. "Do you think we can talk about something else? It's all a bit doom and gloom from now on with what happened next."

"Of course we can . . ." he was about to add more as the door opened and Henry appeared.

Dylan glared at him. "We're just having dinner," which she sensed was a covert way of saying, get lost.

He didn't apologise for interrupting as you would have expected.

"Did Uncle Vic get you?" Henry asked.

Dylan shook his head. "No, I haven't spoken to him."

"He rang the house phone, said he wanted you to ring him back."

"It can't have been urgent otherwise he'd have rung my mobile. I'll call him later."

Henry looked awkward. He clearly wasn't picking up the social clue of his dad wanting rid of him. He stood in the same place, holding onto the door handle with a blank expression which April recognised because she'd been there so many times in her teens. He was lonely.

She cleared her throat. "Have you been anywhere nice this evening?"

He shook his head, again not picking up on the social clue of replying.

Dylan interjected, "You'll not find out where hot-wheels goes to. I got him a car for the purpose of trying to find a job, and granted, he does leave the house each day on the pretext of job hunting, but doesn't seem to come up with one."

Since she'd first met Henry, she'd researched so much on Autism, and it had fascinated her. It appeared everyday life was a significant challenge for those affected. Now she had a better understanding, she could appreciate his odd behaviour and had an unexpected urge to support him.

"I don't suppose there are that many jobs about for young men without experience?" she said sympathetically.

"Exactly my point," Dylan cut in. "There aren't any jobs about for seventeen-year-olds without qualifications, unless you want to be a trainee manager at Burger King or McDonald's," he added sarcastically. "It's for that very reason I'm trying to get him to consider college."

Dylan glared at his son, "Anyway, we're just about to have dessert."

He couldn't have been any clearer he wanted rid of him.

"Why don't you join us?" April invited, knowing that would be the last thing Dylan would want.

She doubted Henry was expecting the invitation, and his father certainly wouldn't be. But Dylan was quick to make an effort. More likely because he desired getting her into bed, so wanted to portray he was a good father.

"Yes, why don't you? Zian will have made plenty."

She willed Henry to come and sit down with them. She now knew those affected with autism don't always pick up on social clues. To anyone else, it would have been obvious his dad didn't want him there. And most males of his age wouldn't want to be anywhere near their dad entertaining a woman either. But Henry came over and dragged out the chair next to her. Even the action of taking his seat was clumsy. His whole persona was awkward.

Zian opened the door and came in carrying a huge plate which she placed on the table.

April widened her eyes, "Another one of your favourites?" she asked Dylan.

He grinned, "They're all my favourites. But this treacle and hazelnut tart has the edge."

"Shall I leave it for you to help yourself?" Zian asked.

Dylan nodded, "Yes that's fine, thank you. Could you bring another plate and spoon for Henry, please?"

April glanced at the cake slice. "Would you like me to?"

Dylan's nod encouraged her. She sliced a large piece and handed it to Henry, and cut a similar sized portion for Dylan.

Zian returned with an extra plate which she used for a small portion for herself. She declined the cream Dylan offered, but watched him and Henry pour a generous amount on theirs.

The challenge now was engaging with Henry. Although she couldn't imagine he'd know anything about his father's activities, he might prove useful, so it was essential she kept that option open.

She took a sip of dessert wine to clear her palate and looked directly at Henry.

"We've spent the evening talking about ourselves, and I've just been telling your dad all about my life which must have been pretty boring for him to have to listen to. So, how about you? Tell me a bit about yourself."

Henry swallowed a spoonful of his dessert. "I used to live with my mum, she died, and I now live here with," he hesitated, "Dylan."

His tone and his reluctance not to call his father, dad, was a clear message.

"I'm sorry to hear that, it's so hard at your age . . . at any age really to lose your mum." She felt his pain. Even though her mother was a drug addict and her parenting capabilities were zilch, she'd still felt so much hurt when she'd died. And anger. She was furious she'd left her and Chloe with nobody.

"My father died," she lied, never having any idea who her father was, "granted I was much older than you, but it's still raw even now. How long ago was it?"

"Before Christmas," he looked down at his food, "I'm over it now."

Are you? I doubt you'll ever be over it.

Best to change the subject.

"So, if you're not keen on going to college, what sort of job do you want to do?"

"Nothing," Dylan threw in, "that's the problem."

She smiled sympathetically. His father had obviously forgotten what it was like to be seventeen.

"What would you like to do?" she asked softly.

"Right now? Go to my room." Henry kicked his chair back and stood up, "If that's okay?"

His father nodded. You didn't need to be a family psychologist to see the tension between the two of them.

Henry didn't nod to her as he left the table. He didn't look back either. He just kept on walking.

She now knew that a trait of autism was being resolute once a decision had been made. So, Henry wanted to leave, and he'd done exactly that. Seemingly many autistic people preferred solitude, and hated socialising.

Dylan's mouth thinned. "Sorry about that. He's a significant challenge. I'm amazed he even sat down with us, he wouldn't have done if I'd asked him to."

"I feel sorry for him, he seems . . . I don't know, tormented maybe. It'll be hard for him losing his mother."

"Yeah, but lots of kids lose a parent. They don't get dragged into drugs though."

"Is that what's happened?"

"Unfortunately, yes. He's clean now . . . as far as I know, that is. I've paid for him to have therapy. Christ knows how long it will last for though. He's a moody little bugger."

She nodded sympathetically. "I can see why you want to get him into some sort of further education."

"Easier said than done, though," he said coldly. "The colleges aren't interested in anyone with a caution for supplying and taking drugs. If it hadn't been for a good lawyer and plenty of money, he'd be in jail right now."

"Oh dear, that is sad. Shame the colleges won't give him a chance. I'm surprised at that. Tons of kids take drugs and have convictions. Surely they can't ban everyone; the colleges would be empty."

"I'm sure money would talk, but he doesn't want to go. It's me pushing it. To be honest, the whole thing is a struggle. I didn't expect to be the soul parent of a seventeen-year-old at my age."

"Did you have a lot of contact when his mother was alive?"

He sighed deeply, "I'm ashamed to say, no. Henry is the result of a brief marriage seventeen years ago. Alicia, his mother and I were young and having a good time. Neither of us was ready for parenthood."

He continued as if he'd read her thoughts and felt the need to explain further.

"She was adamant she wanted the baby. My father felt it was a way to ingratiate her way into the family, but the marriage didn't last long. I've paid of course over the years, and I have seen him, but there's no special bond between us. I might be his genetic father, but that's about as far as it goes."

"But you took him in when his mother died?"

"Yes, and the jury is still out on whether that was the right thing to do." He paused for a moment, she guessed he was contemplating whether to say any more. The wine must have relaxed him.

"He's a troubled soul, spends far too much time messing about on computers. He's a whizz at anything like that."

"Maybe you could get him to study something related to IT then?"

"Doubt it. He'd know more than the teachers. You might well laugh, but I'm telling you, every time I hear about computer hacks like the one that breached the White House, or the recent NHS one, a wave of cold fear runs through me. I think it's him."

She widened her eyes, "He's that good, is he?"

"He is." He took a sip of his drink, "I believe he's drawn towards IT as it's solitary. You don't need to interact," he raised an eyebrow cynically. "I think it's fair to say, social interaction is not his bag. My plan is to get him into work or something, then get him a flat somewhere. I'm sure that'll be the best all round. He hates it here with me."

"Be nice if you could get him into a college though. You don't need me to tell you that education's the key to ambition."

"Yes, but he and I don't even agree on what he should study. I'd like him to do his A levels and go to university . . . he wants to do art," he widened his eyes, "which won't pay the bills. That's why I've suggested going for an apprenticeship, something like plumbing for example. I mean, where in London can you get a plumber these days?" he smiled, "he'd be in big demand and always have work. He's good with his hands so I think he'd be suited to that."

"What does he think about being a plumber?"

"Not much."

"What about the art course, then? I'm surprised you're against it when your occupation is art. Surely he could fit into your world very well?"

"He wants to paint, he thinks he can earn a living from that."

"Is he any good?"

"Lord knows. I've never seen any of his work. I've told him though it's unlikely he'll make a living from that. You'd have to have an amazing talent to get paid for painting."

"I wouldn't rule it out. He could surprise you."

There was a pause as if he was considering what she'd said.

She glanced at her watch. "Anyway, I really think I should be making a move now."

"Surely not?" His gaze fixed on her face, "Can't I tempt you with a nightcap?"

It was tempting, but far too soon.

"No thank you. I think it's time I made my way home."

"But it's early," he cajoled.

"I know it is, but it's still time for me to go. It's been a lovely evening, thank you."

He reached for her hand and she didn't try to pull away. It felt nice.

"I've enjoyed your company tonight. Do you really have to rush off? I can get you a taxi in an hour or two."

She maintained contact with his warm brown eyes, "Shall we cut to the chase. What am I really doing here?"

"I thought this was the chase," he grinned, "a beautiful young woman and an eligible bachelor, enjoying dinner and getting to know one another. I was thinking it was time for us to make ourselves more comfortable. I was about to suggest it, actually."

"I don't think so." Her eyes narrowed, "Look, Dylan, I need to level with you. I'm very flattered that you've invited me here for dinner. I didn't want to accept, but you're a man that's hard to say no to. I've had a nice evening, and I am truly grateful. I've eaten more tonight than I normally do in a week. But as for anything else, I'm really not interested in what you have in mind."

"And what do I have in mind?" he asked innocently.

"Seducing me?"

He pulled a pained face, "I'm more of a *mutual beneficial* man really as opposed to being a seducer," he shrugged, "and I don't understand what's wrong with two people who are attracted to each other, enjoying each other's company."

"No, *you* wouldn't."

"You like men, don't you?" he asked, as if it just dawned on him she might be gay.

"Yes, but not men that employ me."

"I have to say, you're over-thinking this," he splayed his hands, "okay, cards on the table," his eyes suddenly seemed very warm, "I'm not going to deny that right now I'd like to take you to bed. There's nothing wrong with that, is there?"

"No, but I don't want that."

"But you're here?"

"Yes, and I'm not entirely sure why. I admit I was curious, you are an attractive man, and if I'm being totally honest, tonight's dinner has reinforced how attractive you are. But you already know that."

"So? What's the problem with getting to know each other? I'm not in a relationship if that's what you're worried about."

"It's not that. I know you probably find this hard to believe, but I don't actually want to have sex with you."

"Why not? You said you're not involved with anyone."

"No, and that's the way I intend to stay. Let me put *my* cards on the table." She took a deep breath in, "Right now, I need to get my life back on track. I want to do my probation period and then hopefully move on and rebuild my life. It won't be easy with a prison record, I know that, but I'm going to try. So the last thing I need right now is anything complicating that."

"That isn't my intention," he said. "Look, maybe I can help you. If it's a better job you want, and somewhere else to live, then I could be your man. I have tons of contacts."

"And I've got to sleep with you for that, have I?"

The silence between them was awkward.

She stood up. "Could you ring me a taxi please?"

"Don't go like this," he asked, "just hear me out."

She would hear him out.

It was all part of the game plan, after all.

His gaze was steady, "Please."

She sat down again.

He studied her thoughtfully. "I'm sorry if I've offended you. Of course you don't have to sleep with me for me to help you. I do genuinely like you, and I'm not denying that I'm attracted to you." He gave such a sexy smile. "You're on my mind a lot," he widened his eyes, "too much really."

She understood his meaning perfectly, he was a bloke. Their minds were generally linked to their trousers.

"So, how about if we try the *being friends* for now, and see where that takes us? It's three months, isn't it, that you have to stay at the gallery?"

"Yes. I'm going to try and get some money behind me and decide where to go from there."

"Then there's no reason why we can't be friends while you're here. You've already achieved a remarkable feat this evening."

"What's that?" she frowned.

"My son actually sitting down at the table with me; he wouldn't have done that if you'd not been here."

"That's good then," she smiled, "I'm pleased. I guess he's used to me cleaning his room now?"

"Whatever. The main thing is, he seems to like you, and that doesn't happen often I can assure you."

For some reason it pleased her that she'd made an inroad with Henry. Why, she wasn't sure. Maybe she felt an affinity as she'd lost her mother and knew the pain never really went away.

"Okay, what's in it for you? Why do you want to be friends with me? You must have stacks of female *friends*?"

"Now that's where you're wrong. I have stacks of acquaintances, but not many true friends. And I don't like people being down on their luck. That's why I like to try and rehabilitate them by giving them employment at the gallery. So, if you'll let me, I'd like to try and help you."

What a load of bullshit.

"Okay," she nodded, "that would be nice. But can we keep this *friendship* arrangement to ourselves? I would hate anyone to think I was sleeping with the boss to get a rung up the ladder."

"Fine," he agreed and raised an eyebrow, "does that mean there's a possibility you might be sleeping with me?"

"Let's just say *might* is the operative word and leave it at that, shall we?"

He placed his hand on his heart, "At least you have given me some hope."

She couldn't help a smile breaking out. He was far too charming.

"Right," he took his phone from his shirt pocket, "give me your mobile number, and we can conduct our clandestine meetings via text."

"Now you're laughing at me."

"No, I'm not," he said, "far from it, actually. It's refreshing to meet someone like you. So many women would have jumped into bed with me to see what was in it for them. It's unusual to come across someone with principles."

"Unusual for a jailbird, is that what you're thinking?"

"I'm not sure what I'm thinking right now." A vague expression passed across his face as if he was recalling something. It was only for a second, and then just as quickly, he was back with her.

"Right, come on, Cinderella, let's get you that taxi home . . ." He stood up, and then hesitated.

"What?" she asked.

"I was just wondering if Henry would give you a lift. It would give him something to do, and you might be able to talk some sense into him. You know, a female perspective on education being the key to success and all that."

"I'm happy for him to take me home," she agreed, "but I don't suppose he'll take much notice of the cleaner. And I'm hardly a role model for an upstanding citizen, am I?"

"It's worth a try. Maybe listening to how you're struggling might at least give him the wake-up call he needs not to go down the drugs route again."

"No harm in trying," she agreed.

"Okay, if you'll excuse me, I'll go and ask him. He can only say no."

She finished the last dregs of her wine while she waited. Things were going just as she wanted them to. The one thing she hadn't banked on was how attractive she would find him. That was a complete bonus. As far as she was concerned, sex was no longer an option . . . it was a definite.

***

The front door of Rider's house opened, and he checked his watch. They'd been almost three hours.

Three long hours he'd waited in his car. He had to get out and piss in the bushes at one stage he'd drank that much water.

He watched the son come out of the house first and April followed in front of Rider. She looked almost petite at the side of him. She was tall for a female, but not next to Rider.

His gut clenched as he watched him hold her jacket for her to slip her arms into.

He held onto her shoulders much longer than was necessary.

Fucking opportunist.

He wasn't close enough to hear what was being said between them, but he watched Rider walk round to the passenger side and hold the door open for her.

He kissed her cheek and she smiled and said something to him.

Probably thanking him for dinner.

She's playing a part, he reminded himself.

The car pulled away and Rider stood in the doorway and watched her go.

Bet he's desperate to fuck her.

He opened the window to spit out the bile that was clogging his throat.

April Masters was far too good for the likes of Dylan Rider.

Chapter 21

"I feel awful dragging you out like this to take me home," April told Henry, "I did tell your dad I'd get a taxi."

"It's okay," he replied unconvincingly, "I like driving." His demeanour spoke volumes. He might like driving, but taking his dad's date home was probably the last thing he wanted to do.

"I am grateful. Even though it's not far, a taxi would have been expensive." She pulled a face, "I'm afraid money's a bit tight at the moment."

"He'd have paid."

"Yes, you're probably right, but I wouldn't have let him."

"Why?" his eyes were focussed on the road as they joined the mainstream traffic.

"Because I wouldn't. I don't like to be beholden to anyone."

"Yeah, right."

"What's that supposed to mean?"

"He's rich, that's why women go for him. No need to make out you're any different."

She frowned. "You're very cynical for someone your age."

He didn't answer. He kept his eyes fixed on the road. It struck her that driving and talking would suit him as he wouldn't have to interact face to face. She'd read that many with autism found eye to eye contract, stressful.

"Are you angry because your dad likes me, or are you angry because your mum died?"

"I couldn't give a fuck about him," he snapped. "And I told you, I'm over my mother, so I don't want to talk about her."

"I wasn't asking you to talk about her; I was asking if you're angry about her death. She can't have been that old."

"She wasn't," he said coldly.

"Well, all I'm trying to say is, it's understandable you're grieving. It must have been a massive trauma and your life has changed. It must be hard to adjust."

Still no answer. She remembered another autism fact. They were resolute. Once they made their mind up, they rarely budged. He'd said he didn't want to talk about his mother, so he wouldn't.

Try something else.

"Your dad was telling me he wants you to get an apprenticeship. Is that what you want?"

"No."

"What would you like to do, then?"

"It doesn't matter, 'cause he won't let me do it."

"How about telling me anyway, I'd like to know."

"Art . . . I'd like to study Art."

She widened her eyes, "I'm guessing you must have a flair for that, then?"

He shrugged, "Sort of."

"Have you shown your dad any of your work?"

"He wouldn't be interested."

"Why not? Art's his business."

"He wouldn't. Anyway," he scowled, "can we shut up about him?"

"Yeah, that's fine by me. I'm not that interested in him anyway."

"Why are you having dinner with him, then?"

"He asked me. It was hard to say no."

"So next time he asks, you're gonna say no?"

"Probably not. Look, Henry, you're," she tilted her head making out she wasn't sure, "seventeen, right?"

He nodded.

"So, you're not a child?"

The question didn't require a response. He'd know what she was implying.

She carried on. "I've been cooped up in prison for almost two years. I'm only on parole; therefore, I have to make cleaning the gallery, work. I don't mind cleaning your house while your cleaner's off either because I need the money. The fact that your dad likes me is an added bonus because I like him. If something was to happen between us, then that's great. But I'm realistic. I'm an ex-jailbird, and rich men like your dad, don't fall for the likes of me. They just want a bit of fun, and right now, I'm up for some of that. If I get to go out to nice places, and eat good food because your dad's rich, then I'm grateful. If there's anything wrong with that, tell me?"

"No," his voice was low and dull, "I suppose."

He turned right and her flat came into view. An announcement from the sat nav told them they had reached their destination.

"Just pull up on the left past the post box," she directed.

"Which is yours?" he scowled slowing the car down and staring at the rows of pre Second-World-War terraced houses.

She knew why. Notting Dale was hardly a salubrious area. It was an area of high unemployment and headline grabbing crimes.

"The white one at the end," she said and he eased his way towards the pebble-dashed four-storey and applied the handbrake.

He screwed his face up, distastefully. "It's shit round here."

"Yep," she agreed, "it is. But this is all I can afford right now. I'm not living in a dump like this for long, though; I'm going to be moving on soon."

His eyes moved around the dilapidated flats and bedsits. "What if you can't? What if this is it?"

"It won't be. I won't allow it. I've got something going for me that will get me out of here." She paused giving him the opportunity to ask what, but he remained awkward and silent.

Keen to make the point, she carried on. "I've got ambition. I know I've broken the law, but I've learnt from that. That's the thing about mistakes, it's crucial to learn from them." She thought about his drug-taking, "Only a fool repeats the same mistake twice, and I'm determined not to go down that road again. I'm going to make something of my life."

He stared ahead, his hands still gripping the steering wheel. "You think you can move on from a criminal record?"

"I know I can," she answered firmly.

Did he know she was aware of his drug conviction?

He turned his head and looked directly at her which in the short time she'd known him, was unusual. But his eyes looked vacant, empty, almost as if he was looking straight through her. His next statement took her completely by surprise.

"I'll show you some of my paintings if you like?"

Although his expression was pitiful, she caught a glimmer of something else in his eyes.

Hope.

Don't make a fuss. He might change his mind.

"That'd be nice; I'd like to see them." She reached for the door handle. "Right, I'd better get in. Thanks for the lift. I'll see you tomorrow then, maybe?"

"Okay."

She got out of the car and stood to wave him off as he pulled away. He flicked his hazard warning lights back at her, and she watched until he disappeared around the corner before making her way up the endless flights of stairs to her top floor flat.

Would he listen to her advice? Taking drugs was a huge mistake, but not a life sentence. He could move on from it. As a police officer, she spent so much time with young people on the merry-go-round of addiction. By the very nature of being teenagers, many start off smoking cigarettes and enjoying alcoholic drinks, but those with an addictive predisposition quickly move onto harder stuff such as cannabis, ecstasy and cocaine. And once they had, they had a huge mountain to climb down from. Dylan had implied Henry's drug-taking had been serious, but he was now off them, so at least he had a chance. If Dylan was any kind of father, he should be bending over backwards to help him stay off them, yet it was already evident the chasm between him and his son was a wide one.

Her heart went out to Henry. It was the rawness of losing his mother that thumped her hard in the gut. The pain never actually went away.

You just learn to live with it.

But you never truly get over it.

Chapter 22

April stared in awe at the paintings Henry had laid out on his bed for her to look at.

"These are stunning, Henry, they really are." She genuinely meant it. It was obvious he had an incredible talent.

He'd been hovering around most of the morning. Each day she came to clean he was noticeable by his absence. Today, she'd quickly cleaned Dylan's bedroom and bathroom so she could legitimately go to his son's room as Elizabeth had said he was in there.

"May I?" she asked before she handled any of them.

For the first time she saw genuine delight on his young face. It actually transformed him from an awkward teenager, into an attractive young man. It was evident he was Dylan Rider's son. He had the same stature, coloured hair and amazingly long eye lashes like his father. She noticed his skin was much clearer of the acne, so guessed he must have seen a specialist.

She held up a stunning picture of a young boy, no more than five or six, leant against the wall with his face covered by his elbow. The pose reminded her of when her and Chloe played hide and seek as kids. She would lean against the wall in just the same way and count to twenty while Chloe hid.

Although you couldn't see the child's face as he was hiding it, he appeared to be crying, which added a melancholy charm to the painting. The clarity made it seem almost like a photograph.

Was that him as a child?

"Have you shown your dad these, yet?" she asked, convinced his father would recognise his talent immediately.

Henry's expression changed from delight, back to his usual sullenness. Clearly, he hadn't.

"I really think you should," she coaxed, "I'm sure that would influence him to consider you studying Art."

She lifted a painting of a beautiful female with piercing blue eyes. Her blonde hair was piled on top of her head, but it was too thick for the clasp as curly strands had sprung out giving her a messy but appealing look. The smile on her appealing face indicated she was happy, but it was Henry's skill with a paintbrush that captured her joy and transcribed it to canvas. Next to the painting was the same picture as a photograph."

"Did you paint that from the photograph?"

His expression darkened. Gone was the eagerness and brightness from minutes earlier. Now he looked sad and forlorn. She guessed why. The woman must be his mother. The closer she looked, the more obvious it became.

Despite knowing from Elizabeth Lile that Henry didn't let anyone touch him, she put her hand on his arm.

"It's your mum, isn't it?" she asked sympathetically.

He shrugged her hand away and reached for the large portfolio holder alongside the bed. It saddened her more than it should he wasn't going to open up to her.

But why should he? She wasn't his friend.

He took the painting from her.

"You look like her," she told him as she watched him systematically putting each of the paintings in a reinforced compartment inside the holder. "That's a huge holder for storing them, it must weigh a ton."

"It's my portfolio. Mum bought me it so that I could show them at potential interviews."

"Did your mum want you to study Art?"

"Not at first," he shrugged, "she was a bit like him. But in the end, she was okay about it."

"Look, I'm not saying I've got any influence with your father, but do you want me to say something? I'd like to support you."

His expression was indifferent.

"I think you should at least show him them."

"Why do you want to help me?" It was a whisper, almost as if he didn't really want to ask.

"Because I think you have real talent. And as I said before, I believe you can do anything you want to do with your life. It's hard at the moment because you're young and financially dependent on your father, but it won't always be like that. I honestly think you should pursue this, Henry. You clearly have a gift."

He zipped up the holder, "I'd not get in anyway because of my drugs conviction."

"Who told you that, your dad?"

"Yeah."

"Well, I'm not entirely sure that would be the case. But if it is, you mustn't let that stand in your way. If you want to study Art, then make an appointment at the college and speak to the tutors. Plead your case. Tell them you made mistakes, got in with the wrong crowd, anything to make them give you a place. Speak to the college principle if you have to."

Were they tears in his eyes?

Even though she wasn't a particularly tactile person, she had an urge to give him a hug. She'd been where he was. Not the same issues, but the gut-wrenching pain of loss was the same for anyone. And nobody had been there to put their arms around her and say everything was going to be alright. Dylan needed to try harder. He was the adult and should be encouraging his son.

Right now though, she'd said enough. It was up to Henry. There was no point in even trying to hug him, he wouldn't want that. And she was only the cleaner, she reminded herself. All she could do was to encourage him with his dream, but not get sentimentally involved. She wasn't there to sort out the dynamics of the Rider family. Getting emotionally attached and offering support to a seventeen-year-old boy were not options she needed to consider.

Doing so would not bring his father to justice.

This was a job.

She needed to remember that.

Chapter 23

Dylan Rider had been coming home for a late lunch opportunistically the past week since Gemma had been cleaning for him. His housekeeper was too much of an employee to question it. She always left something for his lunch and made herself scarce. Today though, she was hovering.

He eyed up the food on the kitchen table, "That looks lovely, Elizabeth, thank you."

"You're welcome. Before I go, I wanted to let you know Alison rang this morning and is coming back on Monday."

Christ, he didn't want his regular cleaner back.

Not while he was making headway with Gemma.

"Is her wrist okay now?"

"She says it is, yes." She placed a bowl of salad in the centre of the table alongside a plate of ham and pickles. A place had already been set for him.

"Has her doctor said she's fit to return?"

"I'm not sure," Elizabeth frowned, "I doubt whether she's asked him. It was only a sprain after all."

"Yes, but you can't be too careful. The last thing I need is her injuring herself further and me having to pay out on a claim as it happened in my house."

Elizabeth was looking at him as if he had two heads and he fully understood why. But he wanted Gemma to carry on cleaning. She was the reason he'd started to come home from the gallery at lunchtime. He needed to move things on. Sexual frustration at his age, sucked.

He painted a questioning look on his face. "I'm wondering, to be on the safe side it might be best if she takes another two weeks off."

"Two more weeks?" his housekeeper's voice went up an octave, "She's been off long enough as it is."

"I still think longer would be better, you know, give the tendons a chance to heal. It's not as if we haven't got anyone, Gemma might do another couple of weeks. I'm sure she'll be fine."

"What . . . you really want me to tell Alison to have another two weeks off?" her puzzled expression said everything, "And you'll pay her?"

"Yes, do that. In fact, I'll go and ask Gemma now if she can stay on for a bit longer. Is she still here?"

"Yes, she's around somewhere." Her brows puckered further, "Shall I wait and see if she can do anymore weeks, then? She thinks cleaning here's coming to an end."

They both turned their heads as Gemma entered the kitchen.

"I'm not interrupting, am I?" she asked.

"Not at all," Dylan replied. "Elizabeth and I were just discussing you actually."

"Oh," she looked concerned, "is everything alright?"

"Yes, everything's fine," he reassured. "We just wondered," he quickly added, "both of us that is, if you're able to do two more weeks cleaning here so Alison can have a couple more weeks off?"

Gemma looked hesitant.

"I quite understand if you can't," he added, almost holding his breath in anticipation she'd agree.

"It's not that I can't, it's just that," she hesitated as if she wasn't sure how much to say. "To be honest, this house is immaculate. I'm trying to earn my money by cleaning thoroughly, but once I've done the bathrooms, and emptied litter bins, there's not a lot left to do. Henry doesn't like me doing much in his room either, so I'm actually creating jobs for myself until it's time for me to finish."

"We'd still like you to stay," he gave his housekeeper a determined look, "wouldn't we, Elizabeth? Maybe you can draw up some sort of rota of jobs that need doing?" He turned back to Gemma, "How about that?"

He'd caught Elizabeth's expression of, *yes I'll do anything as long as I don't have to do the cleaning.*

"Two more weeks you say?" she asked.

"Yes, certainly no more."

"Okay then, as long as you're sure."

"We are," he nodded, "absolutely."

Elizabeth smiled. "Right, now that's settled, if you'll excuse me. I've got an appointment so I'll have to dash." She looked directly at him. "Shall I give Alison a ring?"

"Yes, if you wouldn't mind."

"Okay, I'll do it later today. I'm back at six to let the caterers in. I've already set up the dining room ready for tonight."

"Thank you. I appreciate that."

He wished his housekeeper would bugger off.

Elizabeth turned to Gemma, "You'll be eating your words tomorrow. There'll be a hefty amount of cleaning up to be done after tonight's soirée."

"That'll keep me busy, then," she smiled, which lit up her beautiful face. "Do you mind if I wash my hands?"

"Of course, dear, help yourself."

Elizabeth picked up her cardigan, "I'll see you later this evening," she nodded to him and smiled at Gemma as she made her way towards the utility room and the back door of the house.

Finally, he was alone with Gemma. She put the towel down she was drying her hands on, and moved towards the door.

"Hey, hang on," he stopped her, "care to share some lunch with me? He nodded to the mini banquet Elizabeth had left him on the kitchen table. "There's far too much here for me on my own."

She hesitated.

"Come on, it's just lunch. Surely cleaners have to eat lunch?"

She gave him a deliberate glare. "They do, yes, but not usually with their boss, and certainly not in their boss's house."

"Can they make an exception to ensure that good food doesn't go to waste?" he asked playfully.

She took a deep breath in. "If you're absolutely sure. But then I really must be going." She widened her eyes in a teasing way, "Even cleaners have a life outside of work you know."

"I'm delighted to hear it." He pulled a chair out for her, "Come on then, I'll get you a plate and we can get stuck in. You can tell me all about your out-of-work activities while we eat."

She walked towards the kitchen table and took the seat he was holding out for her.

"I really don't think that would be of much interest to you."

"You'd be surprised how anything you say is of interest to me," he winked, and she grinned back at him which transformed her eyes into a much richer green.

He was making progress. She was starting to warm towards him, he could tell.

Good.

His cock twitched.

He had great plans for this little beauty.

Chapter 24

April kept her cap on and the large tinted glasses as she asked at the ward reception where Noah's bed was. It would have been polite to have removed her hat, but it was easier to risk someone thinking she was rude than show her whole face.

She poked her head around the bay and saw Noah sat on his bed looking at a comic with her sister sat at the side of him. His face lit up when he spotted her.

"Aunty April," he squealed loudly, and her sister turned around.

April rushed up to the bed and threw her arms around Noah, holding onto him tightly. Her heart constricted; she loved the little fellow and had missed him.

She pulled away. "How's my favourite soldier?"

"Better now. I might be going home."

"Brilliant. Here you are," she handed him a brightly coloured gift bag. "It's a little something for you because I know you'll have been such a good boy." She'd wrapped the box several times for fun. "Unwrap it carefully, won't you?"

She turned and reached for her sister. "Hello, you," she held onto her tightly also. It had been over three months since she'd seen her. She inhaled the familiar scent of her. She loved Chloe. Her and Noah were her only family.

"Are you okay?" she asked, pulling away from her beloved sister who looked exactly the same as she always did. Glamour and make-up were not Chloe, that was for sure. Her hair was tied back in a no-nonsense ponytail, and she was wearing her obligatory tee-shirt and jeans. She always looked that way. On the occasions she dressed up, she looked so nice, but those times were rare.

"Yeah, I'm fine, much better now Noah's on the mend." She pulled a face. "What's happened to your lovely hair?"

"I had it coloured and cut short for a change. She removed her cap and ran her fingers through it, "Do you like it?"

April moved towards a stack of chairs and selected one for herself.

"I'm not sure," Chloe frowned, "I loved your long hair. Did you cut it out of choice, or is it some sort of disguise for your work?"

"Choice, you daft thing," she replied sitting down next to her sister. "What you think I do for living, I've no idea," she pulled a puzzled face, "it's nothing like you imagine. The most I get up to is mixing with unsavoury characters who in most cases owe vast sums of money. All I do is find information to try and get it back for the creditors."

"So, you don't contact me for over three months and I'm not allowed to call you, I have to text first. And that's all because you're a debt collector is it?" Chloe replied sarcastically.

She needed to get Chloe off the scent. If she had any idea she'd been in prison, she'd go ballistic, even if it was undercover. It had been difficult enough. She'd missed her sister and Noah so much. But she couldn't let her know, she'd have been mortified. The police had even sent an undercover officer to visit her in prison, so it appeared she had a relative. It had all been part of the elaborate undercover plan.

"Enough of that Chlo," she dismissed, "I'm here now. Tell me what the doctors have said about Noah.

Noah, interrupted them. "Why is there all this paper, Aunty April?"

"'Cause it's more fun. Like pass the parcel," she smiled watching his tiny fingers deftly opening each layer.

"Go on," she prompted Chloe.

"The usual chest infection, but he's also had a bladder infection as well. That's why he's been so poorly." Chloe turned to Noah, "So that means he has to drink lots of juice, remember buddy."

Noah picked up his glass of orange and took a gulp, before going back to his present.

"But he's fine now?" April asked, looking for anything in her sister's face that implied he wasn't.

"Yes, until the next time."

She squeezed her sister's hand.

"Wow!" Noah squealed, holding up a new iPad minus the wrapping paper, "Look, Mummy, it's an iPad."

Chloe raised her eyebrows, "My goodness, you're a very lucky boy," she gave her a look as if to say it was far too much for a child. "That must have cost Auntie April a lot of money. What do you say?"

April didn't care. Technology was the way forward and she didn't want this little mite to fall behind. He might not be able to walk properly, but she'd be damned if his learning was going to be held back.

His gorgeous little face was a picture. "Thank you," he reached out for another hug and she gladly hugged him back. It was only seconds, but she savoured him in her arms and inhaled his scent as she kissed his little warm neck.

"You're welcome, sweetheart, you deserve it. Here, let me show you something. There are some games you can play on it. And look there are some songs for you to listen to."

April showed him how to click on the music icon, and a catchy melody of a children's song came on.

"How did you know I'd like this song?" he asked innocently, moving his little body in rhythm to the music.

"I asked the lady in the shop what sort of songs were suitable for gorgeous four-year-old special boys, and she told me Paw Patrol was popular. Look in the box, there's some headphones as well for when you want to listen."

"Aw, yeah. Can I play it now?"

"Yes, course you can. Your mummy will charge it up for you at night so it always works when you need it. Here," she passed him the tiny headphones, "try it with these on."

Noah put the headphones in each of his ears. His beaming smile said it all.

"Can I go show Jake, Mummy?" he asked.

"Go on then," Chloe replied, "but don't go any further than the play room as the doctors are coming round shortly. We need to find out if you can go home."

Noah swung his legs to the edge of the bed and reached for his walking frame, securing the iPad underneath his arm. He grinned at them both.

"Mind you don't drop it," Chloe warned, "here, let me put it in the bag so you can carry it."

They both smiled lovingly as they watched him manoeuvre his way out of the bay, the gait of his hips swaying from side to side as the walking frame supported most of his weight, and the small wheels pushed him forward.

"That's far too much for a little boy," Chloe shook her head, "it's not even his birthday."

"Aw, don't be cross. It's just a treat as he's been poorly, and I can afford it."

Chloe reached and clasped her hand, "How can I be cross when I'm so pleased to see you. I've been frantic about you, it's never been as long as this. Please don't do it again."

"I know, and I am sorry. I did tell you it would be a while."

"Yes, but three months without a word. You know that's not fair. What on earth was it? And don't be telling me it was debt collecting again, I don't believe that for a minute."

April scrunched her face up, "You know I can't discuss it. As it is, I shouldn't be here today, so I haven't got long."

"Why? What's more important than your family?"

"Nothing's more important than you two," she stressed, "I'm doing this for Noah. I told you, this is the last job. I want you to have enough money for him to go to the States for his op. That's what's driving me."

"But the fundraising's going okay, so you've no nccd to break your neck. We'll get there, I'm sure of it. Which reminds me, I'm keeping everything crossed Noah's going to be okay for the weekend, there's a *party on the lawn,* this Saturday afternoon. There are loads of stalls, and they're having a band. The blokes are doing barbecue food. Gavin's in charge of burgers," she rolled her eyes, "they're buying two hundred of the things."

"Crikey, I hope they all get eaten."

"Can you come? Noah would be thrilled if you were there."

"I can't, Chlo," she winced, "I'm in the middle of a job. But I promise you, when this is over, I'll be able to see more of you and Noah."

Chloe's expression darkened. "Why is it I don't believe you?"

"You must. Look, at the end of this, I'll have enough money to make a significant difference to the fundraising. When I've finished, Noah is going for that op, I promise you."

"That's brilliant, but I do need to see you, though. And this job worries me. I know you keep saying it's not dangerous or anything, but it must be, or else why all the secrecy?"

"I've told you, I can't discuss it. You just have to trust me on that. I've not come to any harm before, and this is no different."

"You say that, but I'm not so sure. Gavin thinks it's dodgy, he always says something isn't right. You only get paid lump sums of money if you are doing something risky."

"Rubbish. What does Gavin know? I wouldn't do anything dangerous. Why would I?"

"Tell me where you've been for over three months, then? Why all the mystery?"

"You know why. That's the job. I sign a clause to say I won't discuss it. I'm not allowed to."

"I get scared for you, April," her eyes started to well up, "I couldn't bear it if anything happened to you."

"Nothing is going to happen," she reassured, "a few more weeks and it's all going to be finished. And I promise you after that, as I said before, no more secretive jobs. I'll do something different."

"I'll hold you to that," she wiped a stray tear with her finger. "Anyway, tell me, are there any nice men in this secretive world you live in?"

April sighed, "Not so you'd notice."

"I really wish you'd meet someone and be happy like me and Gav."

"I know you do, and who knows, one day I might. I just need to finish this job, then," she paused trying to think of something to cheer her sister up, "I tell you what, just to make you happy, I'll start dating. I'll join one of those internet dating sites, how about that?"

"Sounds good to me, there'll be plenty wanting to take you out."

"Do you think?" she smiled, "I better get on a site quickly then."

Chloe rolled her eyes, "What like you're never asked out?"

"Not lately." She saw the disbelief on her sister's face, "I'm telling you the truth," she grinned, "they're not queuing up I can assure you. Most of the blokes I meet are married or divorced. And they're the worst as they often have kids in tow and want you to spend the weekends at theme parks and Pizza Hut." She shook her head, "Not for me, I'm afraid."

"Yeah, well, maybe you should have found one sooner then."

"That's the story of my life. I'm too late."

"Don't be daft," Chloe dismissed, "it's never too late. When you give up with this secret nonsense, you might find someone."

"Good job this is my last *secret nonsense* job, then."

"Yeah, I'll believe that when I see it." Chloe reached for her handbag, "Anyway, do you fancy a coffee if I nip and get us one from the canteen downstairs?"

"Yeah, a latte would be nice. I'll go and find Noah and spend a bit of time with him. Which way will he have gone?"

"To the next bay on the left, or if he isn't there, there's a playroom at the bottom of the ward. He'll be in there. I won't be long."

Chapter 25

The train was full on the way home, but April managed to get a seat by indicating with her eyes to a young woman to shift her rucksack on the seat next to her.

Her distaste for public transport reared its ugly head and she closed her eyes to shut out the commuters. Today had been just the tonic she needed. Chloe and Noah meant everything to her. Apart from her job, her whole life had been supporting Chloe.

It started when they were very young. Their mother used to put them both to bed, and once she thought they were asleep, she would nip out of the house. April was never asleep although she did a good job of pretending. She would listen for the front door opening and closing quietly, and then run to the window and pull back the ghastly purple material that was supposed to be a curtain, but didn't quite cover the whole window, and watch her mother walk away from the house. It puzzled her why her mother was dressed in flimsy clothes on those cold winter nights and didn't have a coat, and her childish mind wondered where she went to and what was so important that she would leave her and Chloe alone.

Most nights she would get into Chloe's bed with her and cuddle up. As she lay waiting for her mother to return, she would pray that she would change and be like the other mothers.

On a Monday morning at school, her teacher used to give them all a chance to speak at 'show and tell' in the classroom, about the activities they got up to at weekends. How she longed to swap places and visit the special places the rest of the class went to like the zoo, the park, or on a train, or to the cinema. It was baffling why her and Chloe never went on trips like that.

She said her prayers before she went to sleep each night, certain that God would make sure her and Chloe had nice trips, and she asked that her mother would stop in and not go out in the dark when they were in bed. But it seemed that they were not high on God's priority list.

It was a boy at school that alerted her to exactly what her mother was doing. Not that she understood initially what the word prossie meant.

She recalled the summer's day vividly. The sun was hot on the way to school even though it was only morning, and most of the children were wearing pretty sun hats and caps protecting them from the sun, but her and Chloe didn't have hats for the summer, or even in the winter for that matter. They never wore hats like the other children.

On this particular day, she was to receive a certificate for attendance during assembly. The teacher had told her when her name was called out, she was to go onto the stage and take the certificate from the headmaster. She was to thank him and shake his hand.

There was no question of not attending school. Come hell or high water, she had to go. If she wasn't feeling well, her mother would still make her go, and tell her the school would send her home if she got any worse. Many a time she'd be in school and felt poorly, and often the teacher would take pity on her and let her rest in the comfy reading corner. It was as if they knew something she didn't.

At the special assembly, she'd waited while her name was called out and proudly took her certificate from the head. As she turned to walk down the three steps from the stage, she'd eagerly looked around the audience. Most of the children had their mothers there and in some cases, fathers clapping eagerly at their child's achievements, but all she saw was Chloe, beaming away and clapping for her.

Their mother hadn't come.

At playtime, she'd found Chloe in the playground on her own as usual. She sat down with her on the grass. They both wore the pretty hats that they'd been given by the teacher to protect them from the sun. They didn't seem to be in groups like the rest of the girls skipping or playing tag. If they even got close to them, they'd pinch their noses at them and say they had the lergie whatever that was.

A painful image imprinted on her mind was of her and Chloe sat on the grass singing songs together when a couple of the older boys came past and sneered at them, "Your mum's a prossie. Prossie, prossie, prossie."

She'd grabbed Chloe's arm and dragged her towards the school entrance to get away. It felt safer being near where the teacher stood supervising them all.

"What's a prossie?" Chloe had asked.

She shook her head, genuinely unsure. She knew it wasn't something nice though.

"Shall we ask Mrs Green?" Chloe persisted.

April knew whatever it was; it wasn't something they should ask the teacher about.

"No, we don't want to get mummy into trouble. I'll find out what it is and tell you."

It didn't take long to find out exactly what a prossie was. It explained why their mother left them alone each night.

Other things started to fit into place. They'd had a talk from the school nurse about Michael in the class who was poorly. He had a special bag that seemed to go everywhere with him. The school nurse explained that he was often unwell, and they must all make sure they looked out for him and if he appeared poorly in any way, they should let the teacher know.

The school nurse then talked about medicines, and talked about doctors and nurses and how they must try to keep healthy by eating good nutritious food and cutting down on sugary snacks. At the end of the talk, they were asked to draw pictures about anything they'd talked about during the lesson. Some of her classmates on her table drew a bed with a nurse alongside. They put a red cross on her hat, and one boy drew an ambulance with a flashing light. Esme, had drawn a syringe with a needle on it as her mother had been diabetic. April decided she'd do something different. She'd drawn her mother's bedroom. Her colourful picture was a dressing table full of tablets, and she'd even drawn a syringe with a needle on it considering perhaps her mother was diabetic too, not actually sure what that meant but it sounded poorly to her young mind and would explain why she'd seen a syringe. There was an elastic thing she would wrap around her arm. April wasn't sure what that was for, but she included it in the picture.

The nurse came round to each table to look at their efforts and award good work stickers. She said she would take some of the pictures back to her office and put them on the wall. She hadn't taken April's picture though. She'd picked it up, scowled and took it straight to the teacher.

April could remember vividly having to go to the headmaster's office and was asked questions. She knew then that she'd done something very wrong, she just wasn't sure what. But even at that young age, she had an innate understanding to keep quiet.

She continued to make mistakes due to her innocence, but by the time she reached secondary school, she didn't make anymore.

Maturity had afforded her wisdom beyond her years.

Chapter 26

Dylan sat at his desk and his thoughts drifted to Gemma as they seemed to be doing more often than he liked. She was an enigma and occupied his thoughts far too much lately, and he just didn't get it. How come a hard-up cleaner, and an ex-con at that, had him sniffing round like a randy dog? He didn't do desperate.

He'd texted her earlier enquiring how she was as she'd been sick the previous day, but as always her replies to his texts were slow to come, and even though he kept glancing at his phone, he knew she wouldn't respond while she was at the gallery. She never texted during work hours, well not him anyway. Was somebody already sorting her? He wouldn't be surprised. Even in the chain-store clothes she wore, she had an air of finesse and class. His dick twitched at the image of her in the tight cleaning dress she wore at the gallery each night. It was a plain dowdy black overall, which on the other girl looked exactly what it was. But on her, it clung to her generous breasts and nipped-in waist. Not an ounce of fat on her. He loved the shape of her tits and longed to rip the dress off her and bury his face in those pert beauties. He liked generous breasts in a female. Skinny bitches did nothing for him.

He checked his phone again. Still no reply. It was understandable she was working hard to meet the parole conditions so wouldn't want Ingrid to catch her texting. One word from him or Ingrid and she'd be out, but surely she realised that was unlikely to happen? Okay, he was the boss, but she could let her guard down a bit, particularly as he'd made it clear he was interested. Far too interested really. Despite that though, she kept her head down and diligently carried out her work, which not only irritated him, it fascinated him.

He unlocked a drawer and took out the file he had on her. He knew all there was to know about her, so why he was checking it again, he wasn't sure. She'd already explained to him how her head had been turned by an older bloke that led to her stealing money and ending up in jail. She'd been stupid and berated herself for that, but he had a degree of sympathy. Part of the passage of youth was making mistakes. He only had to look at himself getting Alicia pregnant when they were both only twenty and the consequences of that. And then there was Henry and his drug taking which he didn't condone, and sincerely hoped that now he was clean, he'd stay that way, but again youth played a part in the choices Henry made.

But he wasn't actually bothered about Gemma's past, or the fact she'd been in jail. It was the here and now he was interested in. Most women would jump at the chance to be with Dylan Rider, and his sensible head told him to move on to someone else instead of pursuing her. The trouble was, he didn't want anyone else. He wanted her. And the frustration of her keeping him at arm's length was getting to him. Surely she must be gagging for it having been locked up for so long?

The thought again of someone else sorting her, made him uncomfortable. He didn't want anyone else screwing her. He'd been going home for lunch trying to make headway with her. He'd regressed to almost being an adolescent trying to impress her with humorous stories and antidotes that painted him in a good light. Seeing her each day fired him up for more, and images of her invaded his sleep, so each morning a regular wank was the first task of the day. And it didn't stop there either, just a sniff of her within his vicinity, had him hard.

The only certainty he had was his attraction to her was reciprocated. He knew enough about women to know that. But she resisted him and he found that bloody frustrating. He didn't normally have a problem getting a woman into bed.

Some gave a bit of a chase and the run-around, but invariably they gave in. Gemma hadn't though. His patience was wearing thin, and looking at the photos of her in the file, his cock was rock hard again. He really needed to fuck her and get all of this nonsense out of his system. He could move on then to someone more receptive to him, so he didn't have to carry on this juvenile chasing behaviour.

He adjusted his trousers to accommodate the tightness. He could do with tossing it off, but didn't fancy a hand job in the office.

A gentle knock interrupted his train of thought, and Ingrid poked her head around the door.

"Anything I can get you?" she asked demurely.

He knew what she meant. It was what she always meant, and right now, she was going to get it. If her husband couldn't oblige, he could.

"Yes, come in, Ingrid, and lock the door behind you.

Chapter 27

"Anything new?" Paddy asked April as they walked around the boating lake in the park.

"Nothing. The house is clean as far as I can see. I've looked at as much as I'm able in his study, apart from his safe that is. But I'm sure any useful info will be stored at the gallery. He won't have it at his house."

"No, you're probably right. He'd have thought about the ramifications of ever having his house searched."

They halted their steps at a bench. Paddy checked with his hand that the dirty marks were engrained in the wood. It was secluded and away from the others in the park, so they wouldn't be overheard.

She sat down next to him. "It's my so-called birthday tomorrow and I'm going out in the evening with Rachel and Joey. I'll spike Rachel's drink so she won't be in work the following day. She cleans the offices, but if she's off, it'll be down to me, and knowing my luck," she rolled her eyes, "I'll end up doing the bloody toilets as well. But if I can legitimately get into his office, I can have a good root around and see what I can come up with."

"We need something," he screwed his face up in frustration, "anything to lead us to where he's got the Portillo stored. He must have some sort of verification of the painting's validity somewhere . . . and the sales history."

"He's no dummy though," she shook her head, "he'll have that sort of info in his safe at the gallery if he's got any sense, and I can't imagine there's anyone who knows the combination apart from him. He has an admin woman who comes in during the day, but of course I don't see her with my shift not starting until the gallery closes, so no chance of gleaning anything from her."

"What about the supervisor, anything on her?"

"Ingrid? No, nothing. I'm not entirely sure what her role is. I have an inclination she's after Rider for herself."

"Do you think they're involved?"

"I'm pretty sure they are," she nodded. "If he's not already screwing her then she'd like him to be. I've no proof though, so call it intuition. I wouldn't put it past him. Rider's an attractive man and can have his pick of women; he just doesn't get too involved. That's evident from the info we have on him."

"What about you. Is he still keen?"

"He seems to be. It's the chase he's interested in, though."

"Well, don't go down that road with him, whatever you do."

"As if I would," she dismissed, "Rider's not my type, that's for sure. And much as I love my job, sleeping with the suspect is not on the agenda."

"Glad to hear it. We'll just have to see what you can pick up from his office. Tomorrow you say?"

"All being well."

"We'll meet here Saturday, usual time?"

"Yep, that's fine."

"Perfect. See you then."

***

He'd been watching them both sat on the bench engrossed in conversation. She'd been hiding her beautiful face with the obligatory cap and sunglasses, and he noticed she'd taken to wearing a decorative scarf. That'd be to hide her long neck, no doubt. April was a master at blending in and wouldn't want to draw attention to herself in any way.

His fingers had itched watching her brush her fringe off her brow as she was talking. He wished it was his fingers caressing her forehead.

Paddy had stood up and lent forward to kiss her cheek. Bet he enjoyed that, the old bugger.

Her eyes watched Paddy walk away but she remained seated, staring ahead at the ducks bobbing about in the water.

What's going on in that mind of hers?

Bet she knows I'm here.

She's no dummy.

April Masters missed nothing.

She'd know if she was being followed.

Chapter 28

The Italian restaurant April met Rachel and Joey in was crowded. Joey had organised the evening to celebrate her fictitious birthday she'd let slip. That had given them an excuse to go out.

They took their seats in a booth and the waiter handed them a menu each, "Can I get you any drinks while you're looking at the menu?" he asked.

"That'd be great," Joey replied. "What can I get you girls? Do you fancy a beer, or how about a bottle of Prosecco?"

"Oooo, yes please," Rachel smiled enthusiastically. "A bit of bubbly to get the party started."

It was hardly a bloke's drink and April hated it.

"Do you drink, Prosecco?" she asked Joey.

"Nah, but you girls can share a bottle." He turned to the waiter, "A bottle of Prosecco and a pint of lager, please."

"Certainly, sir."

As soon as the waiter was out of earshot, April whispered, "It'll be outrageously expensive in here."

"It doesn't matter," Joey dismissed, "I'm buying."

"No, you're not," April told him, "we'll split the bill."

He frowned, "You're not paying for a meal on your birthday."

She pulled a pleading face at Rachel, but she shook her head, "Don't look at me. I'm happy to pay, but Joey says he wants to, and as he earns twice as much as we do," she smiled cheekily at him, "I for one am happy to let him."

April smiled affectionately at them both. No point in arguing, she knew when she was beaten. In her line of work, she didn't meet people like Rachel and Joey, not often anyway. There were her work colleagues, but on the whole her interactions were with people breaking the law, or subtly dodging it. It was refreshing to be in the company of decent folk.

"Okay, okay," she put her hands up playfully surrendering, "I give in. Thank you, Joey, that is very generous of you. You must allow me to reciprocate when it's your birthday."

"Aw, that's nice then," Rachel turned to Joey, "when's your birthday?"

"Sixth of November, if you'll still be around then?" he asked.

April pulled a face, "Probably not. I'll have to see."

"You're not going yet though are you?" Rachel asked with a wary expression.

"No, course not. I have to do at least three months for my parole, and then I'll see what I'm going to do. I definitely want to move on and get a job where nobody knows about my past, though."

"What did you do anyway?" Rachel asked. "You know . . ." she left the sentence unfinished. Her face had awkward written all over it, as if she knew she shouldn't have asked.

"It's okay," April reassured, "we can talk about it," but the waiter appeared and halted the conversation.

He placed their drinks on the table and took his notepad from his pocket. "What can I get you?"

They'd not even looked at the menu.

"Shall I just get us a couple of large pizzas to share and a bowl of salad?" Joey asked.

They both nodded in agreement and let him order two different types with an abundance of toppings.

As the waiter left, Joey reached for the ice bucket and poured two glasses of fizz and handed her and Rachel one each.

"Here's to us," Joey raised his pint, "good friends."

They all clinked glasses and repeated the toast.

"Go on, Gemma," Rachel prompted, "you were telling us about what you did."

April crumpled her face with a pained expression, "I stole some money. I'm really sorry I did now, but that's no excuse. I shouldn't have done it."

She had their full attention and by their silence she was forced to add to the story.

"I worked in the finance department in an accountant's office. One of the girls suggested I applied for an in-house scholarship to study and become a qualified accountant, which sounded fabulous as they actually paid you to go to college one day a week. I couldn't have afforded to study full-time, so this was a great way to learn on the job. So, I applied, and to my amazement, I was accepted."

They were eagerly taking it all in as she paused. "God, this is so boring . . ."

"No, it isn't," Rachel encouraged, "tell us the rest."

She took an exaggerated breath in. "I was given a mentor, one of the senior staff at the practice who took me under his wing. I had to wait a few months until the course started but he was there to help me prepare. I used to spend a few hours each day with him going over relevant stuff. Stupidly, I fell in love with him and," she added a wounded look to her face, as if remembering was difficult, "I became a puppet doing everything he suggested. Eventually, he persuaded me to steal some money from the firm." She rolled her eyes, "For both of us . . . the company could afford it . . . they wouldn't miss it. He skilfully showed me the way to systematically steal small amounts of money so it wouldn't be missed. Working in finance helped as it gave me access to the company's money."

"How much did you steal?" Rachel asked.

April knew the cover story so well so could have embellished the narrative further, but Joey bailed her out.

"Hey," he interjected, "aren't we supposed to be celebrating your birthday, not looking back on the past?"

"Too right," April went for a relieved expression, "enough of that. I'm just pleased the gallery has given me a chance to redeem myself with the cleaning job, otherwise," she smiled kindly at them both, "I wouldn't have met you two."

Joey lifted his beer, "I'll drink to that," and they clinked glasses again.

"Tell us about Mr Rider's house," Rachel said, "what's that like. Is it a mansion?"

"It's a big place, that's for sure."

"Has it got a pool? You always imagine the rich to have a pool?"

"No, there isn't a pool. He's got a huge Jacuzzi though."

"God imagine that after a long day," Rachel sighed. "Fancy just being able to come home from work, strip off, and jump in your own Jacuzzi. I tell you, next time, I'm coming back as a billionaire or something."

"You'll have to keep buying a lottery ticket," Joey said, topping their glasses up with more Prosecco, "and you might get something in this life-time. You'd have plenty of money for a flash house with a Jacuzzi then."

"Yeah, but knowing my luck, the night I won, there'd be about twenty other people with the same numbers and I'd end up with a measly hundred grand or something stupid like that."

They laughed together at Rachel. April would miss them both when the job was over. She wasn't stupid enough to become attached to anyone while she was undercover, but these two were the salt of the earth.

"How about another toast," Rachel said. "Hey, we'll need another bottle if we carry on like this."

Joey nodded, "We'll get another one when the waiter comes."

"My toast this time," Rachel said and lifted her glass. "To my two besties. I hope one day our lives will be full of money. Oh, and happy birthday, Gemma."

"I'll drink to that," Joey smiled and raised his glass, "Here's to us all having plenty of money. And happy birthday, Gemma."

All three clinked together as the waiter arrived with their food.

The Italian was a good choice and Rachel entertained them with stories about internet dating and some of the choice blokes she'd had dates with.

"What about you, Joey," April said putting her knife and fork together, "have you ever tried internet dating?"

"Nope. Call me old-fashioned, but I like to see what I'm getting. I wouldn't be interested in a blind date. I'd be worried what the hell might turn up."

Joey wouldn't need to meet women on the internet. He was too good-looking to struggle for a date.

"Oh, you'd get plenty of weirdos, I promise you." Rachel rolled her eyes, "They always turn up ten years older than their photos, and ten stone heavier," she giggled. "And you definitely need to half and quarter what they say on their profile."

April needed to get to the bar and get a drink, so she could put the laxatives in Rachel's.

"Anyone fancy a nightcap? I'm buying."

"I thought we'd already had that discussion," Joey frowned, "and we agreed I'm paying."

"We have. But I want to get us one drink at least. Come on, one for the road. What do you fancy?"

He breathed in deeply, "Okay, another beer will do me."

"What about you, Rachel?"

"Er, I don't know. What you having?"

"I might have a Tia Maria and Coke. Do you fancy one?"

"Go on then, that sounds nice."

April stood up and Rachel frowned, "You don't have to go to the bar, the waiter will bring them?"

"I know, but they'll go on the bill and Mr Generous will end up paying. I want to buy us all a drink. I'll be back in a minute."

Chapter 29

April was in the changing room at the gallery removing her coat the following evening.

"Ah, Gemma," Ingrid bustled in, "thank goodness you're here. I'm afraid Rachel's unwell so won't be coming in. You're going to have to clean Dylan's office tonight as best you can before you do the toilets. Joey's going to muck in and start hoovering the corridors. We'll just have to manage and hope she's just off tonight and back tomorrow."

"What's the matter with her?" April asked.

"Severe diarrhoea. Says she's had it all day, thinks it might be something she ate last night."

Great, it had worked.

"Oh dear, that's awful." April put her overall on and fastened the buttons. "I'll make a start straight away, then."

"Yes, do what you can so it looks as if it's been cleaned. Empty the bins, polish his desk etc, and if you could do Dylan's secretary's office too, that would be helpful. If you get chance, run the hoover round, but don't worry if you don't. Then make a start on the toilets. I'll be up shortly to see how you're getting on."

Don't you roll your sleeves up, Ingrid, will you?

April quickly made her way to Dylan's office and closed the door behind her. Her eyes double-checked there was no CCTV in the office. She'd crept in once before to verify there wasn't.

His desk was staring at her like a beacon, and she made her way towards it. She took all the clutter off, resting it on a chair and sprayed generously a layer of furniture polish. If Ingrid came in, it would look like she was in the middle of cleaning.

The top drawer wasn't locked which could only mean there wasn't anything significant for her to see. Dylan Rider wouldn't leave stuff around which was likely to incriminate him. Nevertheless, she quickly lifted a heap of papers out. At a glance, all she could see were receipts and catalogues, nothing appeared to be of any importance, but how was she to know. She quickly took a couple of photos on her phone so the team could analyse them.

She tried the filing cabinets behind his desk. The admin woman couldn't be up to much as the key was in one of them. The alphabetically neatly filed compartments didn't appear to have anything vital in them, but again she took some photos of any documents she could. There wasn't time to rifle through much.

Paddy had asked her to take photos of Dylan's safe so they could scrutinize exactly what sort it was and the level of difficulty of cracking the combination. Her eyes scanned the room trying to locate it, and quickly figured out it had to be in the chimney breast behind the formidable portrait of Carson Rider, Dylan and Victor's father. As she attempted to move the painting, she was surprised it actually opened like a cupboard door and behind it was indeed, the safe. She stepped back to quickly take a photo, and another much closer showing the locking mechanism.

With the painting back in place, she moved back to the desk and rubbed a duster over it. She reached for the ornaments she'd placed on the chair, carefully dusting the framed photo of a much younger Dylan and his parents. It was old, but they all looked happy.

As she replaced the desk blotter, she noted there were a few scribbles, as if someone had been doodling while talking on the phone. Her eyes were drawn to a number 25/5 which had been circled several times. How significant was that? Did that mean the 25th May? If it did, it was almost five weeks away. Was that a deadline?

Her eyes scanned the computer station adjacent to the desk for a diary. There didn't appear to be one, which wasn't a surprise. Men like Dylan Rider would use an electronic diary. But his secretary would have a desk diary to keep track of his appointments, surely? Granted she might be able to access his electronic diary if he wanted her to, but more than likely she would have a paper copy. An admin with any sense would.

She made her way next door to the secretary's office and rummaged through the desk drawers that weren't locked.

Bingo!

There in the central drawer was a large, leather-bound desk diary.

She turned the pages. Friday 25th May. *DR away.*

What was the significance of that date? They knew Dylan needed to move the painting soon. Was that the date, or could he just have something personal on?

The next task had to be accessing his phone to see if there was anything more she could find out. But even if she could get her hands on his iPhone, it'd be password protected.

She hastily dusted around the secretary's office before returning to Dylan's. She was emptying the litter bin as Ingrid poked her head around the door.

"You'll have to get a move on, Gemma," her eyes did a sweep around the office. "It'll have to do in here for tonight."

April tied a knot in the black rubbish bag. "I've done the essentials. Let's hope Rachel's back tomorrow to give it a bit more of a thorough clean."

"Yes, fingers crossed she is."

April followed Ingrid out of the office and closed the door behind her.

How could she find out the password to Dylan's iPhone? Would it be his date of birth?

And more importantly, how could she view his calendar?

Chapter 30

April closed Dylan's bedroom door. She'd just changed the bedding and carried the used sheets downstairs. It was the final day of cleaning at his house. His regular cleaner was coming back.

He'd paid her exactly what they'd agreed for cleaning the house. Mrs Lile, the housekeeper, gave her an envelope each week with the cash in.

Dylan had been coming home for lunch, and Elizabeth Lile was now setting a place for her at the table also. April knew in normal circumstances it wouldn't be right for a cleaner to be having lunch with their wealthy boss. But these weren't normal circumstances and, as she was supposed to be a hard-up cleaner, struggling to make ends meet, why wouldn't her head be turned by the boss's interest?

"Are you about done?" Elizabeth asked as she deposited the dirty laundry in the utility room adjacent to the kitchen.

"Yes, all finished." She fished in her pocket and pulled out a piece of paper and handed it to the housekeeper, "I've made a list so when Alison comes back she can see what's outstanding, and what I've managed to get done."

Elizabeth Lile looked at the list. "You've done so well while you've been here. I've told Mr Rider how efficient you've been, you've literally cleaned every nook and cranny of the house. He says he's going to give you a bonus for all your hard work."

April smiled inwardly.

Yeah, every nook and cranny alright, but I've not been able to access what I really want.

"That'll be nice. I like to do a thorough job, you know . . . I want to try and impress."

"Well, you've certainly done that, my dear. And Mr Rider does like you," she widened her eyes, "I mean really likes you. You can tell."

April managed a coy expression. "Oh, you mean the lunches. They're nothing really. I think he feels sorry for me as I haven't a lot of friends in this area."

"I'm sure there's more to it than that," Elizabeth replied with a knowing look.

"I don't think so," April dismissed, "men like Dylan Rider don't lose their head over a cleaner."

"No, maybe you're right. But you are a stunning girl and no disrespect intended, but I think maybe he's more interested in . . . you know . . ." she lowered her voice, "they're all the same in that department and I'm sure he's no different."

April forced a giggle, "You could be right, but I'm definitely not going there. Oh, before I forget, a couple of the staff at the gallery did ask me to find out if he has a birthday coming up. They're talking about giving him a gift, although what do you give a man who has everything?"

"Yes indeed. But I don't know where they've got the idea it's his birthday coming up. That's not until September. It's on the eighth, the same day as my late mother, that's how I remember it."

So its 8th of the 9th month.
Just need the year now.

"That's odd then," April frowned, "I don't know where they've got the idea from, someone's got their wires crossed. Is it okay to wash my hands?"

Elizabeth nodded, "Please do."

April took her time lathering her hands generously and rubbing them under the warm running tap.

"I'll let them know at work it isn't his birthday then before they rush out and get him something. He is a fit man, isn't he? How old would you say he is . . . mid-thirties?"

"He's thirty-seven, thirty-eight this year. Yes, he does look after his appearance, he exercises every day, and eats healthily. I think alcohol is his only vice," she lowered her voice, "and women. He likes them, as you well know."

They both grinned as they heard footsteps approaching.

"Good afternoon, ladies." Dylan's eyes focussed on her as he came into the kitchen. "Last day then, Gemma?"

"Yes. I've just given Elizabeth the list of what I've done for when Alison comes back."

"Good. You're staying for lunch today though, aren't you? I've asked Elizabeth to make us something."

"If you're sure?" She turned to the housekeeper as she dried her hands, "It really is kind of you. I'll miss your lovely lunches, Elizabeth."

"And I'll miss you, my dear. I can honestly say I've never met a cleaner who works as hard as you."

"Aw, thank you. I try my best. I'm pleased you think I've done a good job."

"You've done more than a good job. I'm going to miss you."

April smiled, she would miss her too. She was a nice lady.

Elizabeth picked up some oven gloves, "Right, I'll just take the quiche out of the oven and leave you both to it. The salad's already on the table."

"Thank you," Dylan smiled, "I'll open some wine." He walked towards an area off the kitchen where the supply of alcohol was stored. It was huge, almost the equivalent of a wine cellar in a restaurant.

"No wine for me, thank you," April called, "I've got the gallery to clean yet."

"One glass won't hurt you," he called back.

Elizabeth placed the quiche on the table. "I'll say goodbye now, Gemma. And good luck with whatever you do in the future. It's been a pleasure having you here."

"Thank you. I've enjoyed it."

It was awkward for a second, and then Elizabeth hugged her. They hardly knew each other, but it was sweet.

"Bye then, dear. You take care of yourself."

"Thank you, I will. You too."

April watched her go and mentally calculated that Dylan was born in 1980. So his birthday in numbers would be, eight, nine, eighty.

Would that be his passcode? It was a bit of a long shot, but worth a try.

Now all she had to do was get her hands on his iPhone. That was going to be a significant challenge.

But there was a way she could get access to it?

Maybe now was the time to step things up a notch.

Chapter 31

The jazz club in Soho was perfect. The dimly-lit basement managed to deliver a surprising level of intimacy and was just the right place to seduce a woman. And Dylan Rider knew just how to do that. He was easy to like, had great charisma, but most important of all, oozed sex appeal. It was no effort to agree to a date. He'd been trying to get her into bed for weeks.

They were in a small intimate booth and April had enjoyed the music while sipping cocktails in the glamorous 1920's surroundings. It had a lot of class, without a hint of pretentiousness.

"Would you like to dance?" Dylan asked when a slow blues song came on.

Why not?

"That would be nice," she smiled and stood up.

He walked with one of his hands on her lower back towards the small dimly-lit dance floor. She'd wager he'd done the seduction routine stacks of times. She easily slipped into his arms and they began moving closely to the music. It actually felt pleasant.

"You smell lovely," he whispered in her ear, "what is it?"

"Nothing you'd be used to buying," she teased. Any perfume he bought for a woman you wouldn't be able to buy over the counter at Boots. He'd be used to buying the high-end stuff.

He grinned. "You're such a tough nut to crack, Gemma, do you know that, mmm?"

"I wasn't aware you were trying to crack me. I thought we'd agreed on being friends."

"I agreed to that because it was what you wanted; I wanted more. But I've respected your wishes, you can't deny that."

"I know you have."

They fitted well, close together. He smelled divine. A subtle oriental fragrance that sent her senses into overdrive. They continued in silence swaying their bodies to the rhythm of the music. Although quiet, a new intimacy was developing between the two of them.

The music eventually stopped, and as he led her to their seats, his hand subtly caressing her lower back. The dance and closeness to him had certainly given her libido a huge kick.

He sat her down before taking his seat and reached for her hand. His warm brown eyes had taken on a sexy, come-to-bed, look.

His lips gently kissed the back of her hand and he held onto it as he rested it down on the table. "I'm wondering if I can persuade you to move things on between us. You must know how attracted I am to you. Dare I say you feel the same way about me?"

Go for it.

"Maybe. But I'm thinking with my head, and not my," she hesitated, "other regions. I still have to work for you. Okay, I'm not cleaning your house anymore, but I'm likely to see you at the gallery."

"So? I'm not just after one night if that's what you're thinking. I'd like to get to know you . . . properly. You're bright, Gemma, you could do so much, especially looking the way you do."

She gave an exaggerated sigh. "I've got to see this rehabilitation period through, and I don't want anything jeopardising that. I'm sure sleeping with the boss isn't exactly what the parole service had in mind when they placed me at the gallery."

"As far as I can see, you're doing a terrific job. Nobody would be questioning your work ethic. I'm pleased with that, and Ingrid is also. I asked her to convey to your parole officer how well you're doing, and I believe she's done that."

"That's kind of her, and you. I am grateful that you've given me this chance. But what if I was caught, you know . . . with you?"

"But you're already here with me, so you're over the first hurdle. I really don't understand what you're worried about."

"Yes, well, I'm hardly likely to bump into my parole officer here, am I? Or Joey and Rachel."

"Is that what bothers you, people finding out?"

"It's a consideration, yes."

"Okay then, what if at the gallery I continue to play your boss, just like I have been doing. How about that?"

"It's a start."

"Right, that's settled then. I can do clandestine, in fact," he raised an eyebrow, "I might actually enjoy it."

She smiled at him. Even though he was good-looking, his charm made him more attractive. He'd know exactly how to please a woman. She had to get to his phone, and the likelihood of getting access to that was much greater if there was some intimacy between the two of them.

That was the only reason, though. Wasn't it?

"Is that a yes smile?" he asked with a cheeky look.

"Sort of."

He leant forward and kissed her for the first time. He didn't make more of the kiss than he had to. She tasted rum. Her tummy flipped, and her pussy twitched. It had been a long time since she'd had sex.

He pulled away. "Are we good to go?"

"Okay, where to?" she asked standing up.

"Well, I have got a table booked for dinner, but I'd sooner scrap that and take you straight to bed."

"Ah, but I need feeding so I'm afraid we're going to have to eat first," she grinned cheekily, intentionally prolonging his wait.

"Right, come on then. How about a McDonald's?"

"A McDonald's?" she repeated.

"Yeah, fast food. That's what I need right now."

She rolled her eyes at him as he helped her on with her jacket.

He'd taken her to a small boutique hotel for dinner. They chatted about the gallery, the weather, and must-see holiday destinations, simply to get through the meal. They both knew dinner was a prelude to sex.

She placed her knife and fork together on an empty plate and smiled at him. "That was a fabulous meal. Thank you."

"Do you want dessert?" he asked.

"Erm, I'm not sure I could eat another thing. How about you?"

"Yeah, I'm fancying something," he grinned seductively, "but it doesn't come out of a fridge and on a plate."

"Is that right? What is it you fancy then?" she asked putting on an innocent expression. "See if you can tempt me, too."

He grinned sexily. He liked this game, she could tell.

"What I want right now is a beautiful woman with a gorgeous figure that I can lose myself with. I want to give her some pleasure . . . until she's begging me for more. I want to bury myself deep inside her until she comes screaming my name. And then I want to fuck her again and again, so tomorrow, she'll be reminded exactly who she's been with."

She crossed her legs. "Well that certainly beats the chocolate torte I had in mind."

He laughed then tilted his head questioningly, "So, what's it to be. My dessert or the chocolate torte?"

She threw him a sexy grin. "Yours has fewer calories . . . and I am watching my weight."

"You are such a bloody tease, Gemma, and there's no way I'm going to make it back to mine. Wait here, while I get us a room."

He closed the hotel room door and pulled her to him, running his fingers through her hair. "You're beautiful," he whispered.

She took a sharp breath and his tongue thrusts between her parted lips. His body was rock-hard against hers, and his spicy cologne filled her senses. She met him kiss for kiss, and the blood rushed downward as his low and deep groan reverberated over the drumming in her ears. One of his hands fisted her hair, tightly, and her mouth opened wider for him as he drove deeper.

He traced his fingers across her trembling lips. "I want you so much," he breathed, "every part of you."

He slipped his finger into her mouth and she curled her tongue around it, sucking and getting more turned on by the second.

"You're so bloody hot," he groaned, slipping in another finger, "so warm, and wet."

His mouth covered hers in another deep, breath-taking kiss. There was an intense throbbing between her thighs, and her legs could barely hold her up.

His passionate tongue dance eased into a gentle nipping of her lower lip with his teeth. He broke the kiss, "Let's get out of these things."

They stripped off eagerly. Even though sex was at the forefront of her mind and pulsating body, she surreptitiously watched where he placed his clothes. He tossed a condom on the bedside table, but left his phone in his jacket pocket.

She kept her purple bra and panties on. They were sexy, and showed off her figure to perfection. Sex with him had been on her mind when she'd bought them.

He took her hand and led her towards the bed, reaching behind her to unfasten her bra. His sexy eyes darkened at the sight of her exposed breasts, and her nipples pebbled with need. She drew in a shuddering breath and closed her eyes as they gently lay down. His palm grazed her breast and cupped its weight, while his fingers pinched her nipple, tweaking and twisting, adding more searing heat throbbing inside of her. She writhed and moaned, incredibly turned on despite him hardly touching her.

His mouth was relentless on hers. "I knew it," he groaned, "you have the most beautiful breasts."

She caressed his thick hair as his teeth worked their magic, grazing her aching breasts, and her head fell backwards as he sucked hard on each nipple. Her belly twisted as the pleasure became stronger and he sunk his teeth into her neck.

He cupped the back of her neck as he licked her collarbone and then slid his splayed hand all the way down, across her tummy until he finally reached where she wanted him to be. She could feel her own wetness and her clit throbbed.

He knew.

He eased her thong slowly down her legs, enhancing the anticipation of touching her where she most needed him to.

It felt like a bolt of electricity when his slick fingers touched her clit, all the time keeping his mouth locked with hers as he started to stroke her.

She moaned as he slid a finger deep inside, and then he added another . . . and rubbed her clit lightly with his thumb. The pressure was pleasurably brutal.

"Yes," she panted as his fingers moved faster and she felt herself rushing towards an orgasm. "Oh God, yes."

"Come," he rasped, pressing his thumb harder against her clit.

Her ears were ringing, and her skin buzzing until she could stand no more. Her pussy clenched as she jerked against his hand and orgasmic pleasure burst through her body.

It had been so long.

She put her hand on top of his, silently indicating it was enough. He held her while her breathing slowed.

"You're so hot when you come, do you know that?" he whispered silkily in her ear, "and I can't wait to be inside you any longer."

He reached for the condom off the dresser, ripped it open with his teeth and handed it to her. She easily applied it to his hard smooth cock, stood to attention with the head glistening.

She began to work him.

"Spread your legs," he demanded.

She did as he ordered and moaned for him when he opened her with his fingers. She squeezed at his cock, at his balls, licking her lips at the thought of him inside her.

"That's enough," he groaned, "anymore and it'll be over before it's begun."

He moved his position, holding his cock and moving it up and down her labia, teasing her entrance and making her pussy twitch for more. His infectious mouth continued to bestow kisses on her as he penetrated her slowly, inch by inch. She adjusted her position to accommodate all of him until he was balls deep inside of her.

They gradually fell into a rhythm where she rocked to meet each powerful thrust. The pleasure was building and becoming stronger with the friction rubbing against her clit.

His pace increased.

"Mmm," she groaned as his hand grabbed her ass, lifting her for better access and filling her to the brim.

She tightened her inner self around him as his cock buried deep inside her, pleasuring her with long, hard and fast stokes, and the bliss was enhanced by her breasts bouncing and rubbing against his chest. She gripped hard as he continued to slam into her.

Every nerve ending was on fire, and her pussy clenched around him trying to suck him deeper. His thrusts became more urgent and relentless, deep and hard into her.

"I can't hold on," he groaned.

She bucked and convulsed around him as a second orgasm hit her. "Yes!" she screamed as pleasure rippled through her again, like a torrent, and he continued to grip her backside, hissing and groaning as his cock jerked inside her with the heat of his own release.

Momentarily, they stared into each other's eyes before he pulled away.

He rolled onto his back breathing heavily and pulled her into the crook of his arm. "I am sorry, that was a bit quick."

She snuggled in, "I'm not complaining."

And she really wasn't. It was divine!

They lay quietly as their breathing slowed.

It felt nice.

Was he as satisfied as she was?

"You are beautiful, Gemma," he whispered, stroking his fingers up and down her arm.

My God, so are you.

He eased himself onto an elbow and unexpectedly she noticed gentleness in his eyes as he stroked the side of her face and tenderly kissed her forehead, nose and mouth in a way more suited to a loved-up union opposed to a no-strings shag. "Excuse me a second while I use the bathroom. Stay right where you are. Don't move."

As soon as he closed the door behind him, she jumped out of bed and fished in his jacket pocket for his iPhone.

She could hear him starting to pee as she keyed in his birthday. Eight, nine, eighty.

Touch ID or enter password again flashed on the screen.

Shit.

It wasn't his code.

Chapter 32

Unexpectedly, April was back cleaning Dylan's house. Elizabeth had telephoned and asked if she could do one more day, as Alison, the regular cleaner had to attend a funeral. It suited her as she'd figured out a possible way of accessing Dylan's phone. She'd asked Paddy to get the IT department to send a couple of random messages to Gemma Dean via Facebook from so called friends, asking if her account had been hacked.

She stood at the door of Dylan's ensuite assessing how clean it looked following the swift whizz round she'd given it. It would have to do, time was of the essence. She knew Henry was usually in on a Monday and she needed to speak to him. She quickly stripped and changed Dylan's bed. There was little else to do. He had a dressing room but that was always clean and tidy. The floor looked fine, so she skipped hoovering, it wouldn't hurt for one day.

She scurried along the landing to Henry's room and gently tapped on the door before going in. It was legitimate that she made his bed each day and cleaned his bathroom.

"Good Morning. Is it okay to come in and make your bed?" she asked.

He was facing one of the computer screens and nodded but didn't turn around. Dylan reckoned he'd told him he had to have his room cleaned, either that, or clean it himself and she saw no evidence he was. It was a typical teenager's untidy room.

She made her way to his double bed and taking her time, stripped back the sheets and tossed the pillows on the floor.

"Can I ask you something?" she said smoothing the bottom sheet so it was creaseless.

"What?" he still didn't turn around.

She continued pulling the sheets up the bed and straightening them. She didn't answer. There was no way she was going to talk to the back of the little sod's head.

He must have got the message as he swivelled his chair round.

"What do you want?" he sighed.

She stopped what she was doing. "I'm not very good with social media and I think someone may have hacked my Facebook account. People have been receiving random messages with attachments supposedly from me, but I haven't sent them."

"You've been hacked, then," he replied indifferently.

"Yes, that's what my friend said last night when I spoke to her. She told me to change my password online, which I've done, but I can't work out how to change my security number on my phone. I'm sure it's simple, but I'm scared I'm going to lock myself out." She put on a clueless face, "I wondered if you could show me . . . if you wouldn't mind?"

His scowl said everything. "Have you got it here?"

She reached in her pocket and walked towards him to hand over the phone.

"It's four-two-ninety," she worked on being embarrassed, "my birthday. I'm rubbish with passwords and security codes. I have to write everything down otherwise I'll not remember."

His face was fixed on her phone. "Pick a number you can remember then, or use the fingerprint recognition."

"Oh, right, I've not done that before."

He shrugged, "Which one?"

"I'll use a number," she pretended to think. "If I can think of a significant one, that is."

"You can still use your birthday," he replied with a hint of irritability in his voice, "just use the current year to remember it."

"There's a thought. Is that what you do?" She'd read up on autism, they tended to be very factual and not lie.

"No."

She paused for him to say more, half expecting he might not, but nevertheless waited.

"I use a date to do with my mother."

"What, her birthday?"

"No. The day she died."

"Oh dear, that's sad." And she meant it. What an odd thing to do. She wanted to hug the poor soul, but she knew that was completely out of the question. What was it about this teenager that got to her?

He shrugged, "Dylan knows my birthday."

"Yes, but I'm sure he wouldn't go into your phone without your permission."

"You don't know him," he sneered, "he's not what he makes out."

She ignored asking the obvious question of, *in what way?*

"Is he a whiz with computers like you?"

"No."

"He's probably like me then and uses his birthday as his code. It seems to be the common thing."

"He doesn't. He'd be too scared someone would suss that out."

"I can't imagine anyone would be interested in looking at his phone, either?"

"You are."

She should have been taken aback by his frankness, but she'd found out autistic people were very direct. They didn't understand social etiquette and tended to come out with whatever was on their mind.

"No, I'm not," she frowned, "why would I be?"

"To check for other women."

She laughed out loud, "Don't be daft. I'm not interested in anything like that. It doesn't matter to me how many women he has on the go."

He shrugged as if he couldn't care less. "He uses Christmas day."

"Oh right," she picked up the pillows from the floor and began fluffing them up. "I wonder what the significance of that is?"

"Who cares? He doesn't celebrate Christmas, not with me anyhow."

"Well, maybe this year will be different now you're living with him."

"Doubt it."

"How come you know his number anyway?"

"I just do." He looked bored with the conversation. "Have you thought of a number?"

"I think I'll go with my mother's birthday, I can't forget that. It's New Year's Day. One-one- sixty."

He fiddled around for a second and then handed the phone back to her. "Try it."

The number worked. "Aw, that's brilliant."

She picked up her caddy of cleaning materials, "I'd better get on, thank you for doing that."

She headed towards his ensuite as he turned back to his computer. So, Dylan's number was Christmas day. Would he use twenty-five and twelve as the month, or twenty-five and eighty, the year he was born? Probably neither. What she needed was an opportunity to at least try both.

Twenty minutes later, she returned to the bedroom and Henry was still on the computer. "I'm done now so I'll get out of your way. I meant to say earlier, your skin looks much better. Did you get Roaccutane?"

"Yeah," he said, his cheeks flushing.

"Good for you. It's made all the difference." His flush intensified.

"What about college, any further headway?"

"No," he said abruptly and then surprised her with his question. "Why are you only a cleaner?"

Christ. What does he know?

She took an exaggerated breath in. "Because it's all I can do right now. There aren't many opportunities for someone who's been in jail. And I need the money. That's why your dad asked me if I wanted to clean here while your cleaner's off."

"What did you do?"

"I got in with the wrong man and stole from our bosses. We both went to prison for fraud."

"What happened to him?"

"Still in jail, his sentence was longer than mine. He was seen as a sort of puppet master, controlling the strings."

"Are you waiting for him to come out?"

"God no. That part of my life's in the past. I'm trying to move on."

"With Dylan?"

She widened her eyes and moved away, "I told you, I'm not bothered about him. If he's interested, that's fine, but if not, it's no skin off my nose."

"Yeah, you are. That's why you want his number so you can check his phone."

"I don't want his number," she scowled, "and I'm certainly not interested in checking up on him. He can see who he likes for all I care. We aren't exclusive. Not that it's any of your business," she said firmly.

"It's twenty-five eighty."

Was that a hint of a smile? As if he wanted her to know.

She silently said a prayer of thanks.

"I think I'm all done here. Your other cleaner is back tomorrow so you'll not be seeing quite as much of me."

"You'll still be seeing him, though."

"For now, if he wants to see me. But if he doesn't, it's no big deal. Like I've said before, it's casual."

She picked up her cleaning caddy and walked towards the door.

He'd given her exactly what she wanted.

She finally had the number to access his father's phone.

Did Dylan have any idea how much his son despised him.

Chapter 33

April had finished in the toilets at the gallery and was wiping down the air conditioning vent when the door opened.

Ingrid smiled. It wasn't a genuine smile. "When you've had your break, Gemma, can you come to my office? I need a quick word."

April wiped the sweat off her brow with the back of her hand. "Sure, do you want me to come now?"

"No, have your break first. Rachel was making the coffees when I poked my head in the staff room." She glanced at her watch. "Come up at half past and we can have a chat."

"Will do," she nodded.

Now, what the hell does she want?

April stood outside with Rachel and Joey while they had their cigarettes.

"Did you see Ingrid?" Rachel asked taking a sip of her coffee, "she was looking for you."

"Yeah, I've got to go and see her at half past." She checked her watch, "I'd better not be late."

"What's it about, do you know?"

She shrugged, "I don't. I hope there's nothing wrong with my work."

"It won't be that," Joey cut in, "nobody works harder than you. I reckon they'll be begging you to stay on here when your twelve weeks are up."

"I doubt it, but I don't really want that, to be honest."

"Why? It's not a bad job," he said.

"And it's good pay," Rachel added.

She needed to choose her words carefully. The last thing she wanted was to offend either of them.

"It is a great job, but I want to move on. I've only ever seen this as a stepping stone. I don't want to stay here indefinitely; I'd like to go somewhere where nobody knows me, you know, doesn't know about my past."

"I think you're being a bit hard on yourself," Rachel said, "everyone makes mistakes, and it's not as if you've murdered anyone or anything. You like it here working with me and Joey, don't you?"

"Of course I do. I love being with you two, but I still need to move on."

"But where will you go? Why don't you stay for a year or so then think about moving? Me and Joey love you being here with us."

"Aw, Rachel, don't say that. You'll make it even harder for me to leave."

"That's exactly what I'm trying to do," Rachel grinned.

April gulped the last of her coffee. "And you're doing a brilliant job," she checked her watch again, "I'd better go and see what Ingrid wants."

"It'll only be about your probation. What else could it be?"

It wouldn't be. Her parole officer, Tom would be there if it was.

"Yeah, I expect so. I'll let you know on the way home tonight."

Joey took a last drag of his cigarette and crushed it against the wall. He put the stub back in the packet.

He let them back into the gallery with the code and his badge.

"See you in a bit." He gave a reassuring wink, "Good luck."

April gave a nervous smile and made her way to Ingrid's office.

The next few minutes were crucial. She couldn't afford to get on the wrong side of Ingrid. Tom had warned her in the beginning she'd be out on her ear if she did, and then it would all have been a complete waste of time.

She tapped on the office door.

"Come in," Ingrid said and she entered. April had never been inside her office as Ingrid cleaned it herself. That seemed to be the only job she did do.

"Ah, Gemma, come and have a seat. Have you had your coffee?"

"Yes, thank you."

She took the seat opposite her. Ingrid would love sitting behind the imposing desk wanting her to feel subservient.

If she only knew.

"Good. I wanted to catch up with you to touch base, so to speak, to see how you're getting on."

Yeah, right.

"Fine." April put on a fake worried expression. "Is everything alright with my work?"

"Your work is excellent as far as I can see."

The relieved expression came next. "Good, 'cause I'm really trying."

"Yes, I can see that. You've made quite an impression with us all . . . especially Mr Rider."

Oh, I get it.

The green-eyed monster rears its ugly head.

"His housekeeper said they were pleased with the work I'd done at his house."

"I'm sure you've done a great job there too, but that's almost finished now, isn't it?"

April nodded, "I've actually finished already. His regular cleaner's back this week."

Come on. Why don't you just cut to the chase?

This isn't about my work.

"I see. Right, well, there was another reason I wanted to have a chat with you," she lowered her voice slightly, "and this is completely confidential, you do understand, just between the two of us."

Cut the crap . . . please.

"Yes, of course."

"How can I say this . . . erm . . . Mr Rider seems to have a bit of an eye for the ladies. I've seen him looking at you on occasions. I don't know whether you've noticed that?"

Well actually we've moved on from the sexy looks.
We're fucking now.

April shook her head vigorously.

"Haven't you? I am surprised. I would have thought a girl with your looks gets lots of admiring glances."

She didn't answer, even though it was yes, she did attract men.

"I just want to say you need to be careful with him, or any man for that matter linked to the gallery."

That must be a warning about Joey, too.

"I think it's important while you're going through this parole period that you don't   . . . how shall I put it . . . don't become emotionally attached to anyone, if you understand my meaning."

Too late.
The horse has already bolted.

Ingrid carried on, "Mr Rider for example. He's a very wealthy man, and wouldn't seriously be interested in a cleaner, not for anything long-term, although men like him do get carried away when there's an attractive female around. And that's what worries me. I'd hate for anything to happen that could jeopardise your rehabilitation. Do you get my drift?"

"I think so." April faked uncertainty. "You're worried I might become involved with him if he showed an interest in me?"

"Something like that, yes."

"I wouldn't," she replied emphatically. "I don't see him much but when I do, he only asks how I'm getting on. He's a perfect gentleman really," *especially with his dick inside me,* "so I can't imagine he's got any designs on me."

"That's reassuring to hear. The last thing I'd want is for you to have your head turned. Mr Rider is a very attractive man."

April nodded her head again, implying she was in agreement with everything Ingrid was saying. She took a deep exaggerated breath in. "I do understand. And while we're talking confidentially," she swallowed, "I don't think I'll be staying on here much longer after my twelve weeks. I want to make a fresh start somewhere else . . . you know, where nobody knows about my past."

Ingrid's expression turned to one of relief. "Very wise. I'm pleased to hear it, and I'm more than happy to supply you with a reference about your work. Anything I can do to help, you just need to say."

"Thank you. That really is kind of you."

"Right then, I'm pleased we've got that settled. And don't forget, let's keep this conversation to ourselves shall we?"

"Of course," April smiled reassuringly and stood up. "Shall I go make a start on the staff-room now?"

"Yes, you do that. Thank you, Gemma."

Stupid cow.

I'll be fucking Dylan Rider as often as I can until I get what I want.

Chapter 34

April was killing time until Dylan arrived to take her out. Chloe answered the phone and she could hear the dulcet tones of Ed Sheeran in the background.

She smiled. "Hello you."

"Hi, April, how's the baddies?"

"Still bad," she laughed. "How did the fundraising event go?"

"Brilliant, loads of people came. Can you believe we sold the two hundred burgers?"

"Really? That's fantastic."

"There was tons of other food left over, though. The organisers gave us stacks to bring home. Even Noah ended up protesting he couldn't eat any more sausages and he normally loves them."

"Aw, God love him. How is he?"

"Much better. You wouldn't even know he's been poorly, he always bounces back. You've just missed him, he's gone with Gavin to his mum's."

"That's great. How much did you raise, do you know?"

"Just over two thousand."

A mere drop in the ocean.

"That's brilliant, Chlo, you must be chuffed to bits."

"I'm stoked. Gav checked last night and we've now got almost thirty-four thousand."

"Brilliant. It's amazing how generous people are, isn't it?"

"I know. We have a sponsored bowling night in three weeks. That should bring in quite a bit, and the website keeps getting donations. We're now wondering if we can apply for some money from Children in Need."

"Isn't that for specific groups of children rather than individuals?"

"I'm not sure. Gavin's going to write anyway. Anything's worth a try."

Gavin was a selfless man. She couldn't wish for a better dad for her son.

"He is good, isn't he? Noah's so lucky to have you both."

"And you. He's lucky to have you, as well. Without you, none of us would have him."

Her insides twisted at the reminder.

"We're all blessed to have Noah. Anyway, like I said, with a bit of luck, I'll have plenty of money soon to add to the pot. Then we can start planning his surgery. It'll be amazing if we can get him walking before he's six."

"Wouldn't it? I have a dream that someone really rich like Elton John or Paul McCartney will come along and pay for it all."

"Yeah, keep dreaming and you never know. You might get it sooner than you think."

Chloe sniggered, "Hey, guess what, a pink pig has just flown past the window."

April smiled, "You wait and see. Right, I'm going to have to go, work beckons."

"What work? I bet you're sat in a comfy office somewhere on a computer trying to catch the criminals out?"

Bless you, sweetie, I wish.

"Yeah, something like that. Anyway, big kiss for Noah, love to Gavin."

"Will do. Take care, won't you? Love you to the moon and back."

"You too."

April ended the call.

Chloe was in for a big surprise when this job was done and they'd have the money for Noah's operation.

It was the only thing spurring her on.

Chapter 35

April looked out of the window and saw the beautiful black Bentley below and waved, making sure Dylan saw her. She needed to get downstairs so that he wouldn't come up for her. Tonight was about seduction and the last thing she needed was for him to see how she lived. He would have an idea, of course, cleaners didn't live in salubrious surroundings, but she wanted to be desirable to him tonight, and a shitty shoebox of an apartment didn't quite cut it.

She moistened a thread of black cotton and placed it in a straight line at the door as she let herself out and headed down the stairs.

"Hi," she smiled as Dylan held the car door open for her.

"Hi to you too," he smiled appreciatively. "You look beautiful."

She might be dressed in chain-store clothes, but she'd worked really hard to look good in her wrap around blue dress and trendy jacket.

"Thank you." She got into the passenger seat making sure she showed plenty of her toned legs.

He got in beside her.

"Where are we going?" she asked as she put her seat belt on.

"I thought we'd go to the theatre and then eat afterwards, if that's okay with you?"

"Lovely. What are we going to see?"

"The Mousetrap," he said. "Unless you've seen it before?"

"No, I haven't."

"Me neither. I've always been promising myself I'll go, and tonight's finally the night. I thought we could get some supper afterwards."

"Sounds good to me."

He gave her a sexy grin as he started the engine. "I've been fancying one of those delicious desserts we had the other night. It's been on my mind all day."

The sharpness of his jaw and the tiny creases at the corner of his eyes when he smiled caused an unexpected shiver to run through her body. She smirked, "Yes, I must admit, it was rather nice. Have you got anywhere in mind?"

"I can easily sort somewhere. I wanted to see how hungry you were first of all."

"I missed lunch," she widened her eyes, "so I'm starving."

"Well, we can't have you starving. Are you okay with the hotel we went to the other night?" He lifted an eyebrow cheekily, "I could phone them from the theatre and book us a . . ." he paused, "table?"

"That would be sensible. Saves time as I bet it's busy on a Saturday night."

"Absolutely."

The car started to move. Her eyes were drawn to the fine dark hairs on the back of his hand disappearing underneath his shirt cuffs as he clutched the steering wheel. In a couple of hours, those hands and fingers as well as his incredible mouth, would be delivering so much.

Her pussy tingled nicely.

She was well ready for him.

He delved into her mouth like a man possessed, his tongue sliding rhythmically with hers. He certainly knew how to kiss. His sensuous lips glided along the nape of her neck before moving on to her ear, sending tickles of pleasure down her spine. She moaned for him as he took the lobe into his mouth, biting down gently with a teasing pull while his dextrous fingers worked their magic caressing her receptive skin.

He cupped her breast with one of his hands as his warm tongue trailed across her skin and circled each nipple; his hot, greedy mouth beyond amazing as it sucked hard.

She whimpered as he continued the pleasurable torture of his lips gliding across her navel, causing her entire body to shudder with need. She groaned as his head curled round the inside of her thighs and his warm breath continued to caress her skin, moving slowly until he reached where she wanted him to be. His tongue lapped her wet pussy, and she gasped as he concentrated on her swollen clit.

He was deliberately slow. It felt incredible. He added a finger, heightening the pleasure.

"Dylan!" she cried fisting his hair, "Oh, god!"

She clung on to the bed sheets, clamping her thighs around his head and squealed as he kept licking and sucking, circling her entrance until her body could stand no more. She bucked and her hips jerked as her orgasm rippled through her. It felt like she was shattering in to a million pieces.

Still drowsy with contentment, she watched him apply a condom over the tip of his already coated dick. The size of him erect, made her eager for more.

He kissed her on the mouth, and she tasted herself on him. "You're beautiful," he breathed in between kisses, "so beautiful."

She took the length of him in her hand, working him. Her legs opened naturally to give him access. Even though she'd come, her throbbing clit still wanted to feel the length of him deep inside her. Her tummy did summersaults as he gently grabbed her by the waist and flipped her over.

He massaged her shoulders and ran his delicious tongue up and down her spine. She moaned when he kissed and bit her ass. Moaned as his fingers stroked through the crease and made its way towards her pussy, and she moaned again when he pushed three fingers into her, stretching her.

"God, Gemma, you're so fucking hot."

He sucked and nipped at her neck, and gently pulled her onto all fours. And then she felt him, his hardness touching against her aching pussy. "God Dylan, just fuck me," she said.

"My pleasure." He took hold of her hips and she cried out as he slammed his dick into her soaking wet pussy. Her internal muscles stretched as he filled her and began to move.

He wrapped an arm around her waist, and pressed down on her lower tummy, his fingers reaching for her erect nub. He rode her harder and harder, strumming her clit, and the pleasure increased with every unforgiving stroke.

She tightened her inner self around him as her orgasm was building, her breath catching as he dove into her again and again; each powerful thrust harder than the last.

The sensation and an awareness of his potent strength had her excitement mounting to fever pitch. She cried out with the pleasure of him filling her to the hilt and his balls slapping her with each thrust.

"Dylan!" she screamed as her muscles contracted around him.

"Fuck!" he yelled out, his hands gripping her backside as he jolted and his cock spasmed deep within her.

They lay together. It felt nice. They weren't a loved-up couple, but it felt right cuddled up beside him with her head resting on his shoulder.

Her only disappointment was, he hadn't put his phone on the bedside table. In the rush to get their clothes off and have sex, he must have left it in his jacket pocket.

Would she have time to go get it while he used the bathroom?

Yes, maybe if he had a quick shower.

"I guess we'd better be making a move," she stretched out, "these hotel rooms are too expensive for this sort of thing really."

"Believe you me, they are worth every penny," he kissed her forehead.

"You know what I mean," she playfully slapped him, "we've moved on now, so you don't need to keep doing this."

"I know. I didn't want it to be awkward for you at the house with a sullen seventeen-year-old prowling around the place."

"Well, I reckon at seventeen he should know the score. Father or no father, he's not a child."

"It's not him I'm worried about. I don't want you feeling uncomfortable in any way."

"And I do appreciate that," she kissed his cheek, "it's very thoughtful of you."

"Thoughtfulness never entered into it, I can assure you," he grinned, "but you're right, there's no reason why we can't be together at the house. If you don't want this to stop, that is?"

"I'm not sure I *could* stop it, to be honest."

He liked that, she could tell.

Typical bloke.

Stroke their ego and they're like putty in your hands.

"Good, 'cause I don't want to either."

He sat up and swung himself over the edge of the bed.

"Are you having a shower?" she asked.

He shook his head, "I wasn't going to. I'll get one at home before I crash."

Shit.

"You have one though," he encouraged, "there's no rush."

"Okay, I will do, after you've used the bathroom."

He stood up and reached for his boxers.

"Can I ask you something?"

"Sure."

"Are you in a relationship with Ingrid?"

"No," he dismissed far too quickly. "What makes you think that?"

"She seems to like you, that's all."

His expression was puzzled, intentionally for her benefit as far as she could see.

"Has she said something?" he frowned.

"God, no, she doesn't have conversations with me. Joey and Rachel seem to think she likes you, and I have seen her watching you sometimes as you leave the gallery."

"She's married," he said as he made his way towards the bathroom.

"Yeah, but when has that ever stopped anyone?"

He paused at the door. "Well if she is screwing outside her marriage, it isn't with me. So you've nothing to worry about."

He closed the door behind him.

You're a liar.

And I'm not one bit worried.

So why was her tummy all knotted up?

Chapter 36

It was her parole officer's visit at the gallery, and they were sat in Ingrid's office. April knew there wouldn't be a peep out of Ingrid since she'd told her she was leaving when her three months was up. Ingrid sat behind her desk presiding over things in her supercilious way

"So, do you want to start, Gemma?" Tom asked. "How are you finding things?"

"Good, thank you. It's actually quite a nice place to work, everyone's friendly. The hours are a bit unsocial, but apart from that, it's fine." She smiled sweetly at Ingrid.

Ingrid smiled back, "As far as I'm concerned, Gemma's doing an excellent job. She's very hard working which is exactly what Mr Rider expects."

Tom Campbell appeared pleased. "That is good to hear. I wish all my clients settled into work as well as you, some are quite a challenge, I can assure you." He gave an encouraging nod, "So, well done, Gemma. You've finished working at Mr Rider's house now, haven't you?"

"Yes, that was only temporary while his cleaner was off. She's back now."

"Good. That extra work is another positive tick for you and makes me think that perhaps it's not necessary to have another visit here at the gallery from me. I can see you are doing really well," he widened his eyes, "as long as you're happy with that, of course."

"Yes, that's fine," April agreed. "Do you still need to come and see me at my flat?"

"I think we can cut that down too. We can chat about that in a minute." He turned to Ingrid, "Is that alright with you? It'll save me keep coming here and disrupting the cleaning schedule."

"That's fine by me," Ingrid nodded, "we know where to contact you if there's a problem, but I don't envisage any. Gemma's fitted in here really well. We're delighted to have her."

"I'm pleased to hear it," he said. "Would it be possible to speak to Gemma alone for a minute and then I'll get out of your way?"

"Yes, of course. I'll leave you both to it." Ingrid stood up, and as if to reinforce her position, she turned to April, "As soon as you're finished with Mr Campbell, can you get the toilets done, we are a bit behind tonight?"

Why does she always mention bloody toilets?

April smiled, "Yes, will do." She looked questioningly at Tom. "I don't think we'll be that long, will we?"

"No, I won't keep you. I only need a quick word and then I'm out of here."

They both smiled at Ingrid as she left the room. Tom turned towards her and April stared into his eyes and shook her head as if to say, *walls have ears.*

He understood. "So, as far as you're concerned, Gemma, you're okay? You weren't just saying that for your boss's benefit?"

"No, not at all. I like it here," she replied enthusiastically.

"Then we'll move on from me visiting your flat to check on things, to telephone contact once a week, unless there are any problems at all. Is that okay with you?"

"That sounds fine."

He passed her a note.

"I'm always in the office on a Friday morning catching up with paperwork, so if you could ring each Friday morning, then I can do the necessary tick list to say we've had telephone contact."

"Yes, I'll do that."

She opencd the note.

There's been an enquiry about you at the office. All the calls are recorded so I've listened to it back. It's a male asking if he could contact you through your parole officer. Reception agreed to pass on a message to me, but the caller hesitated and said he'd leave it for now and rang off. It sounded very much like someone was after confirmation you actually had a parole officer.

Tom stood up. "I've just realised I've forgotten to bring your last assessment document. Typical, it completely slipped my mind. I'll email it to you when I get back to the office. You just need to read through it and keep it for your reference."

She knew he was covertly saying he'd send her the recording to listen to.

"Thank you. I'll do that."

Would she recognise the voice?

"Right," he smiled, "I'll let you get on. You've done really well since you came out of prison. Keep it up."

She nodded and mouthed *thank you.*

She opened the door. "I'll walk with you to the exit. The security man, Joey will be around, he'll let you out."

Who the hell would be asking questions about her?

Who knew something?

Chapter 37

April came out of the changing room in Dylan's house with a towel wrapped round her and made her way towards the Jacuzzi. Dylan was already in and the bubbles were gurgling away.

She removed the towel, slowly, until she was totally naked and stepped into the Jacuzzi.

"Here," he handed her a flute of champagne.

"Mmm, thank you."

"At last," he gave her a sexy smile. "I've wanted to get you in here for a while."

"Yes, well, it's a bit difficult with Henry around. I don't fancy him seeing me in all my glory."

"No, I don't fancy him seeing you either," he smirked taking a sip of champagne. "He's a bloody nuisance skulking around the house. The times I turn around and he's there, in my face. I think he tiptoes around on purpose to have the element of surprise."

"Where is he tonight, anyway?"

"Says he's crashing at a mate's house."

"You don't sound confident he is?"

"Who knows? Long as he's not into drugs, I'm not bothered where he is."

She wrinkled her nose, "I feel a bit sorry for him."

"Well don't. Save your sympathy for me, I have to parent the lazy little bugger."

She sighed, "He seems lonely to me. What about his friends, have you met any of them?"

"No, he wouldn't bring them here. He prefers to go to theirs."

"Aren't you worried who he's mixing with?"

"He's almost eighteen," he frowned, "I can't control who hc sees. All I've asked is for him to focus on getting a job, preferably an apprenticeship as he's not interested in education."

"You've ruled out art totally, have you?"

"He's not mentioned it for a while, so I don't think he's serious about it."

"At least he's kicked drugs, that's a positive. You don't want him going any further down that road."

"Exactly. He's always been a bit of a rebel though, so he does worry me. I remember when he was fifteen and all hell broke loose when he was with a group of older lads who were caught breaking and entering an off-license. My ex-wife was frantic." He shook his head, "I don't really think it was out of choice he became involved, I reckon it'd be more to do with trying to fit in. He's so odd, and never had a lot of friends, but he's very sharp and consequently I know that's why a gang would want him onboard. As I said before, codes and alarms etcetera, are his bag. Fortunately, I have a good lawyer who had the right contacts to keep his name out of it when the police got involved."

"Oh dear, he does seem to have a deviant streak in him. Where does he get that from?"

He gave an indignant look. "Not me I can assure you."

How far could she take this?

"I used to say that," she widened her eyes, "and now look at me."

"Yes, but you've learnt from your mistake."

"I have, but it's an uphill struggle. I wonder if it's a dream sometimes to get myself back on the occupation ladder. You know what I mean, something decent, so I can get a nice flat and maybe buy a car. You know . . . what normal people have."

"You could always bag yourself a rich husband," he smiled topping up their glasses.

"And where do they hang out? I've not met any of them down the pub I go to."

He laughed, "No, I don't suppose they do." He took another sip of his drink, "Tell me, if somebody offered you a way to make some money so things weren't such a struggle, would you take it?"

"Only if it was legit." She shrugged, "But I can't imagine there's an abundance of people out there ready to offer me any opportunities that were going to make me rich, somehow."

"Never say never." He took the drink out of her hand and rested it on the edge of the Jacuzzi. "Anyway, enough about that, I've been thinking about this all day," he started nibbling her neck, "you are certainly getting under my skin, woman, do you know that? I think it must be time to dry ourselves off and adjourn to the bedroom, don't you?"

"Sounds good to me."

"I'll have a quick shower to get the chemicals off otherwise I'll be regretting it later when I'm itching in my sleep." He moved towards the steps. "Do you fancy joining me?"

"No, I'm fine, the chlorine doesn't irritate my skin."

He made his way to the shower room and closed the door behind him.

She quickly got out and reached for his phone resting on one of the wicker tables. She pressed *use passcode* and typed in the access number Henry had given her. Two-five-eight-zero.

Bingo!

She was in.

Thank you, Henry.

Chapter 38

Thursday night and April was back at the Dog and Duck with Joey and Rachel. It was becoming a habit after work. Joey didn't drive to work on a Thursday so they could go out after they'd finished.

They were huddled together around a table enjoying their drinks. Rachel was holding court and moaning there were no decent men about.

"What happened to the last bloke?" Joey asked, "I thought you liked him?"

"I did, but I reckon he had a wife and kids at home. That's the trouble with online dating; you don't really know who you're getting."

"What makes you think he had a wife and kids?" April asked.

"'Cause his profile's gone off the website."

"Jesus," Joey pulled a face, "that's not a great advert for these sites, is it? Don't they do background checks on people?"

"God, how old are you, Joey?" Rachel said scathingly. "They can't check up on everyone registering on a site. There's got to be some trust. And I have met a few nice ones, they never last though, that's the problem. You should go on, Gemma, they'd be queuing up to meet with you once they saw your photo."

"Er, no thank you," she said, "I couldn't be doing with all that. I'd rather meet someone in person and take my time getting to know them."

"Yeah, easier said than done, though. You look round, is there anyone you'd fancy in here?"

April allowed her eyes to wander around the room and they stopped at a reasonably good-looking man propping up the bar and talking in a group."

"He looks okay in the white shirt by the bar."

Rachel turned to see who she meant. The tall man, who appeared to be in his early thirties, looked over at them as if he knew they were discussing him.

"Hey, well spotted," Rachel widened her eyes. "He looks more than okay to me."

Joey sighed, "I'm off outside for a fag while you two are window shopping."

Rachel jumped up, "I'm coming too. I reckon that bloke's clocked Gemma. He'll be over if we're out the way."

"He needn't bother," April said, "I'll go get some more drinks while you're outside, he won't be able to catch me then. Same again?"

April returned to their table with a tray of drinks from the bar.

"Hi," a male voice spoke behind her.

Rachel had been right. It was the man they'd been looking at a few minutes earlier.

"Have your friends gone?" he asked, "I wasn't sure."

"No, they're outside. They'll be back in a minute."

"Do you mind if I join you until they come back? I'm Mike, by the way."

"Yes, I do actually."

He gave her a puzzled look, "Are you with the bloke?"

"No." She took a breath in, "I'm just having a quiet drink with friends and I don't want to pick anyone up. So, it's probably best if you go back to your friends before mine return."

"Okay, okay," he raised the palms of his hands. "I'm only trying to be friendly."

"I know, but I'm not interested."

"Your loss."

"Yeah, right."

She sat down hoping he'd get the message to clear off.

"If you change your mind, you know where I am."

"Thanks, but I won't."

He raised his eyebrows, "You don't know what you're missing."

"I think I can live with it."

"You fancy yourself as something special, don't you," he sneered.

Jesus Christ, she needed rid of him.

She stood up, so she was level with him. "*Mike,*" she emphasised his name, "why don't you piss off and go find someone that might be interested."

His skin coloured, "Oh, I get it," he leered, "you're a fucking dyke. Tell you what, I can fuck you and your friend if you want."

She leant forward so her mouth was close to his ear.

"The only fuck I'm interested in, is you fucking off. So why don't you do that now 'cause I've already had a bellyful of you."

She turned her head towards the door and saw Joey and Rachel coming back.

"Oh, look, here are my friends now. See you around, *Mike.*"

He walked away back to his mates who jeered knowing he'd been knocked back.

"Well?" Rachel asked enthusiastically.

"Well what?"

"I told you he'd come over."

"And I told you I'm not interested."

"You're such a spoilsport, Gemma. Isn't she, Joey?"

He shrugged. "If she doesn't want to meet random men, it's up to her. There's nothing wrong with being single, I like it!" He took a gulp of his pint.

"God you two are so boring," Rachel said. "You should be together, sat at home in your slippers watching telly and drinking cocoa." She craned her neck to see Mike who was back with his friends near the bar. "I think he's fit, and if you're not interested, I might try my luck with him."

April widened her eyes at Joey, "On that note, I'll make this my last and get off. My slippers and cocoa are waiting."

April walked away from the pub towards the bus stop thinking about Rachel. She couldn't help but feel sorry for her life, which sounded a struggle. She worked in a factory packing fish fingers in the day, and cleaned at the gallery each evening five nights a week. There was no way of improving her lot, she wasn't a particularly bright girl, and as far as April could tell, all she did was work and go out with losers. It'd be nice if she could meet a decent man, but being single in London was the norm as most men Rachel's age would be in relationships and bringing up kids. As she knew only too well herself, there wasn't an abundance of single men around, and internet dating wasn't for her. While plenty of it was legitimate, there were some real weirdos out there and she encountered enough of those in the police without dating any of them.

As she turned a corner towards the route to the bus stop, she became aware something wasn't right. She turned around but there was no-one behind her. The street was deserted. Odd that in a city of over eight million, she was all alone. It wasn't much further to walk to the end of the road where it'd be busier nearer the bus stop. She'd be safe then.

The police officer in her sensed something was wrong. Her internal antenna was on full alert. It was quieter than usual down the street. She'd walked the same route several times and there was usually a few people milling about, but not tonight. She increased her pace.

Was someone following her?

She was certain she'd heard someone behind her, or had she sensed it?

A few more paces. Should she run?

She turned again. Her instincts had been right.

A huge fist smacked her hard in the face. She felt herself falling and her head hit the pavement before all went black.

Everything was blurry. She could barely open her eyes. She had an awareness of being dragged, and it only took seconds for her to realise exactly by whom.

Mike, the tosser from the bar.

She started breathing deeply, trying to take in some oxygen so she'd be able to react when he stopped. Her head kept banging on something like soil, but she was too groggy to support it properly.

After a few minutes, he released his grip and she slumped in a heap on the ground. It was dark, almost black. There was a street lamp, however it was too far away to offer much light, but she knew instinctively exactly where he'd dragged her to. It was one of the allotments she passed on the way to the bus stop.

Although she was slightly more alert, she faked being dozy by moving her head from side to side and groaning, as if semi-conscious. It had been a massive punch he'd hit her with. Maybe he boxed or something similar?

He started to fumble with his belt and released his huge dick, glistening in the tiny bit of light.

"Right, bitch, you're going to fucking get it," he was working himself as he moved towards her, "this'll fucking teach you."

He let go of his dick and grabbed her jeans to undo them.

She was ready for him. She reached for his dick and wrapped her hand around it, twisting and squeezing as hard as she could. He gave a high-pitched scream and fell onto his side. She squeezed, harder and harder, and dodged his arms as they lashed out at her, but she wouldn't let go. He wailed like a banshee as she eased herself into a kneeling position.

She held on, and still he screamed.

Her legs were weak, but she managed to get to her feet and as she let go, she stamped as hard as she could on his tackle.

He rolled onto his side with his knees up in a foetal position, groaning. "You fucking bitch."

"Like I already told you, *Mike*, piss off."

She ran.

Adrenaline and shaky legs spurred her on. She kept on running until she was out of the allotments and continued onto the main road. As luck would have it, she spotted a black cab and raised her arm.

The taxi stopped alongside her. She quickly opened the door and checked over her shoulder to see if he'd come after her. All she could see where a couple walking hand in hand.

Where were you when I needed you?

She got in and slammed the door behind her. "Notting Dale, please."

Her face throbbed, and her stomach churned. She let out a deep sigh of relief. She'd just escaped being raped.

What must she look like? She touched her aching cheek.

"Alright, love?" the driver asked looking at her in his mirror.

"I'm okay," she replied, "I fell over."

"One too many?" he asked sympathetically.

"Yeah, something like that."

Shit.

What the hell was she going to look like for work tomorrow?

Chapter 39

April didn't bother trying to cover her face with make-up the following day. What was the point? No amount of foundation or concealer could hide the dark blue bruise around her right eye, or the scratches on her cheeks.

As she stood outside the back door to the gallery waiting for Joey to let her in, she took a deep breath in. He'd see her on the monitor so would be on his way. Although she was dreading seeing him and Rachel, it was Dylan that worried her most of all.

Joey opened the door, concern etched across his handsome face. "What the hell's happened?"

"I'm fine, Joey, honestly," she reassured, "it looks much worse than it is."

"How've you done that?" he asked, tilting her chin to examine it properly.

"I fell outside my flat last night when I got back from the pub."

"It looks nasty," he dropped his hand. "Have you been to hospital to get checked out?"

"No need. It's my pride that's hurt more than anything," she laughed, trying to diffuse the fuss. "I felt stupid as one of my neighbours came out when he heard the commotion. What he must have thought seeing me flat out in the bushes, I don't know."

Rachel appeared and rushed towards them, "Oh, my God, Gemma, what have you been doing?"

"I fell last night near my flat. I'm okay, I was just telling, Joey, it's my pride more than anything that hurts."

"Aw, it looks so sore, poor you . . . come here."

Rachel wrapped her arms around her and hugged her tightly. She was such a sweet girl.

April pulled away, "I'd better get changed before I end up in more trouble."

"Do you think you should be here?" Joey asked. "Maybe you should be at home resting."

"I'm fine, honestly. I'd rather crack on. I've been resting all day and I'm off tomorrow."

"What about Sunday morning though?" Rachel asked, "Will you be okay to clean after Saturday night's function?"

"Yeah, course I will," she smiled.

She headed for the changing room with Rachel and was putting on her overall when Ingrid opened the door.

"Joey just told me you'd had an accident, Gemma, are you alright?"

April turned to face her, "I'm fine, Ingrid, thank you. It's lovely of you all to be concerned, but honestly, I wouldn't be here if I wasn't."

"Well, as long as you're sure," Ingrid's eyes were examining her face. "What happened? Joey said you fell." Her face had disbelief written all over it.

"Yes, I did. It was silly of me, I tripped over a step and it catapulted me forward. Thankfully the bushes broke my fall, but I still caught my face on the wall of the building."

"Oh dear," she frowned. "As long as you're sure you can work. You must say if you don't feel right."

"I'll be okay," April reassured, "but thank you anyway."

April started her usual routine of cleaning the toilets. She crept around on the top floor as she knew Dylan would be in his office until about six. The last thing she wanted was to bump into him.

Would Ingrid say something to him? She doubted it. Why would she? He might send her home, and supervisor or not, she'd have to do some work for a change.

She diligently cleaned the toilets and put bleach down each of them. Although she'd taken some aspirin, her head throbbed. If she could get her hands on that loser, she'd have him arrested for assault and attempted rape. It was unlikely he'd set foot in the pub again, though.

She scoured the vanity units and polished the tiles. Quite how they got in such a mess, never ceased to amaze her. The downstairs toilets yes, as they were open to the public, but not the ones on the first floor.

As she sprayed and polished the mirror over the sinks, she looked at her reflection.

What a bloody shiner.

Please let Dylan have gone home.

She spent as long as she dared cleaning in the toilets praying that Dylan would have left. The last thing she needed was having to embellish the lie. She'd fabricated enough as it was. She checked her watch. It was 6.20 so he should be on his way home by now.

As quietly as she could, she opened the toilet door and made her way along the corridor. She turned onto the office passage way, and there he was in his doorway.

"Hello," he smiled as she walked towards him.

He'd been waiting for her.

There was no way she could hide her face. His concerned eyes were drawn to it immediately.

"What's happened? What have you done?"

She instinctively put her hand up to her cheek. "I tripped over last night just outside my flat. It looks far worse than it actually is."

He moved towards her and put his hand on her chin, examining her face. The sympathy in his eyes caused her tummy to flip.

Please don't let Ingrid see him. She'd be around somewhere.

"That looks sore?" he winced.

"It's not too bad. It'll be gone by this time next week."

"When did you say it happened?"

"Last night."

"Then you shouldn't be here." He stroked the side of her face with the back of his hand. "Let's get you home. I'll take you."

"No, please," she moved her head away so he dropped his hand. "I really don't want a lot of fuss. I'm absolutely fine, I wouldn't have come to work if I wasn't."

She heard footsteps coming along the corridor and knew instinctively who it was.

"Ah, Dylan," Ingrid said, "I was just on my way up to tell you about Gemma. I see you've found her though."

Yeah, right. As if.

You wouldn't have even told him if he hadn't seen me.

"She should be at home," he replied. "You can manage tonight without her, can't you?" he asked but it wasn't really a question.

"Of course, I've said exactly the same myself. Home's the best place for her. Joey's more than happy to take her, and I'll be here until he gets back."

"No need. I'll take her." He turned to April, "Go and get your things and I'll meet you by the door."

There was no point in arguing with him.

Dylan Rider wasn't the type to take no for an answer.

Ingrid would really have it in for her now.

Chapter 40

The car came to a standstill outside her flat. She'd given Dylan directions but closed her eyes on the journey, pretending to doze so she didn't have to speak to him. He'd have more questions, and in her experience of any of the jobs she'd done it was best to keep the lies to a minimum.

She opened her eyes. "Thank you for bringing me home, I am grateful."

"No problem, let's get you inside."

Bugger.

The last thing she wanted was him in her flat.

"There's no need to come in with me, I can manage."

"I know that, but I want to." He opened his door and exited the car leaving her no choice but to follow him.

He'll smell a rat if she protested too much.

"It's quite a hike," she warned knowing how many flights of stairs there were up to her flat.

"Thanks for the heads-up." He took her arm and led her towards the entrance.

"You weren't joking were you," he breathed as they approached the last few steps, even though he'd effortlessly managed them. It was obvious he was fit.

"It's my workout each day, saves me paying gym fees," she smiled.

They reached her door.

"This is it." She willed him to go.

He nodded, "Key please."

She pulled a face. "It's no palace inside."

"I don't expect it to be."

She took the key out of her bag and handed it to him.

"This lock's rubbish," he scowled, "anyone could get in."

"Good job I don't have a lot of valuables then," she shrugged dismissively.

He pushed the door open with his hand and indicated she went in before him. She surreptitiously glanced down at the floor. The cotton was in a straight line.

She made her way towards the lounge and he followed. His eyes travelled around the grubby walls and the sparse tatty furniture. She could only imagine what he must be thinking as he looked around, his eyes glancing at the threadbare carpet from a hundred casual occupants. She was familiar with the shabby dilapidated state; he was seeing it for the first time.

Better appear embarrassed.

"I did warn you."

She saw his chest rise as he took a deep breath in. "Why don't you come and stay at my house for the weekend, you'll be more comfortable there?"

She shook her head. "I don't think so."

"Why not? Just for the weekend, I can look after you then. You can come back on Monday."

"No, it'd be too awkward."

"Awkward?" he frowned, "Why? Nobody would know, if that's what you're worried about."

"What about Henry?"

"I couldn't give a toss about Henry, he'll be out anyway doing whatever shit he gets up to. I have a function on tomorrow night at the gallery, so you'll be on your own. Why not be comfortable?"

"Yes, well, that's another reason not to come. I've got to clean the gallery on Sunday. Ingrid's offered Rachel and I overtime on Sunday morning to clean up after the function."

"Okay. Then come until Sunday morning and I'll take you to work, and after you've finished your shift, come home then."

April found his concern attractive. He hardly knew her, yet he was offering his home for her to recuperate. She gave the appearance of considering. All she'd got from his phone calendar for the 25th of May was the letter 'J' so she still didn't have any idea of the importance of the date even though her instinct told her it was the day they were moving the Portillo. She really needed to know the significance of J and would have greater access to the whole house if he was out for the evening.

"I'd hate anyone to find out. How would that look, one of your cleaners stopping over at yours for the weekend?"

"Who's going to know? I won't tell anyone, and I think we've moved on from you being my cleaner, don't you?" he smiled warmly.

"Okay," she agreed, "if you're absolutely sure."

His nod said he was.

"If you don't mind waiting in the car, I'll throw a few bits together."

She thought he'd want to wait with her, but he was astute enough to realise she needed space to sort her things out."

"Can you manage a bag with the stairs?"

"If I travel light and don't pack my ball gowns, I can," she smiled.

"Okay," he walked towards the door, "No fancy nights out this weekend then, we'll have to make do with stopping in." He grinned, "Right, here I go for the stairs workout. Don't be long."

Chapter 41

Dylan led the way upstairs in his house carrying her bag, and she followed behind. It was nice to have someone taking care of her for a change. It gave her a warm feeling inside which she wasn't used to. As far back as she could remember it had always been her taking care of Chloe. Nobody looked out for April.

He stopped at one of the spare bedrooms and opened the door.

"I thought you'd be comfortable in here," he placed her bag on a chair and nodded towards the ensuite door. "Have a soak in the bath if you want to and come down when you're ready. I'll rustle up something for us to eat."

She widened her eyes, "You cook as well as rescuing damsels in distress?"

He pulled a playful face, "I'd use the word *cook*, loosely. Let's just say there'll be food on the table." His eyes twinkled, "See you shortly, there's no rush."

He closed the door behind him and she sat on the bed. He was full of surprises. She thought he'd be after a night of sex, yet he'd not presumed that. Whoever got him would be one lucky lady. Wealthy, great in bed, and caring.

She chastised herself.

Dylan Rider breaks the law. Your job is upholding it. You'd do well to remember that.

She did as he'd advised and enjoyed the luxury of a warm bath. Her crappy flat only had a shower. The bath reminded her of home. It had been an age since she'd set foot in her own flat. Hopefully it wouldn't be too long now until she was back there.

She took two aspirin to help with her throbbing head and looked at her face in the mirror. The black eye looked unsightly, and there was a long deep-red graze down her cheek where she'd been dragged along the ground. No wonder they were all concerned. She wasn't though, she'd had worse than that during her time with the police. As it turned out, the attack had actually been fortuitous as it got her access to his house for the weekend and the housekeeper wouldn't be around.

She rubbed some moisturiser into her squeaky-clean face, avoiding her eye, and brushed her teeth. Her hair was low-maintenance, so she rubbed a bit of gel into it and fluffed it up. What to wear wasn't a choice. She'd only stuck a tracksuit and a pair of jeans in her bag, but she wasn't there to be dressed up and girly, and they'd already had sex, so she didn't need to work on that. If it happened, it happened. She hoped it would. He was good at that and she did find him hot.

He'd made an omelette and salad. She hadn't realised quite how hungry she was and devoured it. They'd chatted about mundane things as they ate, but once they'd finished eating and were drinking the last of the wine, he looked directly at her with purpose. "Tell me what really happened?"

No surprise he hadn't believed her account.

She placed her wine glass down. "I was attacked."

His eyes darkened, "Define attacked?"

She knew the way his mind was working.

"Not raped, if that's what you're thinking."

"I'm relieved to hear it. What stopped him?"

"I screamed and someone came running towards us."

"Did you inform the police?"

"No." She screwed her face up, "I doubt they'd be interested in me. Ex-prisoners aren't top of their priority list. Anyway, even though I'd spoken to him earlier, I don't think I'd recognise him again."

"What, you mean you'd met him?"

"Sort of. I'd been out with Joey and Rachel and he came onto me in the pub. I knocked him back. He must have waited until I left to catch the bus home and followed me."

"Should you be walking around on your own at night?" he scowled. "You left yourself wide open for something like this to happen."

"Well, I'm afraid when you have to get around on public transport, you have very little choice."

"Surely Joey could have walked you to the bus stop?"

"Joey's not my minder, he can't be escorting me round and about London. It was a night out; he was probably looking to pick up a woman for all I know."

"What, when you were out with him?" he shook his head, "I don't think so. I'm sure if he was after getting laid, he'd be interested in you."

"Don't be silly," she said, "we're friends. He doesn't see me like that."

"Yeah right. Any bloke with blood in his veins would be seeing you *like that*."

She took a sip of her wine, but kept her eyes on his. She liked his company, he was easy to be with.

"You're wrong you know. You might see me like that because we're having sex, but not all blokes do, I can assure you."

"So you're telling me Joey's never tried it on with you?"

"Never."

He raised an eyebrow, "Why don't I believe you?"

"It's true. Maybe he's more interested in Rachel, I don't know. But he and I are definitely no more than friends."

"Maybe on your part, but trust me, I'm a man. He'll be interested."

She laughed, "The way you talk, you'd think blokes were queuing up to take me out."

"Aren't they?"

"No," she rolled her eyes, "I wish."

"Have you had many relationships?"

"Not really, have you?"

"Too many. Although I wouldn't call them relationships," he pulled a face, "more friendships with benefits."

"Why's that, then? Surely over the years you've met some you wanted a long-term relationship with?"

"Honestly?" He shook his head, "I haven't. I think my marriage put me off."

"So you don't want to settle down, and maybe have more kids?"

"Definitely not. I do think sometimes it would be nice to have someone to come home to, but then the urge quickly passes. I think I'm too set in my ways. What about you, is that what you want, marriage and kids?"

"I don't know what I want if I'm totally honest. My priority is getting myself sorted and back on a career pathway of some sort. I'd like to travel though, that'd be nice."

"What about children, do you want them eventually?"

"I'm not sure. I guess that comes into play when you meet the right one. It's certainly not high on my agenda at the moment."

"You're only young, there's plenty of time for that. I personally think kids should come much later in your life. In your twenties you aren't really equipped to deal with them, not men anyway. We're far too immature."

"Yes, but it's nice to be your age now and have a grown-up son?"

"Mmmm," he rolled his eyes, "the jury's still out on that one."

"How is Henry anyway, any further forward with an apprenticeship?"

"You tell me. I hardly see him."

"He did show you his artworks though?"

"No," he shook his head, "I haven't seen any of his art. He's shown you, has he?"

"Yes, one morning when I was cleaning his room. He's very talented."

"You're honoured. He likes Vic, but I don't think he's even shown him."

"Maybe it's because I'm nearer his age?"

He narrowed his eyes playfully. "What are you suggesting . . . that I'm old?"

"Well you are . . . what . . . pushing forty?" She giggled, the wine relaxing her.

"And you're a cheeky mare, I'm thirty-seven. It's a good job you're incapacitated, or you'd pay for that remark."

"And here's me thinking I've only got a black eye, I didn't realise that rendered me incapacitated. What would you have done to me if I wasn't *incapacitated*?"

"Tied you to the bed and tortured you."

Her pussy fluttered at his words.

"Really," she widened her eyes, "shame I'm going to miss that then. I think that might have been just the pick-me-up I needed."

His eyes darkened, as if he was weighing up whether it would be okay to fuck her.

She licked the surplus wine off her lips, staring back invitingly.

He downed the last dregs of his wine, "Your room or mine?"

"Whichever one has the handcuffs."

He'd lived up to his promise. He'd tied her to the bed and blindfolded her and she'd relished his mouth licking, nipping and kissing every surface and orifice of her body. He'd made her come and come again. He'd been relentless.

And she'd played her part. She'd kept him in the bed with her, rather than let him retreat to his own room, for no other reason than it was the only way to get access to his phone.

That was the only reason, wasn't it?

Each time she initiated sex, he complied. He was an unselfish lover, and it crossed her mind she wouldn't have been quite so eager had he not been. Every time he went to use the bathroom to dispose of a condom, she checked his WhatsApp messages. The directive she'd been given was to get as many of them as possible as the force couldn't access them remotely. She couldn't afford the time to be selective, so she randomly opened some and took photos with her own phone. It was painstakingly slow, but she did manage to take pictures of a couple she thought were pertinent.

It was the early hours of the morning when he left her room. She'd made a pretence of dozing which allowed him the chance to slip away. Much as she enjoyed the sex, she didn't want the intimacy of sleeping with him. It would have been awkward in the morning.

Once he'd left her, she checked the photos she'd taken on her phone. One of the WhatsApp messages she'd got between Dylan and Victor mentioned this 'J', but even though they appeared innocuous and were easily interpreted as two brothers discussing a friend, her gut feeling told her that J was relevant to the Portillo.

She eagerly scanned the photo of his recent calls. Even though she knew the police could easily access his call log so getting that wasn't her remit, she'd photographed it anyway. The female inside her wanted to know if he communicated with Ingrid outside of work.

There was no evidence he had.

Why on earth did that make her feel relieved?

Chapter 42

Dylan eagerly made his way upstairs to Gemma's room carrying a cup of coffee for her. They'd had an amazing night of sex and it had been a mistake not spending the night with her. He'd slipped away before dawn and regretted it now. As they'd both dozed, he'd been in two minds what to do, but he'd followed his instinct and gone to his own room. This morning, he couldn't wait to see her again. He had an overwhelming urge to spend the day with her and introduce her to his hobby. Would she enjoy it as much as he did? He hoped so.

He tapped on her bedroom door.

"Come in," she called.

He walked in carrying a latte. He'd made her one before when he first met her and she seemed to enjoy it.

"Morning sleepyhead," he smiled placing the mug on her bedside table.

She pulled herself into a sitting position and ran her fingers through her short hair. No rushing towards the bathroom like women usually did first thing to make sure they looked as seductive as the night before. That wasn't Gemma. He liked that she was sort of quirky and different from the norm.

She leant back against the headboard and pulled the cover around her to make sure those delicious breasts of hers weren't exposed.

"Did you sleep okay?" he asked, knowing neither of them had slept much at all.

"I did, thank you," she grinned, reaching for the coffee, "eventually. Did you?"

"Oh, yes," he winked as he perched himself on the bed. She hitched up towards the middle to give him some room.

He moved her chin with his finger and thumb. Her eye looked yellow as if the bruising was coming out. It must hurt. He'd like to get his hands on the bastard who did that to her.

"Will I live?" she enquired.

"I think so, as long as you keep taking instruction from Dr Rider."

"I thought I already did last night."

She was so sexy. His dick twitched.

"You did, and if I don't get out of here soon, I'll be prescribing more of the same."

Her smile told him she'd be happy to oblige. She took another sip of her coffee.

"But rather than that, as it's such a gorgeous day, I thought I'd take you out for some fresh air."

"That sounds nice. Where?"

"It's a surprise. All you need to do is get ready. Nothing fancy, jeans will suffice."

"Okay, give me five minutes to drink my coffee, ten minutes to shower, and then I'll be with you."

"Great, I love fast women." He spontaneously leant forward and kissed her. It shocked him how easily he'd done so as he wasn't the kissing type. Not for affection anyway, he liked it as a prelude to sex.

Why the hell had he done that?

He stood up and moved swiftly towards the door before he made any other stupid moves.

"I thought you ladies needed time to apply the slap?"

She rolled her eyes, "Not me. I'm a no slap girl, so if that's what you're looking for, then I'm definitely the wrong woman for you."

"Good, you don't need it." He meant it. He hated orange faces, false eyelashes and tattooed eyebrows. "I'll rustle us up something for breakfast and then I'm taking you somewhere you'll love."

"Can't wait," she replied eagerly.

It surprised Dylan that he wanted to take her gliding. It was his bit of escapism from the fast pace of London. He loved to get in the air and escape, but always alone. He'd never had the urge to take anyone with him, let alone someone he was screwing.

It's only to take her mind off being attacked.
That's all it was.

As they'd driven to the airfield at the London gliding club, he felt the need to explain the glider he preferred to use was fitted with a small power unit that could prolong the flight if the conditions weren't ideal. He'd squeezed her leg and reassured her he'd been gliding for years so she had nothing to worry about. But Gemma didn't appear worried at all which was no surprise to him. She didn't seem at all like a usual run-of-the-mill female. Far from it. From what he'd gathered, she seemed ballsy with guts. He wasn't sure how he knew that as he didn't know her well, but he sensed she was no wallflower. She'd have to be tough to have coped with prison. And he suspected the bloke that attacked her, got plenty back. Gemma Dean wouldn't be a pushover. He liked that she was different.

He enjoyed sharing how his father had taken him gliding when he was fourteen and how he'd fallen in love with it. He was quietly confident she would find the experience exhilarating too.

At the airfield, he'd sat and waited while she had to go through the mandatory safety and instruction briefing even though she was just a passenger. It was compulsory as she'd never been in a glider before. His eyes watched as she listened attentively to the chap instructing her. He must have been mid-fifties and as she smiled at him by way of thanks, a stab of jealousy hit him hard. He didn't want her smiling at any man, only him. What was it about her that made him possessive? It wasn't an emotion he was used to feeling. He found himself wanting more from her, and had an overwhelming urge to throw away the casual girlfriend manual, and go for something more in-depth. He'd never felt that way before, so quickly dismissed it. It wouldn't do to get stupid over a woman.

The glider was attached to a motorised plane which towed along the runway and into the sky. He even wanted rid of that as quickly as possible, so he could be on his own with her.

From the minute they were airborne, she seemed to love it. Once they hit a couple of thousand feet, the rope was detached and the silent flight began. Warm thermals pushed the glider upwards, and through her fresh eyes he began experiencing scenery he'd seen hundreds of times. They travelled at speeds of a hundred miles an hour and rode the air currents with scenery stretching to the horizon with barely a sound to disturb the moment. As they glided gracefully over picturesque landscapes, they enjoyed stunning views usually bequeathed to the birds, and her squeals of delight confirmed it had been the right decision to bring her.

Dylan had taken her to a pub for lunch and returned to the table with drinks from the bar.

"So, what did you think?" he asked, sitting down on the stool opposite and passing her a glass of wine.

Her face came alive. "It was incredible. The feeling of flying through the sky and coasting along as free as a bird was exciting . . . amazing . . . spectacular . . . all of those and a whole load more. I'm lost for words to describe it, really." She smiled warmly at him, "I'll never forget today, thank you so much for taking me."

"You're welcome. I'm glad you enjoyed it." His eyes took in her lovely clean complexion from the fresh air; she really was a stunning young woman. And it was a delight to him she'd enjoyed the experience. It gave him a warm comfortable feeling that he was responsible for her happiness. Somehow it pleased him she'd enjoyed the sport he loved. To see the delight on her beautiful face, moved him. She'd had a crap life by the sound of things, so her joy made him feel joyous too.

She carried on, "You're so lucky to be able to escape from the world and do that whenever you want to."

He took his jacket off and tossed it on the seat. "Yes, I suppose I am." He never thought of himself as lucky. But she was right, he was.

"You definitely are," she beamed, "I've never done anything like that . . . nor will I again, I'm sure."

"You can come anytime you want." He meant it. He loved her childish enthusiasm, and wanted more.

"That's a nice thought," she wrinkled her nose, "but I won't be here that long."

Tightness gripped his gut. He didn't want her to go anywhere right now.

"But thank you for taking me. It's an experience I'll not forget in a hurry." She took a sip of her wine. "It was just what I needed after . . . you know."

"Yeah," he knew. "I hate what that loser did to you. The consequences don't bear thinking about."

"Well hopefully it was a one off," she squeezed his hand, "I'll be more careful next time."

He liked the feel of her hand on his. More than he should do. He had the urge to move next to her and hold her hand like lovers do. He really needed to get a grip.

"And thank you for taking me in last night," she continued, "I feel much better now. Which reminds me, after we've eaten; I think I'd better go home."

No way. He didn't want her to go anywhere.

"I thought we'd said you'd stay tonight and I'd take you to the gallery in the morning for your shift."

"I know you said that, but I'm fine now, really I am. And I can't stay at yours on my own when you're out at the gallery function."

"Why not? I'm sure it will be more comfortable at my house than yours."

"I know it is. But you won't be there. It isn't right."

"What's not right? You're my guest."

"It's really kind of you to offer, but you don't know me from Adam. I could take off with the family silver for all you know."

"It's insured," he dismissed indifferently. "I'll only be a few hours, three at the most, and it'll be nice for a change to have someone to come home to." He upped the charm offensive. "Life's not all singing and dancing for a gallery owner you know, it can get lonely sometimes."

"Oh, I bet," she teased. "Come on, a man with your looks and wealth? I can't ever see you being lonely."

"Ah, you don't know that," he took a sip of his wine. "I might appear popular and always be surrounded by people, but more often than not they're only interested in what I can do for them."

"My heart is bleeding for you," she dismissed playfully, "you poor man."

"I am a poor man. I actually need a strategy to cope."

"What sort of strategy?" she grinned.

"Therapy. I need you to take pity on me."

She was so sexy when she smiled.

"You haven't had enough . . . *therapy*?"

"Nowhere near enough," he grinned as the waitress approached the table carrying their meals.

"The lasagne's for the lady, and mine's the fish, thank you."

Chapter 43

As soon as she'd said goodbye to Dylan and he was on his way to the function at the gallery, she made her way to his study. She'd seen Henry earlier on his way out, so she was confident she wouldn't be disturbed. Henry had actually come into the snug where her and Dylan were sat, and exchanged a few words. She'd asked him if there was any news on the job front, but it appeared there was nothing. He was awkward around his father, and Dylan didn't help. You could sense the undercurrent between them both.

She left the door ajar so she could hear if Henry came back, and it would look more legitimate than a closed door. He'd only left an hour earlier so she didn't expect to be disturbed.

The study, like the rest of the house, was a delight. Not one of those stuffy studies you think of by the very nature of the word study, with oak furniture and endless book cases. This room was beautifully designed like the rest of the house. The light grey on the walls, and the contemporary furniture gave it a stylish look and she deduced the room had to be the handiwork of an interior designer as was most probably the rest of the house.

Apart from the huge desk which dominated the room, there was a seating area by the window with modern looking chesterfield type sofas. There were some bookcases, and beautiful art dominating each wall. One particular portrait was clearly Dylan's late father. She could see the family resemblance, but it was Victor that favoured him more.

However, she wasn't there to study the art she reprimanded herself, and started to open each drawer that wasn't locked, carefully photographing its contents so she could put things back exactly as they were. She took out the contents of each individual drawer systematically one at a time, which she'd done before when she'd been cleaning the house, but she'd had to be quick then, as the housekeeper was always hovering. Right now, she had at least three hours before Dylan came back.

Each document she took out, she photographed on her phone. Whoever at the station would have to go through all the data, would curse her no doubt. It was hard to tell what was significant, so she photographed anything she could. It wasn't her job to decide what was relevant.

There were two drawers in the desk that were locked which could easily been broken into, but nothing would be more certain to break her cover. Right now, everything was going according to plan. Dylan didn't suspect a thing. The only complication that she hadn't expected, were the feelings that surfaced within her when she was around him. There was something about him, an evasive concept you couldn't put your finger on, but which she was drawn to. Despite his criminal background, she found him much more attractive than she should and that made her feel uneasy. It didn't pay in her line of work to get attached to anyone. But the sex with him was amazing. He was such a generous lover. Even now she was eager for him to come home so she could have plenty of what she'd got the previous evening. Would he spend the night with her tonight? For some obscure reason, she wanted to wake up next to him, which was ridiculous.

She inwardly chastised herself. She needed to snap out of this romantic bullshit and remember her only chance of success was departmentalising Dylan Rider and keep in mind he was a job and nothing more than that.

Shit. What was that?

She'd heard a noise.

Someone was in the house.

She quickly shoved the contents back inside the drawer and closed it quietly. It was most probably Henry. She glanced at her watch, it was too early for Dylan.

Would Henry think she'd gone to bed for an early night, and carry on to his room?

Should she stay put and hope so?

The study door was ajar. Would he look in? Should she hide?

Footsteps approached. She walked towards the study door just as Henry came into the hall.

"Hi."

He looked towards her, but not directly at her. His glance went past her and into the study. She wasn't sure if it was suspicion, it was hard to tell with him as he didn't have the social expressions people had. But she'd got everything covered for this eventuality.

She held up an iPhone charger.

"I forgot mine, so I just came into the study to borrow your dad's."

He stared at her. Because of his autism, he was incredibly difficult to read.

She looked at her watch. "He said he'd be back around eight thirty."

He shrugged. "So."

"I'm just letting you know," she smiled affectionately; "you don't have to be in your room because I'm here."

"I'm not. I prefer it in my room."

"Okay. Well just so you know, I'll be gone by the morning. Your dad wanted me to stay because of my face. I didn't say earlier, but I was attacked."

No surprise look, or, *are you alright?*

"I was just going to make myself a hot drink, your dad said to help myself. Can I get you one?"

"Okay."

He followed her towards the kitchen and she put the kettle on. "Do you drink coffee, or tea?"

"No." He walked towards the fridge that was so huge, it wouldn't look out of place in a restaurant kitchen. He took out a can of Coke and broke the ring.

"How are you getting on regards the job front?" She selected a mug from the cupboard and put a tea bag in it. "Any interviews lined up?"

He stopped glugging his Coke. "Nope."

"Oh dear, that's a shame, anything more on pursuing college?"

He shook his head.

God, it's like pulling teeth.

"What about your paintings, has your dad seen them yet?"

"I told you, he wouldn't be interested."

"I think he would be once he sees how talented you are."

"No, he wouldn't. He'd be happy for me to go if I was doing business studies or something, but not Art. He's said that a hundred times."

She poured hot water in the mug and used a spoon to stir the tea bag.

"Please don't give up. If you really want to make it happen, you can do. Talk to your dad, tell him how much it means to you."

"What do you care?" he scowled.

"I do care. I know ambition's the key to success. You can make it happen. You're lucky, your dad has money, so many kids don't have that opportunity. Use it. Beg your dad if you have to."

"I wouldn't beg him for anything," he snarled.

"You know what I mean," she glared. *Why was he so literal?* "Make him see this is what you want and that you'll work hard. Try it, Henry, you might be surprised."

He was deep in thought, as if he wanted to say something but wasn't sure.

She took a sip of her tea and waited.

"He's not what you think he is," he said quietly.

"In what way?" she showed genuine inquisitiveness.

"In every way."

Why was he warning her?

Did he know the full extent of his father's business dealings?

"Does it matter?" she asked but he didn't reply. "He's a business man, they don't always play by the rules. That's how they get ahead. You just need to remember, he's your dad and with his help and finances, you can make things happen. You won't always be beholden to him. Utilise him now to get to your goal, which is studying Art." She studied his tortured face, "If that's what you really want to do."

His pitiful nod sliced her in two; he was such a troubled soul.

"Do it," she told him firmly, "and then when your course is finished, you can decide what road you want to take. The way I see it, you're not happy at the moment, are you?"

The shake of his head indicated he wasn't.

"Then what have you got to lose? Go for it," she pushed.

He didn't reply, just stared which she hoped meant he was considering, and then walked towards the bin, depositing the Coke can in the one which was coloured for recycling.

There'd be no more from him tonight.

"I'm going to sit in the snug and watch TV until your dad gets back. Do you fancy joining me?"

It was unlikely he'd want to sit and watch TV with his dad's bit of stuff, but she genuinely wanted him to. Maybe get onto the subject of his mother; she doubted he talked to anyone about her. She could help him as she knew that anguish so well.

Please, she willed, stay and talk.

He shook his head. "I've got stuff to do."

"Okay," she gave in, "but remember what I've said. You've got to make it happen, nobody will do it for you."

He nodded, and for the first time, looked directly at her. But this time it wasn't just a nod to pacify her . . . it looked like an acknowledgment of some sort. Maybe hope? As if she'd finally got through.

Chapter 44

April filled the kettle in the staff room and switched it on ready for their break. A quick glance in the mirror reassured her the bruising and scratches had all but disappeared and had not left any scars. She put a spoon of coffee in each of the three mugs for her, Joey and Rachel. Dylan was still in the building and she'd heard Joey let his brother Victor in minutes earlier. But why was Victor there?

Joey opened the staffroom door, "Great, you're making the coffees."

"I was but I've lost my bracelet," she twisted her hand around her wrist while her eyes scanned the room as if it might have just slipped off. "I think it must have come off upstairs when I was hoovering earlier."

"Do you want me to go up and check round for you?"

"No, it's okay, I'll nip back up. I've left some cleaning stuff in the ladies' toilets I need to bring down anyway. Coffee's all ready if you don't mind making them?"

"No, I don't mind. I need to see Ingrid though, do you know where she is?"

"The last time I saw her was in her office."

"I'll nip there then while the kettle boils," Joey replied, just as Ingrid arrived.

"Ah, just the person," Joey said.

"What's up?" Ingrid frowned.

April tried to squeeze past Joey towards the door.

"Where are you off to?" Ingrid asked.

"I've lost my bracelet. I think the clasp must have come undone when I was cleaning. I'm just going to check the offices."

"Mr Rider's upstairs having a business meeting, so you better leave it for now. I'll have a look when they've finished if you like."

It wasn't a question.

Joey interjected, "Ingrid, can you just come and look at the carpet at the entrance. Some of it has lifted and I'm worried about a visitor tripping on it. You know what Joe Public are like. You could end up with a claim if anyone injures themselves."

"Okay," Ingrid sighed. "I'll come and take a look. Let's hope I can get someone in first thing to sort it before we open."

April waited until they had both gone to inspect the carpet and made her way back upstairs. Dylan's door was slightly ajar. She squatted down with a duster in her hand. If anyone did come out, she could quite easily make it look as if she was dusting the skirting boards.

She hardly dared breathe and strained to hear the heated exchange between the two brothers. It was evident from Victor's tone, he was angry.

"I don't like the involvement between the two of you. Why the hell couldn't you keep your dick in your trousers?"

"For fuck's sake, so I screwed her. What difference does that make?"

"A huge fucking difference. She'll be dreaming of hearts, flowers and a mansion in the country, not shifting an oil painting in the back of a van."

"I'm telling you, she's smart this one. She'll do it."

"You're sure about that are you?"

"As sure as I can be. She's no shrinking violet. She's done time and wants a better life for herself, to move on, and I can help her with that for a fraction of the price we would have to pay someone else. And she doesn't see a future with me, I can assure you."

"How do you know that?"

"I just do. Anyway, what does it matter if she likes me? It wouldn't be the first time she's helped a lover. It might sway her into doing the job."

"You think so? I reckon you'll be shattering her illusion. She'll be thinking she's hit the jackpot with you."

"Look, the way I see it, we've two options. We can use a courier that will cost us big time, or we can use an attractive female again for a fraction of the price. You know the good-looking ones sail through the custom verifications. Last time it went without any hitches."

"Yeah, well you weren't fucking the last one. This one's different," there was a pause, "you're sure everything checks out?"

"Course I am. She's done time, and she's got no real family here in the UK. She's trying to get her life back on track and a lump sum of money will go a long way towards helping her do that."

"What did she do to get banged up?"

"Nicked some money from the company she worked for. It sounds like the old story, an older bloke was the Svengali and orchestrated it all, but she did the actual thieving."

"So, she's not that smart then?"

"Hey, don't knock it. We can only get her to play ball because of it."

"Maybe she's still got some of the money she took?"

"Doubt it. She's pretty poor by the sound of things. It looks like the bloke was the one with the bulk of it. Anyway, it's all there on the internet if you want to read about it."

Vic didn't respond so Dylan continued, "I'm taking her with me to France on Saturday. While we're there, I'm going to suss her out to see if she's willing to play ball."

"Yeah, well, don't go giving too much away, for God's sake." Victor sounded pretty pissed off, "We don't want her running to the cops and getting the finger of suspicion pointed at us before we've even tried to move the painting."

"I won't. But we do need to move it."

Victor's voice again, "Are we still going for the twenty-fifth?"

"Yep. Let me suss her out this weekend and see if she's game. If not, we'll go to plan B and get a driver."

April crept down the rear staircase and made her way back to the staffroom. As she walked along the ground floor corridor, Ingrid and Joey were walking towards her.

Ingrid glared at her with a look that smacked of *I hope you haven't been up to the offices after what I said.*

She held the bracelet between her fingers, "Ta-da. It was in the toilets. I decided to retrace my steps and found it in the first place I looked."

Ingrid looked relieved, "Right, you get your coffee. I'm going to leave a message to see if I can get a carpet fitter to come first thing in the morning to replace the carpet."

April smiled, "I'll go and make them." She headed for the staffroom deep in thought about Dylan and Vic's conversation.

So they were definitely moving the Portillo on the twenty-fifth.

Initially her brief had been to find out where the painting was stored and link the theft of it to Dylan and Victor. Now it was turning into a whole new ball-game. When they'd started out months ago preparing for the operation, none of them had envisaged she'd be asked to be the courier. That was going to be an unexpected bonus, but even so, she still needed to find out where it was stored.

Then hopefully they'd get the lot of them, not just the brothers.

Chapter 45

April gave the impression she was relaxed and enjoying the drive towards the Channel Tunnel in Dylan's Bentley. Paddy had messaged her confirming they'd dealt with customs to okay her fake passport as Gemma Dean.

Henry was on her mind. It didn't do to get sentimentally involved when undercover, but he had somehow got underneath her skin. A woolly unease gathered inside of her when she thought about him. He always appeared so unhappy.

"Have you been through the tunnel before?" Dylan asked, his eyes focussing on the road.

"Yes, not recently though."

"Could you drive it yourself?"

She turned her head and gave him a scathing look. "I think I could just about manage."

"Who were you with?" he grinned, "when you last came?"

"Why do you want to know?"

"I don't know," he shrugged, "you never say much about yourself."

"That's because there's not much to tell."

"What about your family? Have you any in London?"

"No. I'm an only child."

"Parents?" he asked.

He knows all of this. Why's he going over it again?

"I told you, my parents emigrated to Australia years ago. And my dad died."

"That's right, you did. Sorry about your dad. What part of Australia does your mother live in?"

"Melbourne."

Feed him some more rubbish.

"She remarried a widower and became a stepmother to his children. Well, I say children, they're actually adult now."

"When did you last visit?"

She paused giving the impression she was mentally calculating the year, "About five years ago."

"Did she visit you when you were inside?"

"She did actually, yes. Initially I was too ashamed to tell her, but I wrote to her in the end, and fair do's, she came over. We aren't terribly close, if I'm completely honest."

It was time to get him off the subject of her.

"How far is the hotel once we get through the tunnel?"

"About fifty miles. Did I say, when we get to the hotel, I've got some business to attend to? Will you be okay using the spa for a couple of hours?"

Spa?

She hated spas.

"I'm not bothered about anything like that, to be honest."

"It's got a great reputation. You might enjoy it."

"I'd rather go sightseeing for a bit, if that's okay?"

His tender smile caused her tummy to flip.

"You never cease to amaze me, do you know that? I know women that would die to look as good as you, yet you don't seem to work at it. Do you go in for any sort of beauty therapy regime?"

"No, that's not me at all."

"I can see that. Okay, sightseeing it is then. Can you fit in a bit of retail therapy? I'd like you to buy something nice to wear for tonight, my treat."

"There's really no need, I've brought stuff with me," she widened her eyes, "or are you worried I'll let you down in a chain-store offering?"

"I don't think you could ever let me down, Gemma," he squeezed her leg, "you're like a breath of fresh air." He smiled his oh so sexy grin at her, "And you make me feel very horny."

She gave him a suggestive look, "Have we time to do anything about that before your business meeting?"

"I'll make time," he winked, causing an ache deep within her.

He was far too bloody hot for a criminal.

Chapter 46

The waiter removed their dessert dishes. "Can I get you a nightcap to go with your coffee, sir?"

Dylan looked at April, "Would you like a brandy or anything?"

"That would be nice, thank you."

"Two Rémy Martin's please."

The waiter nodded and left.

"It's been a lovely evening, thank you," she smiled. It had. The meal had been a gourmet delight, but it was his company she'd enjoyed. Not only was he incredibly good looking, he had a charming personality and had made her laugh with tales about the all-boys schools he'd attended.

"It has been nice. And much as I've enjoyed imagining getting that beautiful dress off you, I've brought you here to talk to you about something serious."

Her nipples tightened as his sexy eyes devoured her cleavage. The dress was rather a nice prop for seduction. It was black with a low neck edged with tiny pearl beads. It was sleeveless and fitted, so enhanced her waist and hips. She'd made sure when she bought it, she had plenty of flesh on show.

"Go on then, I'm listening."

"Before I do, I want to ascertain something. Where do you see this relationship going between us?"

"I don't really see us as in a relationship to be honest," she frowned, "we're just friends aren't we, enjoying each other?"

"Yes, that's the way I see it. But I do really like you, Gemma, and that makes what I'm about to ask more difficult than I'd expected."

"Crikey, this sounds ominous." She appeared puzzled, "I'm all ears."

His expression was intense. As if he was in two minds whether to ask.

Better throw in some uncertainty.

"Do you want to end it between us? Is that what it is?"

"Absolutely not," he dismissed, "it's nothing like that."

She tilted her head to one side, "What then?"

A muscle in the corner of his eye began to twitch. "I'd like you to consider doing a job for the gallery."

"Not more cleaning?" she pulled a face, "I'm pretty cleaned out to be honest." She lifted her hands, "I've got calluses to prove it."

"It's not cleaning." His expression was serious, as if he was actually in pain asking her.

"What is it then?" She put a questioning look on her face. "It's nothing risky, is it?" she asked cautiously.

"No, it's not *risky* as such."

She blew out a breath, "That's a relief then because that part of my life is well and truly over."

She waited for him to speak again. It surprised her he was struggling.

He cleared his throat. "I wonder if you would consider moving some paintings from the UK over to France for me."

Even though she was expecting him to ask, it hurt.

Stupidly, she was disappointed.

"Me? Don't you have paid drivers to do that?"

"Yes, I have, but I don't trust them with the particular stock I want moving."

"What, you think they might abscond with it?"

"Something like that, yes."

"Well, can't you have a security guard with them?" She frowned hopefully making a good job of looking confused, "Isn't that what you usually do with expensive stock, anyhow?"

"Yes, but these paintings are different."

She nodded, giving the impression she understood, but knew she needed to give more.

"Why don't you move them yourself, then? Can't you and your brother do it between you?"

"No, not this particular stock, we need someone we can trust to move it."

She narrowed her eyes, "I'm not sure I like the sound of this. I've already told you, I'm not getting involved in anything dodgy."

"It isn't *dodgy* as you put it. It's transporting some paintings in a van. Nothing to it really."

"Then why aren't you doing it?"

"The paintings can't be associated with me or the gallery."

"So they're knock-off then, is that what you're saying?"

"I think *highly sought after*, is a better term."

She exaggerated the puzzlement on her face. "So, let me get this right. You want me to transport stolen paintings from the UK across to France?"

"In a nutshell, yes."

"And what if I get caught?"

"You won't. The custom officers will just do a check to see that the paintings match the certification and you'd be on your way."

"Oh, right, easy as that, is it?" She took an exaggerated deep breath in. "I don't know why you think I'd be interested. I get it now why you've been pursuing me. And here's me thinking you liked me."

"I do like you, Gemma. That's why I'm asking you."

"Well I'm not interested. You clearly don't know me very well if you think I'd risk going back to jail. I've told you before; I'm trying to get my life sorted." She kept her voice low. "Why you would even think I'd consider something like this is beyond me. What reason would I have?"

"Twenty thousand pounds."

She visibly swallowed and stared.

The waiter appeared and rested a tray on the edge of the table. She watched him placing the china coffee pot down, and two brandy goblets.

"Anything else, sir?"

Dylan smiled, "We're good thank you."

She watched as he poured her coffee before pouring his own. She broke the silence. "How much are the paintings worth?"

"There's only one of significant value. The others are simply being moved between galleries which is standard."

He sipped his coffee and watched her.

"Is it just you?" she asked.

He raised an eyebrow, "And Vic."

"You two have stolen a painting?"

"No. I meant it's Vic and I that move paintings. We have a buyer for the valuable one, and once it's out of the UK, we'll be paid and that's the end of it."

"It all sounds slick. Have you done this before?"

The aroma of the brandy reached her as he swished his goblet around. "Let's just say we aren't amateurs."

"I can't believe you're telling me all this. Aren't you worried I'll leave here and go to the police?"

He shook his head, "No. People who've been inside rarely confide in cops. And what could you tell them? I'm a respectable business man and there's no link whatsoever to me or Vic to the painting. Anyway, I'm a fairly good judge of character and I don't think you'd do that somehow."

"It's still a massive risk, you telling me."

"I have no choice. I want the painting moved."

"When?"

"Soon."

"I see." She interjected sadness into her tone, "It's all coming together now. You must have done this before. That last girl, what was her name," she purposely got it wrong, "Linda was it? That's why you give the jailbirds jobs at the gallery, isn't it? All this rehabilitation is rubbish. You want them to help you. I bet I'm not far wrong, am I?"

He took a sip of his drink. "Like I said, we are not amateurs. So, are you coming round to the idea?"

"No, I'm not," she snapped. "Tell me, do you sleep with them all. Is that what it's about? Screw the cleaner and turn her head a bit and she'll do anything?"

He took a deep breath in. "It may have been in the beginning, yes. You were easy to screw. You're a very beautiful young woman," he reached for her hand, "but I didn't expect to feel quite the way I do about you."

She pulled her hand away. "Please . . . spare me the crap. You're using me to get what you want."

"Okay, maybe I am a bit, but it needn't be like that. We can still be friends when this is over."

"Oh, yeah right, I bet. And how would that work if I'm handcuffed to a cop?" She shook her head, "I don't think so, somehow."

"Look, all I'm asking is for you to think about it. Twenty thousand pounds would go a long way to getting you that fresh start you want."

"That'll be chicken-feed to what you'll be getting."

"Yes, well, we've done the hardest part. Your bit's relatively easy. It's a regular delivery job."

"What's the painting worth?"

"A lot. But that's split between a lot of people."

"And what will you end up with once you've paid everyone?"

"Does it matter? The question is, will you consider it?"

She took a deep breath in.

You bloody bet I will.

"No."

Chapter 47

Dylan stayed in the bar for a nightcap, and by the time he got to bed, Gemma was asleep. Or pretending to be. She had her back to his side of the bed, and much as he wanted to reach for her, he didn't. Instead, he lay on his back with a hand behind his head and stared around the dark room with just a bit of light from the drapes she hadn't quite closed properly.

Had he said too much?

Surely she wouldn't let on to anyone what he'd discussed? After all, he'd told her nothing really. It was all hearsay. If she did try to expose him, there was nothing tangible to tie him to the robbery. And he'd not specifically mentioned the Portillo by name.

He recalled her saying no, quite adamantly. He wasn't sure if he was pleased. There was a part of him that wanted her to move the painting and take the money, but there was something else simmering away inside of him, almost like relief, that she'd told him to get lost. What an enigma she was. His nostrils flared as he inhaled her sexy perfume.

As if she knew what he was thinking, she turned her naked body over and pressed herself seductively against his thigh. It was the only encouragement he needed.

The kissing dance between them began. His tongue moved inside her mouth and she teased him with hers. His lips trailed down her neck, kissing and biting her smooth skin. He moved onto her breasts and lingered on her nipples, sucking and biting each one in turn.

He took hold of her feet and spread them so her pussy was on display for him.

"You are so fucking sexy, Gemma," he breathed as he flicked his tongue across her folds, like a cat lapping her. Her body quivered and wriggled, but he wasn't going to be hurried. He slipped one of his fingers inside her, and then two, stretching and scissoring her as he forced them deeper. Her body jolted with excitement and she moaned and quivered as he spread her juices all over her clit.

She thrust her pussy in his face. He forced his tongue into her, keeping her on the brink, until finally he ran his tongue up and down, sucking her clit into his mouth and nipping it with his teeth.

"Dylan!" she screamed as he continued lapping and sucking while she writhed.

He moved up to her and kissed her. "You're one fucking hot woman, that's for sure," he smiled.

"And you're one fucking hot man," she purred, "and you taste of me."

"You're killing me," he breathed in her ear, "get on your knees for me, so I can fuck you."

She turned over and he wrapped her in his arms as they knelt together. He kissed and sucked her neck, playfully biting her ear lobes.

The sight of her tight ass on all fours, and the invitation of her wet pussy he'd just tasted, thrilled him. He ran his hand down his long length and pressed his tip to her swollen folds, running it up and down her crease to her clit. She wriggled her ass aligning her wet pussy to him and he pushed forward, sinking his dick effortlessly into her. She tilted her ass up so her pussy sucked him in further, and he held her hips, pulling out slowly, leaving just his tip before sinking back hard and fast.

He forced her legs wider with his knees. He couldn't get enough as her slippery pussy clenched his dick, and he slammed in and out, hitting her cervix relentlessly as he filled her to the brim. Her head dropped and the groans coming from her made him fuck her all the harder.

He cupped her tits and clamped his fingers around her nipples, pulling hard. Her whimpers turned to screams as he pounded her, "Dylan, oh, God, Dylan!" she yelled.

He continued to hammer her relentlessly, until his own body convulsed and he was coming, flesh slapping against flesh until they both collapsed on the bed.

What an incredible fuck she was. He couldn't get enough of her.

*

She snaked herself against his body, throwing one leg over him and resting her hand on his chest.

"Sleep tight, beautiful," he muttered, kissing her head.

Oh, I will.

'Cause you're about to make all my dreams come true.

"You too," she purred.

Chapter 48

"He wants me to move the painting across to France," April told a surprised Paddy at their regular Saturday morning meeting. They were inside the park café to escape a shower.

"Bloo – dy – hell," he took a sip of his coffee. "I didn't expect this."

"Me neither."

He shook his head in disbelief. "You must be convincing, that's all I can say."

You have no idea, Paddy.

He scowled, "But it does put a completely different slant on things now."

April stirred the froth on her latte. "It does, but I think this is our only hope. I know my remit was finding out where the Portillo was stored and linking the brothers, but I can't get anything," she gave a frustrated frown, "you know I've tried. I don't see him any day soon divulging where it is. I think I should go along with this charade and tell him I'll move it. That way, he's going to lead me directly to it."

Paddy added more sugar to his coffee. "He's not going to take you to where it's stored. That's far too incriminating. Those brothers won't have anything traced back to them. We're confident from the coded messages you've managed to get that Jit Monks and his gang carried out the heist, but it's getting the evidence. If we could bring them in also, you and I will be laughing all the way to the bank."

"I think there is a way, but you're going to have to trust me."

"What way?" he asked. "I hope you're not considering what I think you are?"

"Of course I'm not," she dismissed, "I don't need the job that badly."

He widened his eyes. "What were the sleeping arrangements in France, then?"

"Not with him, I can assure you," she lied.

He gave her a look that said he didn't believe her.

"Go on then, what else do you have that's going to get him to open up?" Paddy asked.

"It's only an idea at the moment."

The tone of his voice changed to one of authority. "Tell me what sort of idea?"

"I want to see how the next few days play out. We are this close," she squeezed her thumb and finger together, "I can do this, Paddy, you know I can."

"I don't doubt it, but I need to know exactly how. It's not only tying him to the Portillo, we've also got to get a conviction. And a police officer sleeping with the suspect isn't going to cut it with the Crown Prosecution if that's what you're thinking. You know that as well as I do."

"Yes, and it's for that very reason I've resisted his advances," she lied again, "but he likes me. We have a great rapport. I just need a few more days. Everything we need is in that safe, I can smell it. And remember, unbeknown to him, I know the date the painting is going to be moved."

"He's not mentioned anything to you about the specific date?"

"No, not yet. Right now he thinks I'm not interested in helping him, but all that's about to change. Tonight I'm going to tell him I will."

Paddy checked his watch. "We haven't got long. It's ten days from now if it goes ahead."

"Yeah," she nodded. "Have we got anything from surveillance?"

"Nothing. Wherever he's got it, it's bloody well hidden."

"It's great we're certain Jit Monks and his gang stole the Portillo."

"Yeah, it is. He's got the experience, and done time so knows the score. He's not stupid, either. He'll have an idea he's a prime suspect in the robbery so is lying low."

"Anything from the emails and WhatsApp messages I've sent you?"

"Only Dylan and Victor talk about J and his so-called daughter, which is code for the painting. Nothing that would stand up in court of course."

"You've had a tail on Jit Monks though?"

"Yep, but nothing significant there. No visits to unusual places. He's leading quite a mundane existence." He sighed deeply, "I wish there was something to report."

Paddy's face was a deep red colour, particularly his neck, so she guessed the case was aggravating his blood pressure. He reached for a serviette and wiped his brow and neck.

"I've got the Chief Inspector hassling me, not to mention the insurance company." His tone changed to one of authority, "We need a result on this," he emphasised with an almost painful expression.

"Then trust me to finish it," she pleaded, "let me see what I can do in the next few days."

"We can't let him move that painting out of the country," Paddy warned, "if he does, you and I are finished. We'll end up licking stamps in an office somewhere for the rest of our days."

"I'm going to get him and the painting. I promise you. You know I can do it."

"Yes, but it's how you do it that bothers me."

There was nothing she could say. She wasn't about to divulge anything more to him. She stood up. "I've got to go. I'll be in touch, please try not to worry. I'll not let you down."

Concern was etched on his face. It was sweet that such a tough cop was worried about her.

She leant forward and gave him a hug. "I'll be fine, honestly."

She waited for him to say more, but he didn't. She flung her bag over her shoulder and left him sitting with his empty coffee cup and no doubt his concerned eyes boring into the back of her.

There was work to be done.

Paddy Frodsham was a good Detective, but he really had no idea.

***

He watched her walking towards the park exit chewing her bottom lip. Her fringe kept blowing across her face and she brushed it out of the way with an inpatient flick of her fingertips. The short cut suited her with the decorative earrings showing her pixie-like ears off to perfection.

As always, she was in her blue jeans which clung to her long legs like they'd been painted on, and no make-up. She didn't need it. The pink tee-shirt showed off her generous breasts. Her arms were bare. She could do with some sun on them, she was too pale.

The rain had stopped. People were milling around, mothers with children and pushchairs, and adults clutching coffee cups, hastily making their way through the park.

How he'd love to go over to her. He was close enough to call out hello if he wanted to. She'd be shocked if he did, that was for sure.

The sun was blinding so he pulled the peak of his cap down further so he could watch. She looked over her shoulder as she turned left out of the park.

He knew where she was going now.

He knew all her movements.

Chapter 49

"Come on, you two, some of us have got to be off on time." Joey was standing by the back door of the gallery with his jacket on.

"Okay, okay," Rachel said quickening her pace. "What you in such a hurry for? On a promise are we?"

He rolled his eyes. "Well if I was, at this rate, she'd be gone by the time I got there."

April followed Rachel out of the door. She'd got used to walking with Rachel to the bus stop each evening after work. Joey always came in his car. She watched Joey swipe his badge on his lanyard and then key in a number and close the door behind him.

"I wonder why Dylan's still there?" April asked. "It's late for him to be hanging around, isn't it?"

"Yeah," Joey replied, as they made their way towards his car. "Ingrid said he has a conference call to the US. I think they are about six hours behind us."

"Wonder if Ingrid's part of the conference call?" Rachel giggled, "probably giving him a blow job while he's on the phone."

"Lucky bloke if she is," Joey grinned as they reached his car.

Rachel squeezed his arm, "Have a great night. Make sure you do everything I would, won't you."

Joey opened his car door. "I'll do my best," he winked, "see you both tomorrow."

Rachel linked her arm in April's as they made their way towards the bus stop. This had become their routine four out of five nights after work. Thursday nights, they headed straight for the pub with Joey. It was usual for Rachel's bus to arrive first which was good as April wasn't going home on her bus, not yet anyway. Dylan wanted her to return to the gallery, so they could go over the plan to move the Portillo. She'd given it a few days before agreeing she would transport it across to France. Tonight was about finding out how.

She still couldn't ascertain if he was happy she'd agreed to move the painting or not. His response had been indifferent which unnerved April slightly. She expected him to be pleased. After all, that's what it was all about. *Wasn't it?*

Rachel curtailed any further thoughts on Dylan's reaction.

"Lucky woman whoever she is that's getting to spend tonight with Joey. I think he's dead fit, don't you?"

"Yeah, he is rather."

"But you're not interested?"

"No."

"Even though he likes you?"

"I don't think he does," April dismissed, "not like that. Anyway, he's not my type."

"What's your type then?"

"Oh, I don't know, maybe someone a bit more polished."

"What, like Dylan?"

"Well, he is good looking, you can't deny that."

"So, you wouldn't knock him back if he tried anything?"

"Who would?" April replied, and then nudged Rachel's arm playfully. "I'm only joking. He's nice on the eye, but he wouldn't be for me. I think Joey's nice too, he's just not what I'd go for. Anyway, I've told you, I'm not interested in any blokes at the moment. I just want to get the next few weeks over with, then move on."

"I can't believe anyone that looks like you isn't with someone."

"I've had a bellyful of them," she painted a pained look on her face, "it was a bloke that got me into this mess in the first place. I'm not going down that road again . . . not for a very long time."

Rachel frowned, "What about . . . you know, sex, don't you miss that?"

"A bit. But not so much that I want to get involved right now."

The red number eleven came into sight. "Ah, here it is," Rachel turned and gave her a hug, "I'll see you tomorrow."

"Yep, you will. Unless someone comes knocking who wants to take me away from all this."

"You and me both," Rachel grinned as the bus stopped in front of them. "Or failing that, we might win the lottery."

"Now there's something to dream about," April smiled. "See you tomorrow then, bye."

April waved her off and watched as the bus pulled away. Once it was completely out of sight, she made her way back to the gallery with a smile on her face and a thudding heart.

Tonight, she'd know the whole plan. Everything she'd worked for was coming to fruition.

April sat opposite Dylan in his office with the desk separating them. He handed her three photographs.

"These are the paintings you'll be taking," he passed her another photo, "and this is the van."

She looked at the picture of the van. "That looks rather nice to be transporting paintings."

"It has to be. It's specially equipped with air suspension to mitigate the damaging effects of shock and vibration which can easily be transmitted to a painting on a road journey. It has temperature and humidity controls inside to keep the environment at eighteen to twenty, as close to a museum environment as possible."

She shuffled the pictures of the three paintings and frowned. "They must all be so expensive if you have to go to all that trouble?"

"They are, but that one there," he pointed to a portrait of an Indian lady in a stunning headdress, which she particularly admired when she walked past it each evening in the gallery, "it's fake. The original stays here. I'm giving you the paperwork of the original though, but that comes back."

She examined the picture closely. "It doesn't look fake?"

"That's because it's a particularly good one."

"Why are you transporting a fake, I don't get it?"

"It's going to be hiding the Portillo. That'll be underneath. When they check the UK documentation, they'll see the verifications. They'll have no idea about the Portillo. So, if everything is in order this end, it mitigates any risks."

"Why me then, if there are no risks? Why not just pay a courier?"

"Because it's them I don't trust. They could quite easily take off with the painting."

"And I can't?"

"I don't think you will, no. And you'll have a technician in the van with you."

"A technician?"

"Yes. You don't transport paintings of this value without a technician. Lee will make sure if the van is stopped and the paintings examined, they are handled with extreme care. And that's where you come in. A beautiful woman should be a distraction in itself. If you were stopped, they'd be checking the number of paintings against the description, that's all."

"Right. Is the technician in on it?"

"Not really, no. He's paid well for being the transportation escort, but that's it. He's helped us before, and not the type to ask questions. It's much better for him in the unlikely event of getting stopped, that he knows nothing, just that he's been paid to transport paintings in his role as a technician."

"Unlikely?" she said hesitantly.

"It *is* unlikely, Gemma," he emphasised. "We move expensive paintings all the time for exhibitions. We've rarely been stopped, but if you were, I'm sure a woman with your charm would be a significant distraction for them to not be looking at much more than the documentation tallying."

She widened her eyes, "What if it was a female customs officer?"

He pursed his lips, "The way you look, she'd probably fancy you anyway. And," his eyes softened, "as for you taking off with the paintings, I wouldn't have suggested you if I thought you'd do anything like that."

"You are taking a risk though. I'm already a convicted criminal."

"That's exactly why I want you to do it. You're down on your luck and I'm sure the money will make a difference to your life."

"Yes, I've been thinking about that. How much is this painting worth, exactly?"

"It doesn't matter what it's worth. I've told you before, the money is split between a lot of people. Everyone wants their cut."

"But not everyone's moving the painting through customs like I am."

His eyes darkened. "You've already agreed, Gemma, you can't back out now."

"Who said anything about backing out? I'm thinking more about you increasing my cut."

If he was surprised she'd asked for more, he didn't show it.

"How much?"

Her eyes never left his. "Thirty k."

"Not a chance," he dismissed.

She widened her eyes. "Oh, come on. It's not like you can't afford it. I bet you give more than that to charity each year and claim it back in tax relief."

He stared.

Was that a glimmer of a cynical smile?

As if he'd been expecting all along she'd ask for more?

He stroked his chin with his finger and thumb. "Twenty-five k, and not a penny more."

She stared back, purposely making him wait.

"Okay," she sighed, "twenty-five it is. So, when do I get it?"

"As soon as everything is done. You'll offload the two legitimate paintings at the Musée d' Orsey gallery. Lee, the technician will supervise the handover, and then you'll travel to a hotel with the Portillo still in the van. Once there, you wait in the car park. Vic will be at the hotel waiting for the transfer of money.

"Victor?"

"Yes, he won't allow the painting to go until the money has transferred. Once Vic is satisfied that the bank transfer has gone through, he'll give Lee the nod and someone will come and take the painting from you. You don't need to do anything more after that. Go to the hotel that Lee takes you to, and once you're there, I'll see your money goes into your account."

"Where are you going to be when all this is going on?"

"At the gallery. But whatever you do, don't contact me. If anything should go wrong ..."

"Wrong," she interrupted, "you said nothing could go wrong?"

"And it won't," he reassured, "I'm only saying, if something unexpected happened, don't message me or anything. Lee will know who to contact."

"What if, worst case scenario, they do pull me in and find the Portillo. What happens then?"

"They'll arrest you, and then start questioning you. But you'll say nothing. You won't answer anything, just go with no comment. We'll get you a brief. He will argue you were paid an amount of money to transport the paintings and you had no idea they were anything other than legitimate."

"And that's going to get me out of there, is it?"

"Not initially, no, but eventually it will. But whatever does happen, provided you keep schtum, we'll look after you."

"I don't want to go back inside, Dylan."

"And you won't. I told you. We've done this before, more than once, you'll be fine. As long as the documentation all adds up, you'll sail through the custom checks."

"You better be right," she sighed deliberately displaying a degree of unease.

"I am." His expression darkened and she sensed a warning. "But you do need to know, it's not just me in this operation, there are others involved. It doesn't matter who they are, you only need to be mindful these are not people you cross. You do understand that don't you?"

"I have been inside, remember," she purposely reminded him. "People that have spent time in jail aren't snitches. You know the saying, honour amongst thieves and all that." She paused, "Anyway, that's why you're using me, isn't it? You know I won't grass if I get caught."

"That is a consideration, yes. But you won't get caught. You are delivering paintings, that's all. There's no reason to think you will."

She took a deep breath in, "If there were no risks though, you wouldn't be paying me what you are."

"True." He reached for her hand, "But I'm confident you'll sail through customs. The paperwork is all legitimate. There's no reason to stop you. Trust me," he squeezed her hand gently like you'd reassure a child, "they won't."

She held his gaze for a moment and then glanced down to look at the pictures of the paintings again. Her heart was racing as she calmly asked, "Where is the stolen painting right now, anyway?"

"Don't worry your head about that. All you need to know is the van will be there at your flat at ten thirty on Friday morning, which reminds me, I need a photo of you for Lee the technician so he recognises you."

"Well, I hardly think there's going to be a random woman waiting to travel with him across to France, do you?"

"No, but I still want him to check it's you." He lifted his iPhone to take her photo. "Are you going for serious, or a smile?"

She pulled a get-on-with-it face, and the flash went off.

He tossed the phone on his desk and leaned back in his chair. "Now that's the business side of things concluded, I want to show you what I've been thinking of doing since you first walked into this gallery in that tight little uniform. Come here."

She sauntered over to his chair and eased her body onto his, straddling him. He was already hard. She took his face in her hands and kissed him. Their tongues began sliding together like a rhythmic waltz.

"Have you got out door clothes?" he moaned.

"Yes, I changed when I got here, why?"

"Because I'm going to rip everything off you and fuck you, right now on this chair."

She kissed him, "Good job I've made a start for you then?"

He looked puzzled as she placed his hands around her bare bottom.

A look of surprise passed across his face, "Please don't tell me you clean these offices with no knickers on?"

She grinned, enjoying the power she had over him. "I might do."

"Fuck, Gemma," he breathed, "you shouldn't have told me that."

Still eased herself back so she could unbuckle his fly. Her fingers released his huge dick and she began to work it.

"Why, what difference does it make?" she asked, changing the movement of her fingers to massage the already coated tip.

"You know I'm going to imagine every time I see you what's underneath your uniform. You're not really a cleaner are you," he grinned, "you're a fucking witch?"

She kissed him impatiently. "A witch that's ready for you, right now. So where are the condoms?"

"In that drawer," he indicated with his head and leaned forward holding onto her and opened the drawer, fishing for a condom. She took it from him and tore open the packet. She rolled it on his tip and smoothly sheathed him.

"God, there's only you that can make putting on a condom really hot."

She hoisted her hips upwards, and he held himself as she manoeuvred herself onto his huge dick and slowly eased down, her slick muscles clenching around him, sucking him in before beginning to move gently.

His face looked tortured as he effortlessly ripped open the front of her uniform, exposing her breasts ensconced in a black lace bra. He pulled it down and took her breast into his mouth, hungrily. He sucked on one nipple and then the other, sending sparks to her clit. She continued to ride him, using her knees for leverage.

He buried his face in her breasts, "You have the most amazing tits," he said, almost gobbling them up. He bit, grabbed and sucked, while she rode him, loving the feeling of his dick deep within her.

She clenched her inner muscles around him . . . tightly, enjoying him watching her breasts bouncing up and down as she gained momentum.

He held onto her hips. "You are so fucking sexy, Gemma," he moaned as he licked her neck, nibbling and sucking behind her ear.

He was too. The position was fabulous. He was sinking deeper and further into her and she loved it. He moved his hand towards her clit, which was precisely what she wanted. His magical fingers skilfully circled the erect nub, knowing exactly the amount of pressure she needed as he rubbed and manipulated it in tiny circles.

Sparks ignited, the pleasure was excruciating and her pussy throbbed as she continued to ride him. The tension in her belly twisted as the ecstasy became stronger. Her pussy milked his cock frantically, "Oh, God, yes," her body convulsed as pleasure began cascading downwards.

"Dylan!" she screamed.

"Fucking hell!" he roared as his dick pounded his release at the same time, deep inside her.

She buried her head in his neck and still as one, their breathing slowed together.

He cupped her head and pulled it towards him, kissing her gently, "I'll never be able to look at you again in that uniform without remembering this."

She put a playful surprised look on her face, "Well my parole officer did say I needed to make a good impression on the job."

He threw back his head and laughed making her tummy muscles clench.

What is it about this man?

She was going to miss him when it was all over.

Chapter 50

Dylan was checking his emails in his study and looked up as his son came in and hovered in the doorway, looking his usual broody self. His skin was much better since he'd been to see the private specialist. Cost a bloody fortune though and the miserable little sod wasn't one bit grateful. A word of thanks would have been nice, but as usual, verbal communication between him and Henry didn't happen that often. If the truth be known, he didn't really like him. It didn't sit comfortably with him, but that was the way he felt.

He took a deep breath in, determined to make an effort. "You alright?" he asked.

"Yep."

Henry would want something; he wouldn't be stood there otherwise. Why did he have an irritating way of making him ask questions all the time? Why couldn't he interact like a normal kid? And what the hell was in the huge black folder he was clutching? It looked like an art folder. If they were the paintings he'd done, he certainly didn't have time to look at them now.

"Come and sit down. What's up?"

Henry shrugged his shoulders.

It'd be money no doubt. Even though he gave him a generous allowance, he always needed topping up.

Henry sauntered in and perched his backside on the armrest of the sofa adjacent to the desk. Typical of him, making a point that he wasn't actually going to sit properly and talk to his father. It sort of smacked of, I'll half sit with you and then I'm going. He should have more respect, the spoilt little git.

He ought to remember who puts a roof over his head and food in his belly.

"There's no more money, Henry if that's what you're after," he said firmly, "I told you last month, you need to learn how to manage your allowance."

"I don't want any money."

"What is it then?"

"I want to do a course at college."

Dylan frowned. "What sort of course?"

"An Art course."

"I've told you before, Art won't pay the bills. You do realise that, don't you?"

Another shrug.

"What's brought college on? I've been trying to get you to get back to studying for a while. You said you wanted to get a job."

"I've changed my mind."

"And what's prompted that?"

"I've always wanted to go really. Mum wanted me to."

Any mention of his ex-wife Alicia, irritated him to death.

"It's irrelevant what your mother wanted, she's not here."

He watched his son's expression darken.

Maybe that was a bit harsh.

He sighed, "I've told you before, I'm not overjoyed about you studying Art. But if you really want to go, you'd better contact the college and see if there's some sort of combination degree you can do." He paused trying to think of a suitable option, "Maybe look at business studies so you have something to fall back on when you realise Art won't pay you enough to live on."

No response as usual. Clearly, not what his son wanted to hear.

"Anyway, it's probably far too late to get on the course this year, so you'll need to find some sort of job to tide you over while you wait for a college place."

Henry's face turned smug. "I can get on a degree course at the Chelsea College of Arts starting in September, to do a BA Honours in Fine Art."

Bloody Hell.

Vic must have encouraged him to find a course.

"But you'll still have to go through a selection process?"

Henry shook his head, "No. I've been to see them and they've said I've got to take you to vouch for me," his expression was aggrieved, "because of the drugs. I told them I made a mistake and got in with the wrong crowd, and that I'm clean now. They've said they want to see us both before they can offer me a place."

Dylan rolled his eyes, "Do they, now? These jumped-up college professors get on my nerves. They only want to tick a box to say they've met me."

He thought about Henry having some sort of focus. It was better than nothing. At least by getting on a course, it would mean him getting out of bed each morning with a purpose. And as Vic said, another year or so when he's come to terms with his mother's death, he might be different again.

"I suppose we'll have to play the game," he frowned, "although I don't know what the hell they think I can do with you at your age if you decide to go down that road again."

Henry stared but didn't answer.

"Okay," Dylan sighed, "make an appointment and I'll go with you."

"I have done. It's Friday."

"This coming Friday?"

"Yeah."

The Portillo was being moved. He needed to be free for that.

"I can't make it this Friday."

"It's at eleven," Henry declared.

His son seemed oblivious he'd said no.

"I've just said I can't make it," he said firmly, "ring them up and get another day."

"It's booked."

"Henry, you're not listening. I can't make Friday. Fix up another appointment, they won't mind. Or better still, give me the number of the tutor and I'll ring. That's probably all it'll take. I might not even have to go traipsing down to the bloody college."

"It's Friday the 25th at eleven. We are to meet the course leader in his office. I know where it is."

Henry's face was becoming redder with agitation as he wasn't getting his own way. He'd been like that from an early age. His ex-wife had defended him countless times. She reckoned kids on the autistic spectrum didn't understand anyone else's point of view, and tended to only see things from their own perspective. However, unlike Henry's soft mother, he wasn't about to give in to him.

"I'm not going on Friday. I've told you, I'm busy." He tried to look at Henry's eyes to warn him it wasn't negotiable, but his eyes were focussed on the carpet.

"Look at me, Henry when I'm talking to you."

He waited until his son looked directly at him.

"You need to understand the whole universe doesn't centre around you. I've told you I can't make Friday. Now do as I say, get me the number and I'll call them."

Henry stood up and reached for the black folder resting against the chair. "Forget it," he spat.

"There's no need to be like that. What is that anyway, is it your artwork?"

Henry ignored him and moved towards the door.

Dylan raised his voice. "This is so typical of you. You don't get what you want so you throw a strop. Well, I'm telling you now, that might have worked with your mother, but it won't work with me."

He followed Henry as he made his way into the hall and towards the staircase.

"Come back here, and stop being so bloody petulant."

Henry carried on walking up the stairs.

"I do work you know. I can't just drop everything to suit you."

"Fuck you!" Henry spat.

Chapter 51

April returned from the gallery to her flat and opened the front door. As always she paused, checking for the black cotton on the carpet. And every day, it was there just as she'd left it.

Except today.

The cotton had moved. Someone had been inside the flat.

She took a photo on her phone, and went inside locking the door behind her. Her heart-rate quickened.

Had Dylan and Victor sussed she wasn't Gemma Dean?

Surely not? How could they have found out? Maybe it wasn't them. But who could it be? She knew exactly how she placed the cotton every time she left the flat. She checked the photo she'd taken from the morning when she'd positioned it carefully. The cotton had definitely moved. Someone had walked over it.

Her eyes moved towards the small chest of drawers in the corner of the sitting room and her suspicions were confirmed. The top drawer had been opened. There was nothing of any significance inside, but each time she closed the drawer, she trapped a till receipt which wouldn't be obvious to anyone as only the tiniest corner was visible. The receipt wasn't visible anymore.

She made her way to the bedroom and stared at the ottoman. It didn't appear to have moved. She hoisted it to one side, and gently lifted the loose floorboards. The handbag was exactly as she'd left it. It was an ordinary leather handbag, but it had two tassels hanging from it which she had strategically positioned so she would be able to tell if someone had touched it. The tassels hadn't moved.

She sat down on the floor.

Why had someone been in the flat?

There wasn't anything there that would connect her with April Masters so they'd gain nothing from doing so. She reached for her phone and played the recording again that Tom had sent. It was a male voice asking if they would pass on a message to Gemma via her parole officer. To her, it was obvious they were fishing to see if she did actually have a parole officer. The receptionist didn't give any details away, she'd be too well trained for that. The caller had quickly hung up.

April had listened to the recording so many times. The caller had either made a great effort to disguise his voice, or it simply wasn't one she'd heard before.

Who was it?

There was no point in calling Paddy. Although he was her boss and the expectations were she would report any changes to him, she had nothing to tell him. She went into the kitchenette and poured herself a liberal glass of red wine and took a generous mouthful.

Who had been into her flat, and more importantly why?

She was so close now. Too close to allow anyone to get in her way.

But someone was suspicious.

The question was . . . who?

Chapter 52

Dylan Rider was staying late at the gallery. He took a generous swig of his whisky. Everything was set. All being well, by this time Friday evening, the painting would be in the recipient's hands and he and Victor would be millions of pounds richer.

They'd bided their time as they'd planned from the beginning. Jit Monks had been hassling them, but he and Victor were never going to be rushed. They called the shots, and it was for that very reason things went smoothly. They'd already had to pay a significant amount to the gang that had stolen the painting with the proviso they'd get the rest of their cut when the painting was moved. There was also Jit Monks and the old boy minding the painting left to be paid. Monks was getting his cut when they'd offloaded it, and he seemed content enough with his percentage. The crafty old sod had negotiated a generous amount, but wasn't anywhere near what he and Vic were getting once it was sold on. Monks might know plenty about robbing, but knew very little about the art world.

His thoughts drifted to Gemma, who was going to double-back to the gallery again tonight after she'd gone through the pretence of walking with her mate to the bus stop.

It had been damned hard work getting her to play ball, but eventually she capitulated just as he hoped she would. Women like her responded well to a language they understand . . . money. It amused him though that she'd negotiated a bigger cut for her part. He'd meant it when he'd told Victor she was smart.

Tomorrow, the driver with the van would be waiting outside her flat with everything loaded up. The whole operation had taken meticulous planning and they were now at the final hurdle. He liked the highs that massive heists gave him, and he was damn good at it. It was his attention to detail that ensured the plan worked, and this one was planned to perfection. But now it was almost over, he was considering lying low for a while. He'd analysed why the change of heart, and came up with the reason for the turn of events was Gemma. He wouldn't go so far as to think he was in love with her, as the way he saw it love was for fools, but he really liked her. She was different from the rest and was the first woman to actually get under his skin, and despite him being wealthy and her being poor, she wasn't in awe of him. No, he couldn't imagine Gemma being in awe of anyone. He liked that she was quirky. It made her unique.

Time and time again, he kept telling himself she wasn't for him. He had to let her go. And even though he knew that, somehow, he couldn't see a future without her in it. On hindsight, though, he wished he'd never involved her in the whole operation. That way, she would have no idea about his involvement in the theft of the painting. She'd have seen him as a legitimate owner of a gallery and he might have been able to persuade her to stay on. Not particularly cleaning the gallery, but maybe they could have worked something out between the two of them.

It was too late for that now, of course. He had involved her, so he needed a pragmatic approach to work out what next. He knew his feelings were reciprocated. He was confident she felt the same way about him. The burning question was would they be able to forge a relationship when it was all over?

He had an overwhelming desire to try. Fuck what Victor thought. Dylan Rider always made things happen and right now, he knew categorically he wanted Gemma in his life.

He gulped down the last of his whisky. As soon as they'd offloaded the Portillo as planned, he'd go to her. She'd get her cut, that was only fair, but he'd put it to her that they continue to see each other and see how things developed from there.

He felt slightly elated. He was approaching thirty-eight and could see a whole new chapter in his life emerging.

Now, where was she?

His dick throbbed for her.

He was like a bloody rabbit when she was around.

Chapter 53

They walked around the lake for the last time, and as usual, April linked her arm in Paddy's.

"So, the painting is going to be delivered to you at what time?" Paddy asked.

"Ten thirty."

"And you're supposed to head straight for the Tunnel?"

"Yep. Seemingly I'm going to have a technician with me."

"You're absolutely certain he still doesn't suspect anything?"

"No, not at all."

Nothing to be gained by telling him now that someone had been in her flat.

"He'll have every angle covered though," she reminded him, "anyone with any sense wouldn't let a painting of that value out of their sight."

"Still not an inkling where it could be right now?"

"No."

"We've reached a dead end, too," he scowled, "if only we could have found where it's stored."

"It's unlikely though, now," April said, "but we'll still have enough with my evidence surely, won't we? We said at the beginning we might not get the whole gang. The insurers want the painting, but it's us that want Dylan and his brother."

"Yeah. And we can probably link Jit Monks with stealing the painting. Those emails you managed to get should help. Whether it's enough, we'll have to see."

She widened her eyes. "So we're all good?"

"We are. You've done a great job, April. I never envisaged when we started out, we'd come this far. I hoped, of course, once you came onboard. I knew then if anyone could get us the info, it would be you."

She pointed out the obvious, "It's been a bloody long slog, though. That spell in prison was soul-destroying. It dragged on for so long."

He nodded. "I'm sure. But we wouldn't be where we are now without it. It was absolutely necessary."

"I know," she agreed. "We just need to hold tight and keep everything crossed from now on. The team are all briefed and in place, aren't they?"

"Yeah, they're ready."

"Good. So, once we've got the van with the painting, we'll nick Rider."

"You can bet on it. If anything changes before then, you know how to contact me."

She nodded. "Do you think we'll have enough to get both brothers?"

"I hope so. The main thing is, because of your diligence, we'll get the Portillo back, which the insurance bods will be relieved about, and then we'll have to hope we've got enough evidence to nick both of them. We'll bring in Jit Monks and some of the suspects to see if any will grass."

"Let's hope the final sting goes without a hitch, then."

"I'm confident it will. You've come this far, April, you'll see it through."

She nodded.

Of course she would.

"So," he smiled, "it's a wrap then. Watch your back, though. We don't know how these brothers will react if they suspect they're being double-crossed, or the gang responsible for stealing the painting. Any hint something might be wrong, and they could come for you."

Her gut twisted. Someone was onto her.

"I'll be careful, don't you worry."

"Make sure you are," he warned. "Anything unexpected between now and then, let me know."

"I will."

Paddy hugged her. A proper hug like a father would hug his daughter. It still felt awkward even after all this time. Her eyes followed him as he walked away, and she waited until he disappeared around the side of the park café towards the exit before turning in the opposite direction to head back to her flat.

Detective Inspector April Masters prided herself on being equipped to deal with every eventuality, but nothing had prepared her for the person standing directly in front of her, barring her way.

She reeled back. "What on earth are you doing here?"

Chapter 54

"Following you," Henry replied with a fixed look on his face.

"Following me? Whatever for?"

"I wanted to." His expression was unreadable.

"Well, you've no business doing that. It's not right . . . it feels creepy."

He didn't answer.

What in God's name was he up to?

Getting cross wouldn't help. She needed to find out what was going on, but Henry was a hard nut to crack as his brain didn't work quite the same way as others. She needed to tread carefully.

Why was he following her? And how the hell hadn't she noticed?

"Do you want to get a drink in the café?" she asked.

He shrugged.

"I do. Come on."

They went inside the café and towards the counter. Neither of them spoke. She needed to think. He'd thrown her completely.

"What would you like?" she asked.

"Coke."

"Do you want anything to eat, a biscuit or something?"

"No."

"Okay, you grab us a seat while I get a coffee and I'll bring them over."

As the assistant was fiddling with the coffee maker, her mind was going into overdrive.

How had she missed him?

She'd always been so careful.

She put the tray down on the table and handed Henry a Coke and a glass and placed her own coffee on the table. She sat down and took a deep breath in. "Right, come on, I want to know why you're following me."

"To see what you're doing." He poured his Coke into the glass and she watched it fizz up over the ice.

"What do you mean, what I'm doing? What's it got to do with you?"

He took a mouthful of his Coke, "Who's that bloke you were with?"

"None of your business," she glared.

Silence.

"If you must know, he's a friend of mine."

"He's too old to be a friend."

"He's a friend of my late father, actually. Not that I need to explain myself to you. You need to tell me why you're following me?"

He fiddled with the sugar sachets. "'Cause I don't believe you're a cleaner."

Shit. He could blow the whole operation.

She went for a puzzled expression. "Why are you so interested in me?"

He shrugged dismissively.

The penny suddenly dropped. "You haven't been in my flat, have you?"

Not even a flinch. But no denial, either. It must have been him.

"That's not fair, Henry. How did you get in?"

"Picked the lock."

"You're making me feel very uncomfortable. This isn't on."

She put another indignant expression on her face. "My parole officer says someone has telephoned asking questions about me. Was that you?"

He didn't need to answer, she knew it was.

"I'm going to have to speak to your father about this."

"No, you won't."

"Why won't I?"

"Because I know why you're really with him."

Christ almighty. She'd totally underestimated him.

"And why's that?"

"Because you aren't who you say you are."

Shit, shit, shit.

"And what's that supposed to mean?"

"You're making out you're a cleaner, but I reckon you're from an insurance company."

Thank God.

"Insurance?" She put on a bewildered frown, "Why would I be from an insurance company?"

His look was uncertain, as if he hadn't quite thought it through. "You're something like that, anyway."

"I really have no idea what you're talking about. You've been in my flat, isn't it obvious by the way I live, that I'm a cleaner?"

"You're trying to link Dylan to some stolen paintings."

Oh fuck.

"Stolen paintings?" She put on a fake laugh, "I have no idea what you're on about. I think you've been watching too much TV."

"You know. That's why you meet that bloke here on a Saturday. He's from the insurance company too."

So, he'd seen her with Paddy before. How had she missed that?

"You've got it completely wrong, Henry, honestly. You know I've been in prison. There isn't an insurance company in the world that would employ me, I can assure you. And I know nothing about stolen paintings, in fact you've shocked me. I can't believe your dad would be involved in anything like that."

He wasn't listening.

"I won't tell him," he said nonchalantly, as if they were talking about withholding the result of a football match.

She needed to bluff him out.

"You can tell him what you like but I don't think he'd have any time for this nonsense."

His expression was challenging. "It'd blow your cover if I did."

Find out what he really wants.

"Look, Henry, what's all this about? Tell me why you've taken it upon yourself to be following me and making up these ridiculous stories."

"They aren't stories. It's true. You work for an insurance company," his speech wavered, "or something like that."

She needed to cut to the chase, but she had to tread carefully.

"Is it your dad, is that it?" She threw understanding into her voice, "Are you worried I'm going to hurt him in some way? Because I'm not, you know. Your dad and I aren't a couple. It's just a fling. I'm moving on shortly. He knows that, it's never been anything permanent."

"I don't give a shit about him."

"Then what's this all about? I'm trying really hard to understand why you'd break into my flat and follow me. Surely you can see that that isn't right?"

His eyes drifted towards the huge window overlooking the lake. He said his next sentence to the window rather than directly at her.

"I can tell you where the painting is, if you want."

Christ. The entire police force and insurance company had been looking for the painting since it had been stolen, and a teenager, Dylan Rider's son, knew its exact whereabouts.

"I really don't know what you're on about. What painting?"

"The Portillo."

The police officer in her desperately wanted to know more, but she'd only incriminate herself.

"I've had enough of this," she glanced at her watch, "I think it's time I left."

It was a massive gamble. Would he tell her? She'd underestimated him completely. She stood up.

"So, do you want to know?" he asked and stood up also.

Of course she did. But if she said yes, it would confirm he was right. She couldn't risk that. There was a chance he could go straight to his dad and it would blow the whole thing. He might even do that anyway. This was the first time she'd ever been caught out, and it was by a seventeen-year-old kid.

He then turned his face and looked directly at her, which was most unusual for him. As he stared intensely into her face, it felt like he was challenging her.

"Well do ya?" he whispered quietly.

"No, I don't. Now please, no more following me. I won't have it, Henry. Do you understand? Promise me no more and I'll leave it this time and not tell your dad. But if I find you've been in my flat again . . . " she left the sentence unfinished.

He looked disappointed. Almost as if he wanted her to screw his dad over.

As an afterthought she asked, "Has something happened between you and Dylan?"

Forlorn dark eyes stared. Something significant had happened between the two of them.

In barely a whisper, he added, "There's a barge on the Thames. An old guy never leaves it unattended. Supplies are brought to him every day or so. The Portillo is in a temperature-controlled crate, but they're moving it soon."

She stared. What more could she say without incriminating herself further. He'd provided her with the information she'd been desperately trying to find out for all these weeks.

His sad, pitiful expression hit her hard, but his final words wounded her most of all. And not from a police officer perspective.

"Dylan doesn't keep his phone charger in his study."

She'd lied.

And he knew she had.

She'd been sloppy, snooping round Dylan's office the night she was alone and had unwittingly exposed herself. Before she had chance to defend herself, he hurried away. She thought about going after him, but there was nothing to be gained.

An over-whelming sense of sadness washed over her. It wasn't only that this troubled young man had led her straight to the painting, it was the fact he was willing to incriminate his father.

What had happened between them to make him do that?

Her chest heaved and she swallowed. Unusually for her, she felt emotional. But not so emotional she wanted to abort. They were so close now; all she needed was the final piece on Friday for the jigsaw to be complete.

So, why was it she didn't feel elated?

And why did her gut ache with sadness for a young boy who'd lost his mum.

***

Why was Rider's son with April?

And at the park of all places where she met Paddy Frodsham.

What was that all about?

April had just said goodbye to Paddy, and as she'd turned around, Henry Rider was there barring her way.

Why? What did he want?

She'd taken him inside the café and he'd rushed out ten minutes later on his own. April followed him minutes later, and headed towards the park exit.

She had her head down.
He knew her.
Rider's son would be a complication she wouldn't want.

Chapter 55

Henry Rider meant nothing to April, yet she felt every inch of his pain. Seeing the way he was willing to expose his father had stirred up unexpected feelings. She wasn't a sentimental person at all, but he had had the ability to make her gut twist. Maybe it was the mother-child connection. He'd lost his mum and her heart constricted for him. She remembered the pain only too well.

Her thoughts drifted towards her own son, Noah. She had to compartmentalise him into being her sister's child. It did her no good at all thinking he belonged to her. Dreams of them living a life together had to be stifled. She'd given him away and had to live with that decision.

She pressed Chloe's name on her phone.

Adele's beautiful voice blared out as Chloe answered. "Hi, sis. How you doing?"

"I'm okay, just busy with work. How's things your end?"

"Brilliant. Hey, you know I told you Gavin was applying to Children in Need to see if we could get some help," she didn't wait for April to answer, "well, they've put us in touch with an organisation, and guess what? We've got a donation of ten thousand pounds. We heard on Wednesday and I'm still doing a happy dance."

"That's fantastic. Gosh that must put the total somewhere near fifty thousand."

"It does, just over actually. So we're halfway there. Can you believe it?"

"It's amazing, Chlo. You and Gav have worked so hard, I'm really proud of you."

"You've given us plenty towards it though. It's not all us."

"Not as much as I'd like, but that's going to change soon. I'm almost done here."

"Good, especially if it means seeing more of you. Noah will love it."

"Aw, bless him. I do miss him."

"When we eventually get to the States for the op, I'm hoping you can come and visit us there, the only thing is though, you might have to pay your own fare. I'm not sure how much we would be able to take out of the fund for family visits."

"I could do that, it won't be a problem. We'll see about visiting. If not, then maybe we can all have a holiday together somewhere warm after his surgery?"

"That would be amazing. It wouldn't have to cost a fortune, we could go to Spain or somewhere like that. Maybe in a villa with a pool, I bet that would be great for Noah's physio."

"Sounds brilliant, we'll sort something out. Not long now and I'll be finished on this job. Oh, before I forget, Chlo, remember, if anyone was to contact you, you don't know anything about me. You haven't seen me for years."

"I know, I know. You've told me the drill hundreds of times."

"I just wanted to make sure."

"Well nobody's asked yet, and I won't let you down if they do."

"That's great. Anyway, the reason I rang is to tell you I'm going away."

"When?"

"In the next couple of days."

"Where you going?"

"I can't say, but at least this time I can keep in touch."

"How long are you away for?"

"Not sure, yet."

Chloe sighed out loud, "Do you know, I hope you do actually give this business up. I understand the police force is your life, but all this cloak and dagger stuff is really getting ridiculous."

"And that's why I am giving it up. Don't be cross, I'll keep in touch this time I promise. Put Noah on for a minute before I go so I can say cheerio."

"I'll be furious if I don't hear from you like last time," Chloe warned.

"I'll text you regularly, I promise, *Mother*."

"You'd better. Right hang on a sec," she heard Chloe shout for Noah, "here he is. Please take care of yourself."

"I will. Love you to the moon and back."

"You too."

A child like voice came on and her heart twitched as his tiny voice said hello.

"Is that the best nephew in the world?"

Noah giggled. "It's me, it's Noah."

"I know it is sweetheart, I'd recognise your voice anywhere. What have you been doing?"

"I'm doing a picture for Daddy. He's at work."

"That's nice, he'll like that."

"I want to go out but it's raining so Mummy said I have to stay in."

"Not to worry, it'll brighten up later, then you can go out. If you've got your crayons out, maybe you could do me a picture, too."

"Yeah, I can do you one."

"Can you? I'd love one with lots of colours."

"Do you like dogs?"

"I love dogs."

"I can draw a dog at the seaside."

"That would be a lovely picture to have. I could put it on my wall."

"When will you come for it?"

"Soon. You save it for me, put it somewhere safe. Can you do that?"

"I can put it on my board with a magnet."

"That would be brilliant. You do that."

"Shall I write my name on it?"

"Oh, yes please. Right, I've got to go to work, my darling, and I'll be going away for a while. Can you be a really good boy for your mummy until I see you again?"

"How many sleeps?" She knew he meant how long until he saw her again.

"Quite a few, sweetheart. Perhaps too many to count, but I'll see you as soon as I can. Give your mummy a big kiss and a hug from me, would you?"

"Yeah."

Tears pricked her eyes. She loved him so much.

"Good boy. I'm going to blow you a big kiss too. Can you catch it down the phone?"

He giggled.

She made kissing noises down the phone. "Bye, bye sweetie, love you very much."

A little voice replied, "Bye bye."

She cut the call and swallowed the lump in her throat at the image of him sat at the table with all the bright crayons, colouring a picture for her. Even if he could go outside to play, he couldn't run around like children his age. He had to be content with his walking frame for his mobility. But that was about to change.

She was close to making sure her little boy walked again.

The success of the following day depended on it.

Chapter 56

It was Thursday evening. The club house was in full swing with the usual karaoke singer on the stage thinking she was Whitney Houston.

"Bloody hell," Joey pulled a face, "how much more of this is there? Can't someone shoot her now?"

"Don't be mean, Joey," Rachel tapped his arm, "not everyone can sing like you, you know."

He shook his head disparagingly, "Surely she has someone here with her that could tell her to sit down. My ears can't stand much more of this."

April smiled at Rachel chastising Joey. She was going to miss the gallery despite the bloody cleaning. But tonight she was there for a purpose; she had to tell them she was leaving. There was no coming back after tomorrow. It would be easier to talk without being drowned out by a lousy karaoke singer, so she waited until the audience clapped sympathetically, and the compere came on and said there'd be a break for thirty minutes."

She took a gulp of her beer. "I'm pleased we managed to get together tonight, 'cause I wanted to tell you both something."

That had their attention.

"Tonight was my last shift at the gallery," she pulled a pained face, "I'm leaving in the morning."

"Leaving for where?" Joey asked.

"I've got a permanent job starting on Monday."

"But you haven't done your twelve weeks yet?" Rachel protested.

"Not quite, I know, but it's all okay. My parole officer has cleared it with Dylan for me to go."

"What's more inviting that working with us?" Joey asked teasingly.

"Nowhere will be as good as working with you two," she smiled affectionately, "and it's not the greatest job in the world I'm going to, but it's a means to an end. A mundane job for starters and then I'm hoping to move on when I've saved a bit."

Rachel frowned, "I don't get why you're going then, if it's not for a better job."

"I know you don't, but I want to go, I don't want to stay any longer at the gallery. I associate it with prison and being on probation. My intention was always to move on. I didn't want to just disappear without saying anything as you were upset with the last girl that did that."

"But you don't have to go right away, especially if it's to a rubbish job. Why can't you stay until something good comes along?" Rachel turned to Joey, "It makes sense, doesn't it?"

Joey gave a non-committal expression, "It's up to Gemma what she does."

"Cheers Joey," Rachel snapped, "thanks for your support. Can't you see I'm trying to get her to change her mind and stay?"

Joey shrugged and took a gulp of his pint.

She smiled at Rachel, "I really appreciate you trying to get me to stay. You and Joey have made the last few weeks, bearable, I've actually quite enjoyed cleaning the gallery each night. I was such a wreck when I came out of jail, but you two have actually made things fun."

"You didn't seem like a wreck to us, did she?" Rachel asked Joey.

"Not at all. You've always seemed," he paused, fishing for the right words, "strong and capable."

She smiled affectionately at them both; she genuinely had become fond of them.

"You have no idea," she shook her head. "I was so nervous when I first arrived, but within a day or two of meeting you two, I felt so much better. I'm really going to miss you both."

"We'll miss you too," Joey smiled and stood up. "I'll go get us all another drink, same again?"

They both nodded and Rachel waited until he was out of earshot. "Have you met someone, is that it?"

"No, of course I haven't. I'd be staying if I had."

"I wish you would. It won't be the same without you."

"Aw," April leant forward and hugged her friend tightly. Rachel was a lovely genuine girl and had been so welcoming to her. Of course she didn't know April was only playing a part. She was seeing Gemma Dean, the ex-jailbird who now cleaned for a living.

Rachel pulled away. April was dismayed to see tears in her eyes.

"Hey, you can pack that in or you'll have me at it."

Rachel laughed and reached for a tissue from her bag. "I'm just sad you're going, and I know Joey is. He doesn't say much, but he likes you, Gemma. He's going to miss you, too."

"And I'll miss you both, terribly, but I have to go. You do understand don't you?"

"No, I can't say as I do, but I'll have to try. It's so sudden though, that's why I'm upset."

"I know it is, but it's the way I want it. I need to get off now. I see my next job as a fresh start; I never saw the gallery as that."

"Does Ingrid know you're going, she never said anything tonight?"

"I'm not sure, it's been very last-minute. My parole officer sorted it out with Dylan. He'll tell Ingrid as she'll have to get a replacement. They might already have someone coming from the prison on parole like me, for all I know."

"You will keep in touch though, won't you, to let us know how you're getting on?"

"Course I will," she lied, squeezing her arm. "Excuse me for a second while I pop to the ladies."

She made her way to the bar to catch Joey, who was in a group talking to some of his mates. She had an enormous favour to ask him. It was a big ask, but the final part of the plan had to be to get Dylan to her flat tomorrow morning. The painting was being delivered for her to take across to France, but she needed Dylan there also.

The whole heist depended on it.

Chapter 57

Finally, Friday the twenty-fifth had arrived. Dylan was in his office at the gallery. Everything was in place. He checked his watch again, even though he'd checked it seconds earlier. Any minute now, Lee would take the van to Gemma's flat and she was going to drive to the Channel Tunnel. As a precaution, there was a backup car on hand to follow her.

The office door opened and his secretary came in with his usual morning black coffee. "Good morning, I thought you weren't in today?" she smiled, placing the mug down on the coaster on his desk. "It's a lovely day, isn't it?"

"Yes," he replied, "it's beautiful. I'm not here all day, just for a couple of hours."

"Right," she smiled over her half-rimmed glasses. "Joey Jacobs is outside, can he have a word?"

"What does he want?" He didn't want to be bothered by trivia today of all days, "Can't you sort it?"

"I tried but he's asking to speak to you. He wants Gemma Dean's home address. I've told him we can't give details out like that, but he seems keen and asked if you would be able to give him it?"

"No, of course I won't," he said irritably, "just tell him that."

Why was he sniffing round for Gemma's address?

"Why does he want it, anyway?"

"He wouldn't say, just that it was important."

Gemma had said she was going to tell Joey and Rachel last night she was leaving the gallery, so what did he want her for now?

He sighed, "You'd better show him in then."

Seconds later, there was a tap on the door. "Come in."

Joey entered and closed the door behind him. "I'm sorry to bother you about this. I know it's irregular, but I thought I'd give it a try."

"It is irregular. If Gemma wanted you to have her address, she would have given you it."

"I know that. I've got her phone number but she's not answering. I've tried texting too but still no luck."

"Well she's either busy, or . . ." he shrugged and left the sentence unsaid. No need to add *she might not want to speak to you.*

She'd better not be speaking to him, either. Today was a big day.

The penny must have dropped as Joey raised an eyebrow. "Ah, I see what you're thinking. No, it's nothing like that," he shook his head, "I think she already has a boyfriend, anyway. The reason I want to speak to her is she's been looking for a job so she can stay in the area and my sister is desperate for a chambermaid as hers has disappeared today. She owns a small hotel with her husband in Shepherd's Bush. The woman she had was a bit highly strung and it sounds like she's run off with the breakfast chef, as he's gone too."

Dylan's stomach clenched.

What boyfriend?

Joey rattled on. "He's married, so it's one hell of a mess and my sister is struggling and needs someone at short notice."

What the fuck was he on about?

Joey looked directly at him as if he knew he was hardly listening. "I thought it was worth letting Gemma know before she leaves. To be honest, I don't think by the sound of things it's much of a job she's going to, she's being very vague about it all."

Dylan sighed, he didn't need this today of all days. It never occurred to him that Gemma might have another bloke on the go as well as him. It thumped his gut, hard.

"I still can't give her details out," he dismissed, "you'll just have to hope she responds to your text messages. She could actually be long gone by now."

Maybe she's told him she has a boyfriend to keep him at arm's length.

He made the pretence of shuffling some papers around on his desk, but had to ask, "You say she has a boyfriend, she's probably gone off with him. It did seem sudden, her wanting to leave."

"Yeah, you could be right," Joey agreed, "probably best to leave it, then. Thanks anyway."

Dylan watched Joey walk towards the door. He couldn't resist. "Have you met her boyfriend?"

"No. She's quite a private person so I've never let on I know. I only found out as I stumbled across her in the park with him one Saturday morning when I was walking my dog. I've seen her with him a few times, she's never seen me though, so I haven't mentioned it. To be honest, he looks a lot older than her. Probably married for all I know."

The pain in Dylan's gut was radiating through the rest of his body.

Surely she wasn't fucking two of them at the same time?

Jealousy wasn't an emotion he was used to. In fact, it was the first time he'd ever experienced it. An image of Gemma meeting an older bloke flashed before his eyes. Why would you meet your lover in the park of all places? Surely if he was married, you'd be somewhere fucking, not walking around the park? Unless . . .

Fuck.

No.

He stood up. "You said you've seen her a few times?"

"Yeah."

"Were they, you know, kissing? Holding hands?"

Joey shrugged. "I don't know. Maybe not kissing."

"An older man you said. How much older?"

Another shrug. "Old enough."

"Well, as I said, I can't help, now if you'll excuse me, I really do need to leave for an appointment."

"Oh, yeah, sure. No problem. It was just a thought." Joey opened the door, "Thanks anyway."

He nodded at Joey as he left and closed the door.

Rage erupted inside of him. He needed to get to Gemma's flat . . . quickly.

I'll fucking kill her if she's crossed me.

He waited until Joey was out of earshot and picked up his mobile. He keyed in Victor's name.

Come on, come on.

His fury was like a red-hot torrent flooding through his body. His heart was pounding so much, it must surely be visible. He ran his hand across his sweaty brow.

Victor answered on the fourth ring.

"We need to abort," his voice didn't sound like his own, "that bitch is about to double cross us."

"What!?"

"She's been meeting some bloke in the park. I reckon they're going to take the painting."

Let this be a mistake.

"You *reckon.* What proof do you have?"

What proof did he have, other than his aching gut and the fury running through his veins?

"Call it gut instinct," he said, "everything feels wrong about this now and we just can't take any chances. We need to abort."

"Fucking hell," Victor spat, "how the hell did you let this happen?"

He had no defence.

"I'm on my way to her flat right now. I'll strangle the fucking bitch when I get my hands on her."

"Hang on," Victor snapped, "the van will be on the way to her flat, if it's not there already. We can't put ourselves anywhere near the painting. No brief in the world would be able to get us off that. I'll ring Jit to abort."

"I'm sorry, Vic . . . I had no idea."

"There's no time for this shit right now," Vic dismissed, "let's try and sort this fucking mess out. You can't go near her or the painting, do you hear me?"

"I'm going to kill her."

"Don't go . . ."

Dylan cut the call.

The bitch.

She'd played him and he'd fallen for it.

She'll pay for this.

He'd make sure of it. If it was the last thing he ever did.

Chapter 58

April watched the Transit van approach that contained the paintings she was meant to transport. She was already waiting at the front door with a rucksack on her shoulder. She needed to move quickly. Time was of the essence. Joey would be asking Dylan for her address right now. Everything was meticulously in place. She couldn't allow anything to go wrong.

She took a deep breath, held it, and slowly exhaled. Her heart was racing as she approached Lee, the driver. He had the window down and his elbow was casually leaning out.

"Hi," she smiled.

"Hi," he nodded, "you all set?"

"Sure." She turned her head towards the back of the van and frowned, "Is that tyre alright?"

Lee leant his head out of the window towards the back tyre. "What's wrong with it?"

She moved towards it kicking it gently with her foot. "It's almost flat."

"What?" He opened the door, stepped out of the van and walked towards the back tyre.

Within seconds, two men in plain clothes appeared. One grabbed his arm and pushed him towards the van, kicking his legs apart and grabbing his hands, pulling both his arms behind his back.

"Jesus Christ," Lee yelped, "what the hell's going on?"

April cuffed him. "You're under arrest for possession of stolen goods. You do not have to say anything, but it may harm your defence if you do not mention when questioned something which you later rely on in court. Anything you do say will be taken down and may be used as evidence against you . . ."

She reached in his trouser pocket and removed his phone.

"What the fuck . . ."

"You'll get it back at the station."

He shook his head incredulously, "*Stolen goods*. These are paintings we're transporting to France."

She ignored him, "Take him away."

"You've got this all wrong," he shouted as she watched him being led towards the waiting van, "I don't know anything about stolen goods."

One down.

One to go.

April got into the driver's seat of the van and tossed Lee's phone on the passenger seat. It was ringing. The caller id was Jit Monks. The answer phone clicked in, but Jit Monks whoever he was, wouldn't speak into an answer phone. He'd be trying to tell the driver to abort.

She turned on the ignition. Her intention wasn't to go far, she just wanted to make sure the van wasn't outside her flat. She was banking on Dylan arriving in the next few minutes.

She glanced at her watch, needing to get a move on as he should be there very shortly if Joey had done as she'd asked. She moved the van along the road and turned right. Earlier she'd cordoned off an area with police cones so she had somewhere to put the van out of Dylan's sight. It would be a disaster if he made straight for the van and took off with it. She had no idea if he had another set of keys.

She secured the van and ran back to her flat, making her way up the endless stairs. She had simultaneously had the tailing car pulled up and the driver arrested. He'd be in the van alongside Lee right now heading away. Both drivers would be incensed knowing the plan had been thwarted and there'd be no pay-out for them now. They'd know their future most probably meant a period of time behind bars. The bloke driving the tail car would be calculating how he might be able to escape a prison sentence. He'd be thinking a good brief could get him off that, but Lee would be shitting himself. He was in possession of stolen goods and was looking at a long stretch. Was he completely innocent, or did he really know what he was transporting? Dylan had implied he didn't, but she wasn't so sure.

She entered her flat and the four uniforms were sat where she'd left them having a coffee.

"It's time. Remember, it's most likely there'll only be Dylan Rider, but if his brother comes, we want both of them. Don't, whatever you do, allow either of them to make a run for it."

They nodded and moved towards the kitchen adjacent to the lounge. The last uniform closed the door behind him. They'd struggle in the kitchen as it was so tiny, but it would only be for minutes.

Now all she had to do was wait.

Dylan should be here any minute now.

She was confident of that if nothing else. All the months of planning had been for this moment. But now it was time for the execution of the plan, her tummy was doing somersaults.

Thank Christ for adrenaline.

Lee's phone rang. And again Jit came up on the screen. She let the answer phone kick in, but he hung up. They'd be desperately trying to abort the whole operation.

Please let him come.

The whole plan depended on Dylan entering her flat. Surely his bruised ego would bring him?

Everything depended on it.

April waited.

Each second was painful. Even though she was an experienced police officer, she was on edge. She was so close now. Nothing could get in the way.

Five – long – minutes.

Where was he? The bay window gave her a panoramic view of the street, which was why this particular flat had been chosen.

There was movement outside. Victor Rider was on foot, making his way towards her flat.

He must have left his car further down the road.

Her heart rate accelerated.

What a bonus getting him too.

Seconds later, Dylan's black Bentley mounted the pavement and screeched to a halt. Victor turned towards the car and opened the door to let Dylan get out. Both brothers visually scanned the immediate area. It was obvious from their body language they were arguing.

Dylan shook his head and made a move towards her flat. Victor grabbed his arm. She hardly dared breathe. So much was depending on Dylan's rage.

Come on. Come on.

Dylan shrugged Victor's arm away and headed through the entrance gate to her flat. Victor hesitated for only a second, then followed.

She held her breath. *That's it. Come to Mummy.*

Her heart-rate accelerated even further, if that was possible, as she pictured the brothers climbing the endless stairs. She opened the kitchen door, the uniforms had been well-briefed, but now Victor had arrived, it was a new ball game.

"The brother is on his way up as well, so, two of you for Dylan, two for the brother."

She positioned herself as far away from the lounge door as she could, but facing it so they'd see her when they came in. The front door was locked but it could easily be forced. Dylan had complained it wasn't secure. *Stupid bugger,* she'd purposely had it set up that way.

Minutes later, she heard one of them kick the front door open and within seconds they both appeared in the lounge doorway.

"You fucking bitch!" Dylan yelled and lunged for her, closely followed by his brother.

April stood her ground.

The kitchen door burst open and the uniforms rushed out. Two of them grabbed Dylan and the other two his brother. They held onto them just as she'd instructed and cuffed their hands behind their backs. As they did so, she repeated the arrest spiel.

"Dylan and Victor Rider, you are both under arrest on suspicion of theft and attempting to move stolen goods out of the country. You do not have to say anything, but it may harm your defence if you do not mention when questioned something which you later rely on in court. Anything you do say may be given in evidence . . ."

Dylan stared in disbelief, "You're a fucking cop?"

The question didn't need an answer.

Victor was shaking his head furiously.

She indicated with her head towards the door. "Take them away."

Dylan snarled. "Do you really think any of this is going to stick when I tell them a police officer opened her legs to get justice? Not a fucking chance. We'll be out before the end of the day."

"Whatever." She nodded to the uniforms, "Now."

"You'll be fucking sorry. You can't hide. Remember that."

She turned her back on them as they were led away.

The flat was eerily empty. She moved towards the window and waited until the brothers came into view. They were unceremoniously chucked into the back of the waiting van and the door secured behind them. Only when it moved away did she allow herself to breathe out.

It was over.

She'd done it.

Well . . . almost.

Chapter 59

Dylan sat opposite his brother in the back of the van, both of them with their hands cuffed behind their backs.

"Shit, shit, shit," Dylan said, shaking his head, "I can't believe this. An undercover cop. Why the fuck didn't I see it?"

"Cause your eyes were in your bollocks that's why," Victor spat.

Perspiration trickled down Dylan's back. "We'll ring Stephen Wallis when we get to the station. He'll have us out by the end of the day. And I swear, I don't care how long it takes, I'll get her. She'll pay for this."

"It's not the fucking courts we need to worry about," Victor groaned, "now they've got the painting, how the hell are we going to pay everyone? I can't see Jit Monks and the gang being fucking delirious about this."

Dylan wasn't listening. "She was so convincing. She's just come out of the nick, for Christ's sake."

Victor's face was full of venom. "Yeah, obviously a set up. They must have had us in their sights for a while. She was bloody convincing, I'll give you that. They needed someone as slick as her to pull it off."

"Wait till I get my hands on her," Dylan said. "I never suspected a thing. Not once until the security bloke mentioned seeing her in the park. I knew then something was wrong. I'd never have guessed she was a cop though. Even on my way to her flat, I was convinced it was an insurance job. Those cops coming out of the kitchen and handcuffing us was a shock. I still can't believe it."

"I told you not to go after her," Victor said, "but you wouldn't listen."

"Nobody said you had to come," he snapped back.

"What the fuck did you expect me to do? You left me no choice, racing round to her flat."

Victor was right. He had been a bloody fool. He was normally so measured, but he'd let his guard down. Gemma Dean, or whoever she really was, had played him every step of the way.

He felt nauseous. Vic looked ashen. He watched his brother try to wipe the sweat running down his face, on his shoulder. They had a long road ahead of them now.

"Anyway, you're right," Vic said, "we'll be out by the end of today." But he didn't sound convincing. They'd prepared for eventualities, but not for this. Vic carried on, "The brief will sort this. But once we're out, we're still in deep shit, that's for sure."

"Do you reckon they've picked Jit up as well?"

"I reckon, yeah," Victor said, "they'll not get anything out of him though. He's no grass."

Dylan shook his head, "What a fucking mess."

The van started to slow down.

"Where the fuck are they taking us?" Victor frowned, bending his head to look through the windscreen. The view was obscured by the visor separating them from the cops, but he could just about see the road ahead.

Dylan ducked his head also. "Christ knows. Not Kensington, that's for sure." He scowled, "Maybe they're taking us to Fulham?"

Both of them continued to watch.

"Why are we stopping?" Dylan frowned.

Victor shook his head, "Where the hell are we, anyway?"

The van entered a car park and came to a halt. One of the cops got out and moved a couple of cones that had reserved a parking space. The second cop manoeuvred the van into the space and applied the handbrake before cutting the engine. The cop got out of the van and slammed the door, leaving him and Victor alone.

Dylan looked around incredulously. "Where the fuck are they going?"

Why would two police officers leave prisoners unattended in the back of a van?

Okay, their hands were cuffed, but nevertheless.

Both he and Vic's eyes were focussed on the officers as they let themselves into a parked Ford Focus. The one in the driver's seat started the engine and slowly moved the car forward towards the car park exit. He didn't look back.

Victor screwed his face up. "They're not fucking cops. They're just dressed as cops."

Dylan looked disbelievingly at his brother and his expression mirrored his own. "Shit."

Victor's face twisted, "Yeah, and she's got the fucking painting."

Chapter 60

April stared around the pristine and tranquil Simpson Bay on St Maarten's beach in the Caribbean. The vibrant golden sun shone on the sparkling water. The waiter had walked down to the beach from the bar and placed April's two margarita's on the small wooden table beside her lounger.

She rooted in her bag and handed him a couple of dollars. "Thank you."

"You're welcome." He flicked the small arrow down on the back of lounger she'd used to highlight to the barman she needed a drink.

"I'll keep an eye. Flick it up when you want more."

She smiled, "I think this will probably be the last. They're not both for me anyhow. I'm expecting someone."

He nodded and walked away, no doubt thinking, yeah, that's what they all say. But she meant it. She reached in her bag for her phone and keyed her sister's number.

Chloe answered after a couple of rings. "Hello you?"

"Hi Chlo. Are you okay?"

"Fine. Are you?"

"Never better. How's my favourite nephew?"

"Great. It's Book Day at school and they all have to go as a character from a book. He's gone as Willy Wonka. He looks so cute with his black top hat Gavin made."

"Aw, WhatsApp me a picture, would you?"

"Course I will."

"Right, listen, 'cause I haven't got long."

"I'm listening."

"I've got the money for Noah's op. You can go ahead and tell the consultant you can take him to America."

"What money? What are you talking about?"

"I've got enough for you to go to the US for as long as it's going to take. Gavin as well."

"How? Even I know the police force don't pay that sort of money."

"They have for the job I've just done, and I've also taken redundancy."

"Redundancy, you? The police force is your life."

"I've got it, Chlo, I promise you. Now don't waste any more time, get Mr Adams to make the arrangements. I've enough for you to get a place out there close to the hospital to stay for as long as it takes until Noah is walking."

"I don't know what to say. I can't believe you've got the money."

"Well you better, 'cause it's true. I'll be in touch over the next few days to get your bank account details so I can send the money to you."

"You've really got it?" Chloe started to cry, "You mean it, April, the police force has given you that much?"

"Yes, I mean it. I have the money. Make the arrangements."

"But you'll need that money won't you, to live? I can't believe you'd leave the police force, you love it so much."

"I did love it, but I'm looking to do other things now."

"Will there be enough money left for you to come to America while we're there?"

"I'll see. I'll need to look around for another job, so it depends on if I can get away."

"But you'll get holidays, won't you, surely?"

"Yes. I'll sort something. It might be you all come to me, wherever I am."

"What do you mean, wherever you are?"

"I might not come back to the UK."

"Not come back? Where are you now?"

"On holiday."

"Who with?" Chloe didn't wait for an answer. "Don't tell me you're with someone?"

"I'll tell you all about it later. Right now, I want you to make arrangements for you to go to the States and Noah to have his op. And don't worry about the money, I have more than enough. Just get it sorted."

"We already have fifty thousand from the fundraising."

"Yes, I know, and I can make up however much more you need."

"Is this really happening, April? I can't believe it. You're sure?"

"Of course I'm sure. When have I ever let you down?"

"Never."

"Well, there you go then. I've made it happen. Now you need to go and do the rest."

"I will, April, I will. I'm going to ring Gavin right now and get onto the hospital."

"You do that. And give Noah a great big kiss from his auntie and tell him I love him."

"I wish he was here, so you could tell him."

"You and Gavin tell him, you're his mummy and daddy. I'll be in touch in a day or so and you can tell me then what you've got sorted. I can speak to Noah then."

"Am I going to wake up in a minute and find this is all a dream? Is it really happening?"

"You bet your life it is. Right, I've got to go. You and Gav open a bottle tonight and celebrate, I know I'm going to."

"We will. You are so good, always taking care of us. We do love you for it, you know."

"'Course I know," she swallowed the lump in her throat, "you're my family, and I love you too. Very much."

She heard the tears in her sister's voice as she croaked, "Love you to the moon and back."

"Me too," she swallowed and cut the call.

She blew her nose. She wasn't normally emotional. It must have been the strain of the last few months, and knowing finally, that her son was going to get the surgery he needed which would enable him to walk. Then he could live his life to the full, just as she'd intended.

Minutes later, she saw him. She'd know that swagger anywhere. She placed her hand over her eyes to shield it from the sun, so she could get a better look at him. As he got closer, she saw he was grinning, and she grinned back.

They were such a brilliant team.

Without him, she couldn't have pulled it all off. He'd watched her back the whole time. Would he suspect she'd slept with Rider? Of course he would. But she was a master at lying, and she'd deny it. Maybe he wouldn't ask. Who knows? Dylan Rider had been good in the sack, but he'd been a means to an end. Thank God he was attractive, that made it much easier. If he'd have been ugly, the job would have been so much harder.

The man she was waiting for approached her lounger and his athletic physique blocked out the sun. Her eyes met his and she stood up directly in front of him, but not touching.

"Hello . . . Joey."

Familiar lips covered hers. She kissed him back as if she was a drowning woman.

He pulled away. "God, April, I've missed you so much."

"I've missed you too. Is it done?"

"It is."

He'd offloaded the painting. They were rich beyond their wildest dreams. No police pension for her, but she wouldn't need that now. She felt a slight pang when she thought of Paddy. It had been easy to dupe him by giving him Saturday the twenty-sixth, a day later for moving the painting opposed to the Friday. By the time he'd have the team assembled, she had been long gone. He'd be devastated by her betrayal, and no doubt be pensioned off by the Force, but he hadn't been astute enough. He'd even cleared with customs her fake passport on the previous run across to

France, so there was no chance of being stopped when she fled to the Caribbean the previous day.

A warm feeling wrapped around her heart as she recalled her sister's voice when she told her she was sending the money for Noah's operation. Somehow, that made the whole thing okay. The fact she wouldn't be able to visit them in the UK ever again would be difficult, but she'd have them visit her wherever she was in the world. There was plenty of money for that now.

Joey Jacobs had been watching her back from the very beginning. She knew he'd been out there keeping an eye on things, covertly spying on her. Knowing that he was there had spurred her on. She knew exactly when he was following her . . . she wouldn't have been much of a police officer if she hadn't.

And he'd played his part of being a security officer at the gallery so well. He'd managed to get the fake police officers and the uniforms. His dummy run had been the full Monty he'd done at the club. For a few grand, the blokes had willingly agreed to play the part of arresting the Rider brothers and dumping them in the car park miles away.

She handed Joey the margarita. "There you go."

He clinked her glass and smiled lovingly at her. "It's been an absolute nightmare being so close to you the last few weeks but not being able to touch you. I hated it."

"Me too." She widened her eyes, "Especially as you look so hot in your security guard's uniform."

They kissed again.

"Can you believe we've pulled it off?" she grinned.

"I believe you can do anything you put your mind to, April Masters." He raised his glass slightly, "Here's to our future together."

She clinked her glass with his, "Yes, our future. Cheers."

Chapter 61

Joey opened his eyes and it took a second for him to become accustomed to where he actually was. He'd been dreaming about the gallery and April cleaning the toilets. God, she'd been convincing as Gemma the cleaner, and he'd fancied her rotten in that tight little uniform.

His head was thumping.

Fuck, how much had they drunk last night?

He reached an arm out for April, but the bed was empty. He'd really missed her. He'd vowed that he was going to wake up every morning from now on, with her by his side. He'd speak to her about that. He didn't want her getting up before him. He was determined that each morning when he opened his eyes, she was the first person he saw.

Christ, his head hurt.

He must have slept solidly not to have heard her get out of bed. He could hear the shower running and would love to join her, but needed to gather himself a bit first. The roof of his mouth was dry and his breath smelt sour. He licked his dry lips.

He reached for his watch, surprised to see it was ten o'clock. He sat on the edge of the bed and felt woozy.

What the hell had they had?

He waited for a few seconds before heading across the room to the fridge for a bottle of water. He unscrewed the top and glugged nearly the full bottle. The movement of tilting his head backwards made it throb even more than it was already. He grabbed the unit to steady himself as a wave of dizziness rushed over him.

April had opened the patio doors and the sea was crashing only a few metres away. He'd have a dip in there later once he'd eaten and hopefully cleared his head. No more alcohol today though, better give that a rest. He slowly finished the water, gently titling his head this time.

The view was spectacular. He took a few paces to stand on the patio and gazed at the cruise ships in the distance with the passengers herding off and into the smaller boats taking them to shore. St Maarten was paradise for duty-free shopping.

They'd decided to have a few days there and then would be moving on. He wanted to spend some time with April as they'd been so long apart. The sex between them last night had been amazing. How many times had they fucked? He couldn't remember much, only flashbacks to various positions. It was almost as if he'd blacked out.

What a remarkable woman she was. They'd met at work, he was a police sergeant, and April had been assigned to him as a mentor as he was under review by the Independent Complaints Commission. They'd launched an investigation into a whole bunch of them for supposedly taking back-handers. Instead of being suspended on full-pay while they concluded on the investigation, the force had introduced a new regime where any officer under investigation was not suspended, but allowed to work under supervision until it was concluded. The writing was on the wall, though. He knew he would lose his job.

He'd been attracted to April from the beginning. At first they were just casual, fuck buddies, but their relationship developed at a fast pace. Not in work. There they had to behave professionally, and did that very well. Nobody suspected they were an item.

He was bitterly disillusioned with the Force and dreamt of owning some land and working for himself. He'd been brought up in the country and after the cut and thrust of the Met, he yearned for life at a slower pace.

As the internal investigation had progressed, April confirmed it was highly likely he was going to be sacked, and it was by chance she spotted an advertisement for a security officer at the Carson Rider gallery. She teasingly said he ought to apply for it – it was one way of getting out of the police force before he was pushed.

They'd joked he was over-qualified to be a security guard, and messed about online producing a CV which indicated he'd spent some time in the police force, but they were creative about him being disillusioned with it and had fled to the country and joined his parents on their farm where he'd worked for five years. Coincidentally, during this period, April had been part of a team looking at the Rider brothers and their possible involvement in the theft of paintings.

The light-hearted application turned into reality and he applied for a job at the gallery. Although it was half the money he was earning in the Met, it was a means to an end. He was likely to be dismissed from the force anyway; it seemed only a question of time. His reasoning was, if he got the job and did it for a while, then he could use them as a reference for another position. April, as a senior officer, gave him the reference to say he'd previously worked in the Met, but had left five years earlier.

Dylan Rider and Ingrid had interviewed him and offered him the job. Seemingly the insurance companies preferred security guards with a background in policing.

The job worked out well as he became quite useful to April keeping her informed about the gallery, which she used at work to push the investigation into the Rider brothers further. Eventually, a covert operation had been facilitated by the Met in conjunction with the insurance company, to carry out an undercover operation at the gallery. For it to be authentic and subject to scrutiny, it was necessary for April to spend three months in the open prison. During that period of time, he hated not being able to see her or hear her voice. He missed her. But he always knew they'd get to this point. Nothing was more certain with her at the helm. She was a master at planning.

Once the covert operation began, he watched her regularly, always when she was meeting Paddy in the park and on a couple of other occasions. He liked to feel close to her. He was sure she would know he was out there watching. Not much got past April.

Each evening at the gallery he saw her, and on the occasions they met as a threesome at the pub with Rachel, he savoured being close to her even though he couldn't be familiar with her. Nobody suspected a thing. She'd insisted on virtually no communication between the two of them, not even texting until right near the end.

On the day April was supposed to be moving the painting, they needed a distraction so they could still move the painting to France, but just a different way. Taking the technician, the tailing car, and the Rider brothers out of the equation, gave them time. The fake police officers were a master stroke. While that was going on, he'd collected the van around the corner from April's flat where she'd parked it and conveniently left the van keys in her mail box. He'd driven the van to Portsmouth and across to Le Havre where he offloaded it to the original buyer. All the paperwork was in order, they'd just cut the Rider brothers out, perfectly. The painting was stolen anyway, so the hard work had been done for them. The buyer didn't care how he got the Portillo, as long as he did. And he'd paid handsomely for the privilege.

Joey thought about April and how she'd masterminded the whole plan. She was incredibly astute. What a future to look forward to with her in it. If he didn't know in the beginning he was in love with her, he did now. The thought of spending the rest of his life together with enough money to enable them to do whatever they liked, gave him a huge adrenaline rush. And, headache or no headache, he wanted her again.

He tapped on the bathroom door, "Coming in, ready or not."

She didn't answer. He tried the door, but it was locked.

Christ, she'd been in a long time.

"April, are you okay?"

No answer.

He shook the handle. "Let me in, April."

Still no answer.

Something was wrong.

Fuck, how long had she been in there?

The lock was a disabled one which could easily be turned from the outside. He quickly used his thumb nail to open it. The bathroom was full of steam and it took a second for his eyes to become accustomed to the fog in front of him.

The hot water was running in the shower, but the cubicle was empty.

The bathroom was empty. April wasn't there.

His blood pressure plummeted. He felt light-headed. His chest tightened.

She'd gone. And he knew with absolute certainty, the money had gone also.

His stomach heaved.

He screwed his face up as he recalled her sending for champagne and him telling her not to bother as it was almost morning. But she'd insisted. She must have drugged him.

He turned the shower off and rubbed his throbbing temple.

Fool.

It had been him that had taken all the risks and moved the painting. It had been him that had sold it on. All for what? Here he was, standing alone in a bathroom with no painting, no money, no nothing.

And she'd got the lot.

How had he not seen it coming?

His brain went into over-drive. She'd masterminded it all from the very beginning. His job at the gallery. The undercover operation. Paddy Frodsham. Dylan Rider. They'd all fallen for it, hook, line and sinker . . . she'd made fools of all of them, him being the biggest fool of all.

About the Author

I sincerely hope that you have enjoyed reading April Fool as much as I have enjoyed writing it. Any feedback would be greatly appreciated; I'd love to hear your thoughts. My email address is joymarywood@yahoo.co.uk.

If you are interested in reading any more of my books, I have written three other romances which are standalone books and can be read in any order.

For the Love of Emily
Knight & Dey
Chanjori House.

Lightning Source UK Ltd.
Milton Keynes UK
UKHW010110080222
398328UK00001B/142

9 781788 765725